Léon Delbos

The Student's French Prose Composition

Léon Delbos

The Student's French Prose Composition

ISBN/EAN: 9783337366278

Printed in Europe, USA, Canada, Australia, Japan

Cover: Foto ©Andreas Hilbeck / pixelio.de

More available books at **www.hansebooks.com**

THE STUDENT'S
FRENCH PROSE COMPOSITION

WITH AN

INTRODUCTORY CHAPTER

AND

NUMEROUS NOTES

BY

LEON DELBOS, M. A.

OF KING'S COLLEGE, LONDON.

WILLIAMS AND NORGATE,

14, HENRIETTA STREET, COVENT GARDEN, LONDON;
AND 20, SOUTH FREDERICK STREET, EDINBURGH.

1887.

CONTENTS.

Contents.

Contents.

page

Part III.

INTRODUCTORY CHAPTER.

No one who has learnt a foreign language, be it a modern or a dead language, and who has become a proficient scholar in it can undervalue the use of composing into that language. This is true of Latin and Greek, and those who are set to write Latin and Greek composition are required to do so, solely to enable them to gain a deeper insight into the very spirit of those languages, than could possibly be acquired by mere translations from Latin and Greek into English. No one now uses, or intends to make use of Latin as a medium of intercourse between persons of different countries, but in the case of a modern language this is not so. Those who imagine that a person who cannot turn a few lines of plain English into anything like idiomatic and fairly grammatical French, can read even the simplest French novel with a full understanding of every portion of the text, labour under an illusion which nothing will dispel better than the utter failure which will attend their efforts at rendering a passage of good French into readable English. How many French books of sterling worth have been spoilt by translators is not a question easily answered, and yet professional translators are generally persons who have spent some time in France, and who are tolerably ac-

quainted with the spoken language. What we say of translators of French books into English applies equally well,
or rather better to translators of English books into French.
Those who, like Alexander Dumas think that English is
nothing but French badly pronounced, or that French is
nothing but bad English are invariably those whose knowledge of either language is extremely superficial and in-
accurate. We cannot too strongly admonish those who
desire to learn a language not to make too light of the
apparent simplicity of its grammar. Foreigners generally
think English Grammar can be mastered in the course
of a few days or weeks of desultory study, and that is
undoubtedly the reason why there are so few who can
write a page of fairly decent English. Those who know
most about languages always find plenty of difficulties in
the easiest tongue, and if they succeed in becoming
proficient scholars it is solely because they are aware of
that fact, and that they set to work with the determination of studying everything thoroughly. Determination and
persevering study will make even Sanskrit easy of attainment. Therefore we advise all those who wish to ac-
quire a thorough and really useful knowledge of French
to devote a portion of their time to the translation of
English into French.

In the first part of this work we have given an almost word for word imitation of the English as it should
appear when turned into French, and as that imitation
is on the same page as the correct English text the
student will have something more than notes to guide his
faltering steps. We must add that all the pieces contained in Part I are the result of actual class work and
that most of those contained in Part II have also been

used with the advanced pupils. For the benefit of any critic who may feel inclined to censure us either for giving too many notes, or not enough notes, or useless notes, we wish to say that every careful teacher has found by experience that the most puzzling things to pupils are often those which would have been thought the plainest, and that, may be to his disappointment, he has also found that certain portions which he had taken care to illustrate with notes required scarcely any elucidation.

Lastly we have found that the best and most successful plan is to make pupils commit the notes to memory and also to make them go over pieces previously done in class not only once but twice, thrice and even oftener. We speak with confidence of this method which to the more go-ahead teachers may seem rather antiquated, and not in keeping with the so-called modern improvements, because long experience in teaching either classical or modern languages has convinced us that apparent slowness of work, frequent repetition and learning by heart never fail to give the best practical results.

REMARKS ON PART I.

1. Words linked together are to be translated into French by one word only, thus

to_see   = *voir*

to_see_again = *revoir*

to_him   = *lui*, not *à lui*.

2. When the word *to* before an infinitive is not linked to it, it is to be translated by a preposition which will be found by a reference to the tables of prepositions governed by adjectives or verbs pp. XII. XIII &c. thus

he liked to see = *il aimait à voir*.

3. When *y* should be used in French, before the verb, we have represented it by the English *there* whilst we have made use of *of_it* for *en*.

PART II.

HINTS ON FRENCH COMPOSITION.

THE ORDER OF WORDS.

1. The order of words in French is generally as follows:

I. *Nominative* called in French *Sujet*

II. *Verb*   „   „   „   *Verbe*

III. *Accusative*   „   „   „   *Régime direct*

IV. *Dative*   „   „   „   *Régime indirect*

Sujet	*Verbe*	*Régime direct*	*Régime indirect.*
Le Général	envoya	un ordre	aux troupes.

2. If the accusative has a complement, the dative, if shorter, generally precedes it.

	Dative	*Accusative with extension*
J'ai donné	à mon frère	un livre contenant des gravures superbes.

3. The order of the pronouns will be best ascertained by means of the following examples which should be committed to memory.

he gives	*it to me*	= il *me le* or *la** donne
„ „	*them to me*	= „ *me les* „
„ „	*it to thee*	= „ *te le* or *la** „
„ „	*them to thee*	= „ *te les* „
„ „	*it to him*	= „ *le* or *la* lui* „
„ „	*it to her*	= „ *le* or *la* lui* „
„ „	*them to him*	= „ *les lui* „
„ „	*them to him*	= „ *les lui* „
„ „	*it to us*	= „ *nous le* or *la** „
„ „	*them to us*	= „ *nous les* „
„ „	*it to you*	= „ *vous le* or *la** „
„ „	*them to you*	= „ *vous les* „
„ „	*it to them* (m)	= „ *le* or *la* leur* „
„ „	*it to them* (f)	= „ *le* or *la* leur* „
„ „	*them to them* (m)	= „ *les leur* „
„ „	*them to them* (f)	= „ *les leur* „

	me			moi
	thee			toi
	him			lui
	her			elle
with	it	= avec		lui or elle*
	us			nous
	you			vous
	them (m)			eux (m)
	them (f)			elles (f)

4. In the imperative the order of the pronouns is reversed except in the case of pronouns of the third person singular or plural. In such cases, *me* becomes *moi* and *te, toi*.

| Give *it to me* | = donnez *le* or *la moi* |
| „ *them to me* | = „ *les moi*. |

---

* As there is no neuter gender in French *it* always refers either to a masculine or feminine noun; therefore *le* or *la, lui* or *elle* must be used to suit the gender of the word represented by *it* in French.

5. If a sentence contains an interrogative pronoun or adverb, the nominative may be placed before or after the verb.

Quand mon ami viendra-t-il? or
Quand viendra mon ami?

6. However the second construction must not be used when the verb is in a compound tense, or when the word *pourquoi* begins the sentence. We must then write

Quand mon ami est-il venu?
Pourquoi mon ami viendrait-il?

7. An inverted construction is required after

aussi { accordingly / consequently / therefore
à peine hardly, scarcely.
au moins, at least.
à plus forte raison, so much the more.
en vain, in vain.
encore, besides, even then.
peut-être, perhaps.

I. Nous partîmes trop tard aussi *manquâmes-nous* le train.
II. Peut-être *viendrait-il* s'il savait que vous êtes ici.

8. After a relative pronoun such as *dont lequel, duquel &. &. où que,* the subject comes after the verb, if the nominative, followed by an extension of meaning, is longer than the predicate:

On ne sait d'où lui *vient* son *immense fortune.*

But without the extension *immense* the phrase might be construed thus:

On ne sait d'où sa *fortune* lui *vient.*

9. The same thing takes place after *ainsi, tel, quel, ici, là.*

Tel fut Turenne.
Là tombèrent les 3oo Spartiates.

and after adverbs or adverbial expressions of time or place or *c'est .... que* followed by a neuter verb, and after *quel* in indirect questions

C'est le vendredi *que part la malle des Indes.*

THE ARTICLE.

10. Words in apposition require no article.

Louis XVI, *roi de France*, mourut &c.
Shakspeare, *poète anglais*, naquit &.
not *le roi, le poète.*

TO DO.

11. *to do* when it means 'to make', 'to perform', is translated by *faire* otherwise it is not translated at all.

What are you doing == *que faites-vous?*
I do not know you == *je ne vous connais pas.*

12. If *to do* is used elliptically the understood verb must be expressed in French:

Do you swim? *Nagez-vous?*
Yes I do. *Oui, je nage.*

13. If a noun has been used in the question, the pronoun taking the place of the noun, and the verb must be both used.

Are you M. C.?, *Etes-vous Monsieur C.?*
Yes I am. *Oui je le suis.*

14. This rule applies equally well to the verbs "to have", "to be", "will", "shall", "would", "could", "might".

TO HAVE.

15. To have, expressing supposition must be rendered by *si* followed by avoir in the imperfect Indicative.

Had he not been in the boat they would have perished.	*S'il n'avait pas été dans le bateau, ils auraient péri.*
Had he known it &.	*S'il avait su cela &.*

16. 'Had it not been for' is translated by *n'eut été* or simply by *sans*

Had it not been for the general, the army would have been massacred.	*N'eut été le général l'armée aurait été massacrée;* or *Sans le géné ral &.*

REFLEXIVE VERBS.

17. Remember that a reflexive verb is always con-jugated with *two* pronouns and that its compound tenses are conjugated with *être.*

THE PRESENT PARTICIPLE.

18. If the English present participle becomes a noun and is used as the nominative to a verb, or if it is the object to a verb it is translated, either:

I. by a noun: —

Walking is the best exercise.	La *marche* est le meilleur exercice.

II. by an infinitive: —

I intend *writing* to him.	*J'ai l'intention de lui* écrire.
You should not go out without *telling* your master.	Vous ne devriez pas sortir sans le *dire* à votre maître.

19. When preceded by *my, thy, his, her, our, your, their* the English present participle is translated by a noun, an infinitive, or some other tense of the verb.

His coming surprised me.	Son *arrivée* me surprit.
I did not reckon upon his pay-ing me.	Je ne comptais pas *qu'il me paierait.*
I am surprised at your speaking to him in such a manner.	Je suis surpris *que vous lui ayez parlé* d'une telle façon.

THE PASSIVE VOICE.

20. French, unlike Latin and English prefers the active to the passive voice and in many cases where the passive is almost indispensable in English it cannot be used in French.

I have been told, = one has told me	= on m'a dit.
I had been forbidden to go out = one had forbidden me to go out	= on m' avait défendu de sortir.

It had been forbidden to go out = one had forbidden &. &. | = *on avait* &.

This man is seen everywhere = one sees this man everywhere | *on voit cet homme partout.*

21. The English passive is also frequently translated into French by a reflexive verb used only in the 3rd person.

This article is sold in all London shops. | *Cet article se vend dans toutes les boutiques de Londres.*

This writing is easily read. | *Cette écriture se lit facilement.*

THE ADVERB.

22. Adverbs generally follow the verb.

23. They are sometimes placed at the beginning of a sentence but never between the pronoun and verb as is the case in English.

PREPOSITIONS.

24. All prepositions govern the infinitive except *en* which requires a present participle, therefore,

after having given must be translated by | *après avoir donné* and not *après ayant donné.*

25. The preposition except in certain cases must be followed by its complement.

He went to and returned from London in two hours, | must be translated as if we had in English: he went to London and returned from it in two hours = *il alla à Londres et en revint en deux heures.*

MISCELLANEOUS REMARKS.

26. When an English word implying a negative has no corresponding word in French the phrase must be turned in such a manner as to make the sentence negative whilst using the affirmative word. e. g. *He was disbelieved by all.*

As there is no corresponding word in French for 'to disbelieve' except a verb *décroire* which is now obsolete the phrase must be turned by:—

No one believed him —	*Personne ne le crut*
or by	
He was not believed by any one	*Il ne fut cru par personne.*

27. *Having*, followed by *become*, is often omitted in French at the beginning of a sentence.

| Having become rich he retired from business. | *Devenu riche il se retira des affaires.* |

28. If followed by a transitive verb the object comes first and is followed by the verb in the past participle.

| Having made my purchases I prepared to leave the town. | *Mes achats faits je me préparai à quitter la ville.* |

29. Pay special attention to the rules on *en* and *y*.

30. Also to those on the use of the Imperfect and Perfect.

31. Study carefully the rules of the subjunctive and the sequence of tenses.

32. AN ALPHABETICAL TABLE OF ADJECTIVES REQUIRING DIFFERENT PREPOSITIONS IN FRENCH AND IN ENGLISH.

adroit *à*	skilled *in*
affable *envers*	affable *to*
affligé *de*	afflicted *with*
altéré *de*	thirsting *for*
ami *de*	friendly *to*
bon *à* or *de*	good *to*
bon *pour* or *envers*	good *for*
charitable *envers*	charitable *to*
comblé *de*	filled *with*
couvert *de*	covered *with*
ennemi *de*	hostile *to*
esclave *de*	slave *to*
étonné *de*	astonished *at*
exact *à*	exact *in*
fâché *de*	sorry *for*
fâché *contre*	angry *with*
fort *à*	clever *at*
fort *sur*	skilled *in*

fou *de*	mad *with*
habile *à*	clever *in*
inexact *à*	inexact *in*
inhérent *à*	inherent *in*
libéral *envers*	liberal *to*
patient *à*	patient *of*
pauvre *de*	poor *in*
propre *à*	fit *for*
ravi *de*	delighted *with*
rempli *de*	filled *with*
riche *de* or *en*	rich *in*
voisin *de*	next *to*
zélé *à*	zealous *of*

AN ALPHABETICAL TABLE OF VERBS REQUIRING DIFFERENT PREPOSITIONS IN FRENCH AND IN ENGLISH.

33. FRENCH VERBS GOVERNING NO PREPOSITION BEFORE THE INFINITIVE.

abuser	to *deceive*
aimer mieux	to *prefer*
aller	to *go*
appeler	to *call*
applaudir	to *praise*
avouer	to *confess*
compter	to *purpose*
confesser	to *acknowledge*
croire	to *believe*
daigner	to *deign*
déclarer	to *declare*
désirer	to *wish*
devoir	*must*
entendre	to *hear*
envoyer	to *send*
espérer	to *hope*
faire	to *do*
falloir	to *be necessary*
s'imaginer	to *imagine*
laisser	to *leave*
se laisser	to *allow one's self to*
nier	to *deny*
oser	to *dare*
paraître	to *appear*

penser	*to think*
pouvoir	*to be able*
préférer	*to prefer*
prétendre	*to pretend*
se rappeler	*to remember*
reconnaître	*to recognize*
regarder	*to look at*
retourner	*to return to*
savoir	*to know*
sembler	*to seem*
sentir	*to feel*
souhaiter	*to wish*
soutenir	*to affirm, to support*
valoir mieux	*to be better*
venir	*to come*
voir	*to see*
se voir	*to see one's self*
vouloir	*to wish*

34. PRINCIPAL VERBS GOVERNING À BEFORE AN INFINITIVE.

s'abaisser à	*to stoop to*
aboutir à	*to result in*
s'accorder à	*to agree in*
s'acharner à	*to be intent on*
accoutumer à	*to accustom to*
s'accoutumer à	*to get used to*
s'aguerrir à	*to inure one's self to*
aider à	*to help*
aimer à	*to like to*
s'amuser à	*to amuse one's self in*
appeler à	*to appeal to*
s'appliquer à	*to apply one's self to*
apprendre à	*to teach*
s'apprêter à	*to get ready to*
s'attendre à	*to expect*
autoriser à	*to authorise*
avoir à	*to have to*
se borner à	*to limit one's self to*
chercher à	*to seek to*
commencer à	*to begin to*
se complaire à	*to delight in*
condamner à	*to condemn to*
consentir à	*to consent to*
consister à	*to consist in*
contraindre à	*to compel to*

contribuer à	to *contribute to*
convenir à	to *suit*
convier à	to *invite to*
se decider à	to *determine one's self to*
demander à	to *ask to*
se determiner à	to *resolve upon*
se disposer à	to *prepare one's self to*
se divertir à	to *amuse one's self in*
donner à	to *give to*
employer à	to *use in*
encourager à	to *encourage in*
engager à	to *invite to*
enseigner à	to *teach to*
s'épuiser à	to *exhaust one's self with*
être à	to *be occupied in*
exceller à	to *excel in*
exercer à	to *exercise in*
s'exercer à	to *exercise one's self in*
exhorter à	to *exhort to*
exposer à	to *expose to*
se fatiguer à	to *tire one's self in*
gagner à	to *gain in*
habituer à	to *accustom to*
s'habituer à	to *accustom one's self to*
se hasarder à	to *venture to*
hésiter à	to *hesitate to*
inviter à	to *invite to*
se mettre à	to *begin to*
montrer à	to *show how to*
s'obstiner à	to *persist in*
s'occuper à	to *be occupied in*
s'opiniâtrer à	to *persist in*
parvenir à	to *succeed in*
perdre à	to *lose by*
persister à	to *persist in*
se plaire à	to *delight in*
prendre plaisir à	to *take pleasure in*
pousser à	to *urge to*
se preparer à	to *prepare to*
reduire à	to *reduce to*
renoncer à	to *give up*
se résigner à	to *be resigned to*
se résoudre à	to *determine one's self to*
rester à	to *remain to*
réussir à	to *succeed in*
servir à	to *be of use in*
songer à	to *think of*
suffire à	to *suffice to*

tarder à	to *delay in*
tendre à	to *tend to*
tenir à	to *value*
travailler à	to *labour in*
venir à	to *happen to*
viser à	to *aim at*

35.   PRINCIPAL VERBS GOVERNING DE BEFORE AN INFINITIVE.

s'abstenir de	to *abstain from*
abuser de	to *misuse*
accuser de	to *accuse of*
achever de	to *complete*
affecter de	to *affect*
s'affliger de	to *grieve at*
s'agir de	to *be in question*
ambitionner de	to *aspire to*
appeler de	to *appeal against*
s'applaudir de	to *congratulate one's self on*
avertir de	to *warn to*
s'aviser de	to *take it into one's head to*
blamer de	to *blame for*
brûler de	to *be anxious to*
cesser de	to *cease*
charger de	to *commission to*
se charger de	to *take upon one's self to*
commander de	to *order to*
conjurer de	to *beseech to*
conseiller de	to *advise to*
se contenter de	to *be content with*
convenir de	te *agree, to own to*
craindre de	to *be afraid of*
dédaigner de	to *disdain*
défendre de	to *forbid to*
défier de	to *defy to*
demander de	to *ask to*
se depêcher de	to *hasten to*
désespérer de	to *despair of*
déferrer de	to *delay*
dire de	to *tell to*
discontinuer de	to *discontinue*
dispenser de	to *exempt from*
dissuader de	to *dissuade from*
empêcher de	to *prevent from*
s'ennuyer de	to *grow tired of*
entreprendre de	to *undertake to*

essayer de	*to try to*
s'étonner de	*to be astonished at*
éviter de	*to avoid*
excuser de	*to excuse for*
s'excuser de	*to apologize for*
exempter de	*to exempt from*
feindre de	*to feign*
féliciter de	*to congratulate on*
finir de	*to finish*
se flatter de	*to be sanguine of*
frémir de	*to shudder at*
se garder de	*to beware of*
gémir de	*to lament*
se glorifier de	*to glory in*
se hâter de	*to hasten to*
importer de	*to be important to*
s'indigner de	*to be indignant at*
jurer de	*to swear to*
louer de	*to praise for*
manquer de	*to neglect*
méditer de	*to plan*
menacer de	*to threaten to*
mériter de	*to deserve to*
négliger de	*to neglect*
offrir de	*to offer to*
omettre de	*to omit*
ordonner de	*to order to*
oublier de	*to forget to*
pardonner de	*to forgive for*
parler de	*to speak of*
permettre de	*to allow to*
persuader de	*to persuade to*
se piquer de	*to pride one's self on*
plaindre de	*to pity for*
se plaindre de	*to complain of*
presser de	*to urge to*
se presser de	*to hasten to*
prier de	*to ask, to beg to*
promettre de	*to promise to*
proposer de	*to propose*
se proposer de	*to propose*
punir de	*to punish for*
recommander de	*to recommend to*
redouter de	*to dread*
refuser de	*to refuse to*
regretter de	*to regret to*
se réjouir de	*to rejoice at*
remercier de	*to thank for*

se repentir de	*to repent of*
reprocher de	*to reproach for*
résoudre de	*to resolve to*
rire de	*to laugh at*
risquer de	*to risk*
rougir de	*to blush at*
sommer de	*to summon, to command to*
se souciar de	*to care*
souffrir de	*to be pained at*
soupçonner de	*to suspect of*
se souvenir de	*to remember*
suffire de	*to suffice to*
supplier de	*to beseech to*
tenter de	*to attempt to*
trembler de	*to tremble at*
se vanter de	*to boast of*
venir de	*to have just.*

FRENCH COMPOSITION PART I.

1. THEMISTOCLES.

When Themistocles was a boy, he was once, on returning from school met by Pisistratus. "Stand out of the way", said the master of Themistocles, "and give place to the prince." "What!" replied the boy boldly, "has he not room enough?"

2. ADMIRAL DRAKE.

Admiral Drake, when a young midshipman, on the eve of an engagement, was observed to shake and tremble very much: and being asked the cause, he replied: "My flesh trembles at the anticipation of the many and

---

1. THEMISTOCLES.

When Themistocles was child he met once, in returning from the school, Pisistratus. (Stand out of the way = *dérangez-vous*) said the master of Themistocles and make place to the prince. "What!" replied boldly the child, "is it that he has not enough of place."

2. THE ADMIRAL DRAKE.

When the admiral Drake was a young midshipman one remarked the eve of an engagement (that he shook and trembled very much = *qu'il tremblait de tous ses membres*) and to him of it having asked the cause, he replied: "My flesh trembles at the thought of the great

I

great dangers into which my resolute and undaunted heart will lead me."

3. THE MURAL CROWN.

The first among the Romans who was honoured with the mural crown was Manlius Capitolinus. When he was, as yet, not more than sixteen years of age, he had won the spoils of two enemies; and he lived to gain no less than thirteen civic garlands, and thirty other military rewards. It was this Manlius who defended and preserved the Capitol, when the Gauls had almost become the masters of it; and hence it was he received the surname of Capitolinus.

4. EPAMINONDAS.

Darius, king of Persia, sent great presents to Epaminondas, general of the Thebans, with a design to bribe him: "If Darius," said this great captain to those

───────────────

and numerous dangers in the midst of which my heart resolute and undaunted me will lead.

3. THE CROWN MURAL.

The first who among the Romans was honoured with (*de*) the crown mural was Manlius Capitolinus. At sixteen years he had obtained the spoils of two enemies and he lived (long enough = *assez longtemps*) to win at least thirteen garlands civic and thirty other rewards military. It was this Manlius who defended and preserved the Capitol when the Gauls (had almost made themselves the masters of it = *s'en étaient presque rendus maîtres*), and it was from there that he drew the surname of Capitolinus.

4. EPAMINONDAS.

Darius, king of Persia, sent some great presents to Epaminondas, general of the Thebans with the design of him to bribe: If Darius, said this great captain to

who brought these presents, "wishes to be a friend of
the Thebans, he needs not to buy my friendship; and if
he has other intentions, he has not riches enough to
bribe me," and he sent them back.

5. SOBRIETY.

One of the kings of Persia sent to the Caliph Mu-
stapha, a very skilful physician, who, on arriving, asked
what was the style of living at that court. He was
answered that they only ate when hungry, and never
entirely satisfied their appetite. "I may withdraw," said
he, "there is nothing to be done here."

6. HONOUR.

King Pyrrhus's physician having proposed to Fabricius, the Roman general, to poison his master, Fabricius
sent to Pyrrhus that traitor's letter, with these words:

---

those who brought these presents, wishes to ‿be the friend
of‿the Thebans he needs not (he needs not = *il n'a
pas besoin d'*) to‿buy my friendship, and if he has some
other intentions, he has not enough of riches for me
(*me* is the object) to‿bribe, and he them sent‿back.

5. THE SOBRIETY.

One of‿the kings of Persia sent to‿the Caliph Mu-
stapha a physician very skilful, who in arriving asked
which was the manner of to‿live of the court. One
to‿him answered that one not there (*y*) ate but (but =
que) when one had hunger, and that one not there
(there = *y*) satisfied never entirely his appetite. I can
me withdraw, said-he, there is nothing (there is nothing
= *il n'y a rien à*) to‿do for me here.

6. THE HONOUR.

The physician of‿the king Pyrrhus having proposed
to Fabricius general of the Romans of to‿poison his
master, Fabricius sent the letter of that traitor to Pyrrhus with these words: Prince, for the future (for the

"Prince, learn better for the future how to choose your friends and your foes". To requite this benefit, Pyrrhus sent back all the prisoners; but Fabricius received them only on condition that he would accept the like number of his; and wrote to him: "Do not believe, Pyrrhus, that I have discovered this treason to you from a particular regard to your person, but because the Romans abhor base stratagems, and scorn to triumph otherwise than by open force."

7. HUMANITY.

A friend of the Duke of Guise frequently represented to him the necessity there was for putting his affairs into better order, and gave him a list of useless people that he entertained about him. After the prince had examined it: "It is true," said he, "that I can live

---

future = *à l'avenir*) learn better how (*à*) to‿choose your friends and your foes. To requite this benefit, Pyrrhus sent‿back all the prisoners, but Fabricius not them received but (but = *que*) at condition that he would‿accept the same number of his (of his = *des siens*), and to‿him wrote: Not believe not, Pyrrhus, that I you have discovered this treason because I have a regard particular for your person, but because the Romans abhor the base stratagems and scorn (scorn = *dédaignent de*) to‿triumph otherwise that by the force open.

7. HUMANITY.

A friend of the Duke of Guise to‿him represented frequently the necessity that there was (there was = *il y avait*) of to‿put his affairs better order, and to‿him gave a list of‿the people useless that he entertained (entertained = *entretenait*) around of him. After that the prince it had examined: It is true, said he, that I can very well to‿live without these people, but, I you

very well without these people, but pray how will they
live without me?"

8. SHERIDAN WITTY TO THE LAST.

This great dramatic writer, orator, and wit was requested when dying to undergo "an operation." He
replied, that he had already submitted to two, which
were enough for one man's life-time. Being asked what
they were, he answered, "having his hair cut, and sitting for his picture."

9. BURKE.

This celebrated orator, the pride and glory of the
English parliament, being one day at church, was unexpectedly saluted with a political sermon, which, though
complimentary to his own views of public affairs, was

---

pray, how will they live (will live = the future of
the verb live placed before they) without me?

8. SHERIDAN WITTY UNTIL THE END.

When this great author dramatic, orator, and wit
(wit = *bel esprit*) was dying (was dying = *était à la
mort*) one him requested of to undergo an operation. He
replied, that he had already submitted to two (that he
had already submitted to two = *qu'il s'était déjà soumis
à deux opérations*) and that it was enough during the life
of a man. To him having asked what they (what they
= *ce qu'elles*) were, he answered having had his hair
cut (having had his hair cut = *se faire couper les cheveux*) and sitting (sitting = *poser*) for his picture (*portrait*).

9. BURKE.

This celebrated orator, the pride and the glory of the
Parliament English, being one day at the church was
unexpectedly (unexpectedly = *sans s'y attendre*) saluted
of a sermon political, which though, complimentary to
his own opinions on the affairs public was according to

in his opinion, so little suited to the place, that he displayed unequivocal symptoms of disapprobation by rising frequently, taking his hat as if to depart, and reseating himself with evident chagrin. "Surely," said he, on another occasion, "the church is a place where one day's truce may be allowed to the dissensions and animosities of mankind."

10. ERASMUS.

When Erasmus was a poor student at Paris, he was indeed very anxious to be a little richer; but, almost in rags as he was, it was not fine or even comfortable raiment after which he principally longed. "As soon ϗ as I get money," says he, in a letter to a friend, "I will buy first Greek books, and then clothes." "It is the mind," says Shakspeare, "that makes the body rich;" and so the young scholar felt. Of his two contemplated

---

him so little suited (so little suited = *si peu approprié*) to the place (place = *endroit*), that he showed some symptoms unequivocal of disapprobation in rising (*se levant*) frequently, in taking his hat as if he wished to‿depart, and in reseating (*se rasseyant*) with a chagrin evident. Assuredly, said he, another time (*fois*) the church is a place where one can allow a truce of a day to‿the dissensions and to‿the animosities of‿the mankind.

10. ERASMUS.

When Erasmus was a poor student (*étudiant*) at Paris, he desired much of to‿be a little richer, but although he was in rags (in rags = *en haillons*), it was neither (it was neither = *ce n'était ni*) some beautiful or even some comfortable raiment which he desired the most ardently. "As soon as I shall‿have some money", says he, in a letter to a friend, "I will‿buy first (*d'abord*) some books Greek and then some clothes." "It is the mind", says Shakspeare, "which renders the body rich;" and the young student it felt. Of his two purchases

purchases, it was not the clothes, he knew, but the Greek books, that were to bring him any thing permanent, either of enjoyment or distinction.

11. GENEROSITY OF DUGUAY-TROUIN.

In 1707, after the famous engagement between the English fleet and the combined squadrons of Duguay-Trouin and de Forbin, the king granted Duguay-Trouin a pension on the treasury of a thousand livres. Duguay-Trouin wrote to the minister begging him to bestow this pension on Mr. de Saint-Aubain, his second captain, who had lost a thigh in boarding the Cumberland and who had more need of a pension than himself. "I am too highly rewarded," added he, "if I obtain the promotion of my officers."

12. EXTRAORDINARY EFFECT OF ELOQUENCE.

The following anecdote is given as a proof of the

---

contemplated (*projetés*) he knew, that it was not the clothes, but the books Greek which to him would bring something of permanent either (*soit*) as enjoyment, either as distinction.

11. GENEROSITY OF DUGUAY-TROUIN.

In 1707, after the celebrated engagement between the fleet English and the squadrons (*escadres*) combined of Duguay-Trouin and of Forbin the king granted to Duguay-Trouin a pension of thousand livres on the treasury. Duguay-Trouin wrote to the minister him praying to bestow this pension on Mr. de Saint-Aubain, his second, who had lost a thigh at the boarding of the "Cumberland" and who of it had more want than himself. "I am much too rewared", added he, "if I obtain the advancement of my officers."

12. EFFECT EXTRAORDINARY OF THE ELOQUENCE.

One gives the anecdote following as a proof of the

irresistible power of Sheridan's speech in the House of
Commons on bringing forward his charge against Warren Hastings, a speech the effect of which upon its hearers has no parallel in the annals of ancient or modern
eloquence, when, as Mr. Pitt expressed it, all parties
were brought "under the wand of the enchanter." Mr.
Logan, well-known for his literary efforts, and author
of a most masterly defence of Warren Hastings, went
that day to the House of Commons prepossessed for the
accused and against his accuser. At the expiration of
the first hour he said to a friend: "All this is declamatory assertion without proof." — When the second
was finished: "This is a most wonderful oration." —
At the close of the third: "Mr. Hastings has acted very
unjustifiably." The fourth: "Mr. Hastings is a most
atrocious criminal;" and at last: "Of all monsters of
iniquity the most enormous is Warren Hastings!"

---

power irresistible of Sheridan in the House of Commons
(House of Commons = *chambre des communes*), when he
accused Warren Hastings, speech of which the effect
on its hearers has not of parallel in the annals of the
eloquence ancient or modern, when (*lorsque*) as it said
Mr. Pitt all the parties fell under the charm of the
enchanter. Mr. Logan well known by his efforts literary
and author of a defence of Warren Hastings, of the
most masterly, went that day to the House of Commons,
prepossessed in favour of the accused and against the accuser. At the expiration of the first hour, he said to a
friend: "All this is an assertion declamatory without
proof." At the end of the second hour: "It is an oration of the most marvellous." At the end of the third:
"Mr. Hastings has acted of a manner very unjustifiable."
At the fourth hour: "Mr. Hastings is a criminal of the
most atrocious" and at last: "Of all the monsters of
iniquity Warren Hastings is the worst."

13. COLLIN-HARLEVILLE.

One of Collin's old fellow-collegians meeting him by chance after thirty years' separation and availing himself of their former acquaintance, went to see him and confessed that he was in necessitous circumstances. Collin gave him not only money, but likewise many articles of his own wearing apparel; he supported his school-fellow some time in Paris until at length the latter determined to return to his department. Collin paid the expenses of the journey, conducted his friend to the coach-office and saw him take his seat inside; when the vehicle was just going to start (it was in the early part of November and the weather was beginning to get cold) Collin stepped aside, pulled off a good great-coat he had on and threw it in at the coach-door on the knees of the traveller, saying: "My friend, you

13. COLLIN-HARLEVILLE.

One of the friends of college of Collin-Harleville, him meeting by hazard after thirty years of separation and availing himself of (availing himself of = *profitant de*) their acquaintance of former times (of former times = *d'autrefois*) went him to see and confessed that he was in the want. Collin to him gave not only some money, but also many articles of his own clothes; he supported his school-fellow during some time, at Paris until, at the end the latter determined (*se décida*) to return in his department. Collin paid the expenses (*frais*) of the voyage, conducted his friend to the coach-office (*bureau des voitures*) and him saw take his place at the inside; as the vehicle was just going to start (was just going to start = *était sur le point de partir*) (it was at the beginning of November and the weather was beginning to be cold) Collin stepped aside (stepped aside = *fit un pas de côté*) pulled off a good great-coat which he wore, and it threw inside by the door (*portière*) of the coach, on the knees of the travel-

have forgotten your great-coat." This delicate manner
of giving rendered it impossible for the person obliged
not only to refuse, but even to return thanks for the
benefaction.

14. JEFFERSON'S OPINION ON THE FRENCH PEOPLE.

I cannot leave this great and good country without
expressing my sense of its pre-eminence of character
among the nations of the earth. A more benevolent
people I have never known, nor greater warmth and
devotedness in their select friendships. Their kindness
to strangers is unparalleled, and the hospitality of Paris
is beyond any thing I had conceived to be practicable
in a large city. Their eminence, too, in science, the
communicative dispositions of their scientific men, the
politeness of the general manners, the ease and vivacity
of their conversation, give a charm to their society to

---

ler in saying: My friend, you have forgotten your great-
coat. This manner delicate of to‿give prevented the
person obliged not only of to‿refuse but even of to‿thank
the benefacter.

14. OPINION OF JEFFERSON ON THE PEOPLE FRENCH.

I not can (not generally followed by *pas* after the
verb) leave this great and good country, without to‿ex-
press my sense of the pre-eminence of its character
among the nations of the Europe. I have never known
a people more benevolent or of whom the friendship
select was (*fût*) endowed of a warmth or of a devotedness greater. Their kindness towards the strangers is
without parallel and the hospitality of Paris is superior
to all that which I had believed possible in a great
town. Their eminence in the sciences, the disposition
communicative of their men of science, the politeness
of the customs (*mœurs*) general, the facility and the
vivacity of their conversation give also to their society
a charm that one cannot find elsewhere (that one cannot

be found nowhere else. In a comparison of this with other countries we have the proof of primacy which was given to Themistocles after the battle of Salamis. Every General voted to himself the first reward of valour, and the second to Themistocles. So, ask the travelled inhabitant of any nation, "In what country on earth would you rather live?" — "Certainly in my own, where are all my friends, my relations, and the earliest and sweetest affections and recollections of my life." — "Which would be your second choice?" — "France."

15. NAPOLEON.

While the French troops were encamped at Boulogne, public attention was excited by the daring attempt at escape made by an English sailor. This person having escaped from the depot, and having reached the sea

---

find elsewhere = *que l'on ne peut trouver autre part)*. When we compare this country to the others, we have the proof of the primacy granted to Themistocles after the battle of Salamis. Each general voted to himself (voted to himself = *se vota*) the greatest part of courage and granted to Themistocles the second. Ask also to the travellers of the other nations in which country they would prefer to live they will answer: "In my country where are all my friends, my parents and where are also and the sweetest affections and the most sweet remembrances of my youth. Which is that that you would choose after: "The France."

15. NAPOLEON.

When the troops French were encamped at Boulogne, the attention public was excited by the attempt daring that made (*fit*) a sailor English for to escape (*s'échapper*). This person having escaped from (having escaped from = *s'étant échappé du*) depot and having gained the

shore, the woods on which served him for concealment,
constructed, with no other instrument than a knife, a
boat entirely of the bark of trees. When the weather
was fair, he mounted a tree and looked out for the
English flag; and having at last observed a British
cruiser, he ran to the shore with his boat on his back,
and was about to trust himself in his frail vessel to the
waves, when he was pursued and arrested. Every
body in the army was anxious to see the boat, and
Napoleon, having at length heard of the affair, sent for
the sailor and interrogated him. "You must," said Napoleon, "have had a great desire to see your country
again, since you could resolve to trust yourself on the
open sea in so frail a bark. I suppose you have left
a sweetheart there." "No:" said the sailor, "but a poor
and infirm mother, whom I was anxious to see." "And

---

border of the sea, of which (*dont*) the woods to him
served for to hide (*se cacher*), constructed without other
instrument but (*que*) a knife, a boat made entirely of
the bark of the trees. When the weather was fair, he
mounted upon a tree and sought the flag English and
having at last observed a cruiser English, he ran on the
shore of the sea with his boat upon the back, and
was going to trust himself (to trust himself = *se con-
fier*) to the waves in his frail vessel, when one him
pursued and him arrested. Everybody in the army
was desirous of to see the boat and Napoleon, having
at last heard to speak of the affair, sent for (sent for =
envoya chercher) the sailor and him interrogated. You
must have had (you must have had = *vous avez dû
avoir*) said Napoleon, a great desire of to see again your
country, since you have been able to resolve (since you
have been able to resolve = *puisque vous avez pu vous
résoudre à*) you to trust at the sea in a bark so frail.
I suppose that you there have left a sweetheart. No,
said the sailor, but a poor mother infirm whom I

you shall see her," said Napoleon, giving at the same
time orders to set him at liberty and to bestow upon
him a considerable sum of money for his mother observing, that she must be a good mother, who had so good
a son.

16. CHARITY.

An old Austrian officer, who had but a small pension that was insufficient for the demands of his family,
came to the Emperor Joseph, exposed his indigent condition, and entreated his sovereign's compassion, adding
that he had ten children alive. Joseph, desirous to
know the certainty of this affair, went to the officer's
house in disguise, and instead of ten, found eleven children. "Why eleven?" said he. "It is a poor orphan,"
replied the soldier, "that I took into my house from

---

was⁀desirous of to⁀see. And you her shall⁀see, said
Napoleon, giving at the same time (at the same time
= *en même temps*) the order of him to⁀put in liberty and
of him to⁀bestow a sum of money considerable for his
mother, remarking that the⁀one (*celle*), who had a so
good son, must be (must be = *devait être*) a good mother.

16. THE CHARITY.

An old officer Austrian, who not had for the wants
of his family but (*que*) a small pension, which was insufficient, came to⁀find the emperor Joseph and to⁀him
exposed his condition of poverty and besought his sovereign of to⁀have pity of him adding that he had ten
children all living. Joseph desiring to⁀know the truth
of that affair disguised himself (disguised himself = *se
déguisa*) and went at⁀the⁀house⁀of⁀the officer, and
instead of ten children he of⁀them found eleven. "Why
are there (are there = *y en a-t-il*) eleven," said he.
"It is a poor orphan, replied the soldier, whom I have
taken in my house (in my house = *chez-moi*) by cha-

motives of charity." The Prince immediately ordered
a hundred florins to be given to each of his children.

17. SUCCESS IN THE NAVY.

John Bart commenced his career as a fisherman and
ended it as commander of a fleet; Ruyter, from a cabin
boy became Vice-Admiral of Holland. Van Tromp so
celebrated by his victories in the war with Spain and
England, was also the architect of his own fortune. Duquesne, who was the son of a captain, likewise succeeded
by the force of his merit. Born in 1610, he served
under his father at the age of 17. He fought sixty
years at sea, and his whole life was one continued series
of intrepid actions or signal victories. But it is his
wars in Sicily that have most contributed to his reputation.

There he had to encounter an enemy no less formi-
dable than the great Ruyter; and although inferior in

---

rity. The prince commanded that one might give, immediately hundred florins to each of the children.

17. SUCCESS IN THE NAVY.

John Bart commenced his career as fisherman and
it ended as commander of a fleet. Ruyter of cabin boy
that he was became Vice Admiral of Holland. Van
Tromp so celebrated by his victories in the war against
the Spain and the England, was also the architect of his
own fortune. Duquesne who was son of a captain succeeded likewise by the force of his merit. Born in 1610
he served under his father at the age of 17 years. He
fought (*combattit*) during sixty years in sea and all his
life was a series of actions intrepid or of victories signal. But it is (it is = *ce sont*) his wars in Sicily which
have the most contributed to his reputation.

It was there that he had to encounter (that he had
to encounter = *qu'il eut à en venir aux mains*) with
Ruyter; and although inferior in number, he defeated

number, he defeated the combined fleets of Holland and
Spain, on the 8th of January, the 22nd of April and
the 2nd of June 1676. In the second of these engagements Ruyter was killed. Asia, Africa and Europe witnessed in turn his valour. Duquesne became Admiral
of the French naval forces and died on the 2nd of February 1688, at the age of 78. Duguay-Trouin too, the
commencement of whose career was still more obscure,
rose to the highest ranks in the Navy. Such examples
cannot be too frequently laid before the public in general and young mariners in particular, in order that all
may learn that great talents may lead to the highest
places and that merit has no need of ancestors.

18. A PROMISE IS SACRED.

A Spanish cavalier, having assassinated a Moorish
gentleman, instantly fled from justice. He was vigorously

---

the fleets combined of Holland and of Spain, the eight
January, the twenty two April and the two June 1676.
Ruyter was killed in the second of these engagements.
The Asia, the Africa and the Europe were, in turn (in
turn = *tour à tour*) witnesses of his valour. Duquesne
became admiral of the forces naval of the France and
died the two February 1688 at the age of 78 years.
Duguay - Trouin of whom (*dont*) the beginning of the
career was still (*encore*) more obscure rose (*s'éleva*)
to the highest ranks in the navy. One cannot too often
to place of such examples before the public in general
and in particular before the young mariners, in order
that (in order that = *afin que*) all may learn that the
great talents may lead to the highest places and that
the merit has no need of ancestors.

18. A PROMISE IS SACRED.

A cavalier Spanish having assassinated a gentleman
Moorish fled (*s'enfuit*) instantly for to escape to the
justice. He was pursued vigorously, but availing him-

pursued; but, availing himself of a sudden turn in the road, he leapt unperceived over a garden-wall. The proprietor, who was also a Moor, happened to be at that time walking in the garden, and the Spaniard falling upon his knees before him, acquainted him with his case, and, in the most pathetic manner, implored concealment. The Moor listened to him with compassion, and generously promised his assistance. He then locked him up in a summer-house, and left him with the assurance that, when night came, he would provide for his escape. A few hours afterwards, the dead body of his son was brought to him, and the description of the murderer exactly agreed with the appearance of the Spaniard whom he had then in custody. He concealed the horror and suspicion which he felt, and, retiring to his chamber, he remained there till midnight. Then going privately into the garden, he opened the door of

---

self (availing himself = *profitant d'un*) turn sudden on the road he leapt without to be seen over a wall of garden. The proprietor who was also Moorish was walking (was walking = *se promenait*) then in the garden, and the Spaniard throwing himself upon his knees (upon his knees = *à genoux*) before him, acquainted him with (acquainted him with = *lui fit part de*) his case and him implored of the fashion the most pathetic of him to conceal. The Moor him listened with compassion and to him promised generously his aid. Then he him shut into a summer-house and him left in to him assuring that, when the night should come, he to him would give the means of to escape. Some hour after one to him brought the body dead of his son and after (*d'après*) the description of the assassin which agreed (agreed = *s'accordait*) exactly with the appearance of the Spaniard that he had taken under his guard. He did not showed the horror and the suspicion which he felt and withdrawing (*se retirant*) in his room he there remained until midnight. Then going in secret into the garden he opened the door of the summer-house, and thus accosted the cavalier: "Christian, the youth whom you have murdered was my only son. Your crime deserves the severest punishment. But I have solemnly pledged my word not to betray you, and I disdain to violate a rash engagement even with a cruel enemy." He then conducted the Spaniard to the stables, and furnishing him with one of his swiftest mules: "Flee," said he, "while the darkness of the night conceals you. Your hands are polluted with blood; but God is just, and I humbly thank him that my faith is unspotted, and that I have resigned judgment to him."

19. CORREGIO.

This celebrated painter sold, at a very moderate price, some of those master-pieces which now adorn the galleries of amateurs. His greatest enjoyment consisted in relieving the unfortunate, and the consequence was

---

the summer-house and accosted thus the cavalier. "Christian, the young man that you have killed is my only son (only son = *fils unique*). Your crime deserves the punishment the most severe. But I me am engaged solemnly to not you betray and I disdain of to violate an engagement rash, even with an enemy cruel." He conducted then the Spaniard to the stables and to him giving one of the mules the most swift. "Save yourself" (*vous*), said he, "whilst the darkness of the night you conceal. Your hands are polluted of blood, but God is just and I him thank humbly of that which (*que*) my faith is not polluted and that I have left the judgment between his hands."

19. CORREGIO (*LE CORRÈGE*).

This painter celebrated sold at a price very moderate some (*quelques uns*) of the master-pieces which adorn to-day the galleries of the amateurs. His greatest pleasure was of to relieve the unfortunate and in conse-

that he lived and died in a situation bordering on
poverty.

The end of this great genius commands respect, and
claims our sincere regret. Having gone one day to
Parma, in order to receive the value of a picture, instead of being paid in gold or silver, he was presented
with an enormous bag containing twelve hundred francs
in copper. He durst not refuse it: his family was in
extreme want, and his sick mother had been confined
to her bed during several weeks. "O my good mother,"
cried he, "this is for you." In order to afford her immediate assistance, he would carry the money himself;
but the ardent zeal which animated him, and the burden
with which he was laden, overcame him.

Arriving exhausted and covered with perspiration,
he embraced his mother, took to his bed, and died a
few days after of an inflammation of the chest.

---

quence he lived and died in a situation neighbour of
the poverty.

The end of this great genius commands the respect
and claims our regrets sincere. Being gone one day to
Parma (*Parme*) in order to receive the amount of a
picture instead of to͜be paid in gold or in silver, one
to͜him presented a bag enormous containing 1200 francs
in copper. He durst not (*n'osa pas*) it to͜refuse: his
family was in a poverty extreme and his mother sick
had kept the room during several weeks. "O my good
mother," cried he (*s'écria-t-il*), "this is for you." In
order to to͜her to͜procure (some assistance = *des secours*) immediate, he would (*voulut*) to͜carry the money
himself, but the zeal ardent and the burden with which
he was laden him overcame.

Being arrived exhausted and covered of perspiration
he embraced his mother (took to his bed = *se mit au
lit*) and in a͜few days he died of an (inflammation of
the chest = *fluxion de poitrine*).

20. ADMIRAL BLAKE'S HONOUR.

In February 1650, Blake, still continuing to cruise, in the Mediterranean sea, met a French ship of considerable force, and commanded the captain to come on board, there being no war declared between the two nations. The captain, when he came, was asked by him, whether he was willing to lay down his sword, and yield, which he gallantly refused, though in his enemy's power. Blake, scorning to take advantage of an artifice, and detesting the appearance of treachery, told him, "that he was at liberty to go back to his ship, and defend it as long as he could." The captain willingly accepted his offer, and, after a fight of two hours, confessed himself conquered, kissed his sword, and surrendered it.

21. ROBERT BURNS.

Robert Burns, the author of Tam O'Shanter and the Cotter's Saturday-night, was about thirteen years of age,

---

20. HONOUR OF THE ADMIRAL BLAKE.

In February 1650 whilst that Blake was‿continuing to cruise in the Mediterranean he met a ship French of a force considerable and commanded to‿the captain of to‿come on board (*à bord*) as there was not (there was not = *il n'y avait pas*) then of war between the two nations. When the captain came he to‿him asked if he was‿willing render his sword and yield, that which he refused gallantly although at‿the power of his enemy. Blake scorning of to‿profit of an artifice and detesting the appearance of the treachery to‿him told, that he was free of to‿return to his ship and of it to‿defend as long as he it could. The captain accepted willingly his offer and after a fight of two hours he (confessed himself = *se reconnut*) vanquished, kissed his sword and it surrendered.

21. ROBERT BURNS.

Robert Burns, author of Tam O'Shanter and of‿the "Cotter's Saturday-night" had about (*environ*) 13 years

when Murdoch was appointed parish school-master of
Ayr, upon which Burns was sent for a few weeks to
attend his school. He was now with me, says Murdoch,
day and night, in school, at all meals and in all my
walks. At the end of one week, I told him that, as he
was now pretty much master of the parts of speech,
etc., I should like to teach him something of French
pronunciation; that when he should meet with the name
of a French town, ship, officer, or the like, in the newspapers, he might be able to pronounce it something
like a French word. Robert was glad to hear this proposal, and immediately we attacked the French with
great courage. Now there was little else to be heard
but the declension of nouns, the conjugation of verbs,
etc. When walking together, and even at meals, I was
constantly telling him in French the names of different

---

when Murdoch was appointed (parish school master =
maître d'école communale) at Ayr upon what Burns was
sent to his school during a few weeks. Then, says
Murdoch, he was with me day and night, at the school
at all the meals and in all my walks. At the end of
a week I to him told that as he knew pretty (*assez*)
well the parts of the (speech = *discours*) etc. I should like
(*voudrais*) to him to teach something of the pronunciation
French, in order that when he should find the name
of a town French or of a ship or of an officer or (the
like = *quelque chose de semblable*) in the newspapers,
he might be able it pronounce nearly as a word French.
Robert was content of that proposal and we attacked
immediately the French with a great courage. Then
one not heard hardly more than some declensions of
nouns and some conjugations of verbs etc. When (we
walked = *nous nous promenions*) together or even at the
meals, I to him said constantly in French the nouns
of the different objects which (presented themselves =

objects, as they presented themselves, so that he was hourly laying in a stock of words, and sometimes little phrases. In short, he took such pleasure in learning, and I in teaching, that it was difficult to say which of the two was the more zealous in the business; about the end of the second week of our study of the French, we began to read a little of the "Adventures of Telemachus," in Fenelon's own words.

Another week, however, was scarcely over, when the young student was obliged to leave school for the labours of the harvest. I did not, however, lose sight of him, but was a frequent visitant at his father's house, when I had my half-holiday; and very often went, accompanied by one or two persons more intelligent than myself, that good William Burns might enjoy a mental feast. Then the labouring oar was shifted to some other hand. The father and the son sat down with us, when

---

se présentaient) of such fashion, that at all hour he accumulated a provision of words and sometimes of little phrases. In short he had so much of pleasure to learn and I to to him to teach, that it was difficult of to say which of the two was the more zealous. Towards the end of the second week of our study of the French we began to read a little of the adventures of Telemachus in the language even of Fénélon. One other week (had scarcely = *s'était à peine*) passed that the young student was obliged of to leave the school for the works of the harvest. However I not him lost of sight and I used to go often at the house of his father, when I had a holiday and I was often accompanied of one or two persons more intelligent than I (in order that = *afin que*) the good William Burns might be able to enjoy of a feast of the mind. Then the work passed into some other hands. The father and the son (sat down = *s'asseyaient*)

we enjoyed a conversation wherein solid reasoning,
sensible remark, and a moderate seasoning of jocularity
were so nicely blended as to render it palatable to all
parties. Robert had a hundred questions to ask me
about the French, etc.; and the father, who had always
rational information in view, had still some question to
propose to my more learned friends upon moral or
natural philosophy, or some such interesting subject.
It is delightful to contemplate such scenes of humble
life as these, showing us, as they do, what the desire
of intellectual cultivation may accomplish, in any circumstances.

22. GALILEO.

A very beautiful example of the way in which some
of the most valuable truths of natural philosophy have

---

with us and then we enjoyed of a conversation where
the reasoning solid, the remarks sensible and a quantity
moderate of jocularity (were mixed = *se mélaient*) so
well, that it was at the taste of everybody. Robert
had hundred questions to me ask at the subject of the
French and the father who had always in view the
knowledge rational had also some questions to ask to my
friends more learned, on the moral or on the natural philosophy or on some other subject as interesting. It is a
pleasure of to contemplate of such scenes in the life
humble, to us showing as they it do (what can = *ce
que peut*) accomplish the desire of the culture intellectual
in (any circumstances = *n'importe quelles circonstances*).

22. GALILEO (*GALILÉE*).

The discovery of the regularity of the oscillations
of the pendulum by Galileo to us offers a very fine
example of the manner by which the discovery of the
truths the most precious of the natural philosophy have

been suggested for the first time by the simplest inci-
dents of common life is afforded by Galileo's discovery
of the regularity of oscillations in the pendulum. It was
while standing one day in the metropolitan church of
Pisa, that his attention was first awakened to this most
important fact, by observing the movements of a lamp
suspended from the ceiling, which some accident had
disturbed and caused to vibrate. Now this, or something
exactly similar, was a phenomenon which, of course,
every one had observed thousands of times before. But
yet nobody had ever viewed it with the philosophic
attention with which it was on this occasion examined
by Galileo. Or if, as possibly was the case, any one
had been half unconsciously struck for a moment by
that apparent equability of motion which arrested so
forcibly the curiosity of Galileo, the idea had been
allowed to escape the instant it had been caught, as
relating to a matter not worth a second thought. The

---

been suggested for the first time by the accidents the
most simple of the life of all the days. It was during
that he was once in the church metropolitan of Pisa,
that his attention was attracted towards that fact very
important in observing the motion of a lamp suspended
at the ceiling that an accident whatever had moved
and made to vibrate. Now (*or*) this accident, or something of similar was an accident which all the world
had observed some thousands of times. And however
nobody not it had yet remarked with the attention philosophical that Galileo to it put. Or if as it is possible
one had been unconsciously struck of this equality apparent of motion which stopped so forcibly the curiosity
of Galileo one had left the idea to escape (*s'échapper*)
as soon as caught as an affair on which (it was not
worth the trouble == *il ne valait pas la peine*) of to stop
(*s'arrêter*). The young philosopher (*physicien*) of Italy

young philosopher of Italy (for he had not then reached
his twentieth year) saw at once the important applications which might be made of the thought that had
suggested itself to him. He took care, therefore, to
ascertain immediately the truth of his conjecture by
careful and repeated experiments; and the result was
the complete discovery of the principle of the most perfect measure of time which we yet possess.

23. CHARLES IX OF FRANCE.

This prince was only ten years of age, when he was
crowned. His mother, Catherine de Medicis, mention-
ing her apprehension that the fatigue of the ceremony
might perhaps be too much for him; he replied, "Madam,
I will very willingly undergo as much fatigue, as often
as you have a crown to bestow upon me." When the
Constable de Montmorency died, the young prince, then

(he had not yet reached his twentieth year) saw
(at‿once = *de suite*) the applications important that
one could make of the thought which itself (*s'*) was
presented to him. Therefore he took care of to‿prove
at‿once the truth of his conjecture by some experiments
made with care and often repeated and the result of‿it
was the discovery complete of‿the principle of the most
perfect measure of‿the time which we have (*ayons*) until
this day.

23. CHARLES IX OF FRANCE.

This prince (had but = *n'avait que*) ten years, when
he was crowned. As his mother Catherine of Medicis
to‿him made part of the fear which she had that the
fatigue of the ceremony (might he = *ne soit*) too strong
for him, he replied: Madam, I shall‿endure willingly
the same fatigue all the times (*fois*) that you shall‿have
a crown to me to‿give. When the Constable of Mont-

only seventeen, did not immediately appoint another person to that high office, saying, "I will carry my own sword in future." And to his mother, who wished to keep him under her own direction, he said, that he would no longer be kept in a box, like the old jewels of the crown.

24. HOW TO ASK FOR A PENNY.

It has often been said, that the Members of the Society of Friends are possessed from their youth of more than an ordinary share of acuteness. The following fact may serve as a proof of this assertion: — Some time ago, Mr. —, a most respectable ironfounder, of Birmingham, discovered that his son, a boy five years of age, was accustomed to ask gentlemen who came to his house, to give him money. He immediately extorted a promise from him, under a threat of correction,

---

morency died, the young prince, then aged of 17 ans (did not name == *ne nomma pas*) immediately an other person to that high employ, saying, (In future == *à l'avenir*) I shall⁀carry my own sword. And to his mother who desired to⁀continue to him to⁀direct he said: that he (would not == *ne voulait pas*) to⁀be longer shut⁀up in a box like the jewels of the crown.

24. HOW ONE ASKS A PENNY.

One has often said that the members of the Society of⁀the Friends possess as⁀soon⁀as their youth a share more than ordinary of acuteness. The fact following can serve of proof to this assertion. (Some time ago == *il y a quelque temps*) Mr. — ironfounder of Birmingham very respectable, discovered (*s'aperçut*) that his son a boy of 5 years had the habit of to⁀ask to⁀the (gentlemen == *messieurs*) who came (to his house == *chez lui*) of to⁀him to⁀give some money. He to⁀him made to⁀promise immediately, him threatening of a punishment that he not it

that he would not do so any more. The next day Mr.
—, his father's partner, called, and the boy evaded a
breach of his promise by saying, "Friend, dost thou
know any one who would lend me a penny, and not
require it of me again?"

25. LIBERTY OF THE PRESS IN ENGLAND.

Till the revolution of 1688, the liberty of the press
was very imperfectly enjoyed in England, and only during a very short period. The Star-chamber, while that
court subsisted, put effectual restraints upon printing. On
the suppression of that tribunal in 1641, the Long Parliament, after their rupture with the king, assumed the
same power with regard to the licensing of books; and
this authority was continued during all the period of
the republic and protectorship. Two years after the

---

would do more. The day next Mr. —, partner of his
father, came and the child avoided of to break (*manquer à*)
his promise in saying: "Friend knowest thou anyone
who (would be willing = *voulût*) me to lend a penny
and who not me it (would ask again = *redemande-
rait pas*).

25. THE LIBERTY OF THE PRESS IN ENGLAND.

Until the revolution of 1688 the England enjoyed
very imperfectly of the liberty of the Press or (it =
elle) (of it = *n'en*) enjoyed but very little of time.
So long as the Star Chamber existed it put a restraint
effectual to the press. At the suppression of this tribunal in 1641 the Long Parliament after its rupture with
the king, (took possession = *s'empara*) of the same power
in that which concerned the authorisation of the books
and that authority continued during all the period of
the Republic and of the protectorship. Two years after

' Restoration, an act was passed reviving the republican ordinances. This act expired in 1679; but was revived in the first year of king James. The liberty of the press did not even commence with the revolution. It was not till 1694˙ that the restraints were taken off, to the great displeasure of the king and his ministers, who, seeing nowhere, in any government, during present or past ages, any example of such unlimited freedom, doubted much of its salutary effects, and probably thought, that no books or writings would ever so much improve the general understanding of men, as to render it safe to entrust them with so easily abused an indulgence.

26. SINCERITY.

A Corsican gentleman who had been taken prisoner by the Genoese, was thrown into a dark dungeon, where he was chained to the ground. While he was in this

----

the restoration one passed an act which (revived = *remit en vigueur*) the ordinances republican. This act expira in 1679 but was revived during the first year of the reign of (James = *Jacques*). The liberty of the press not commenced even not at the revolution. It not was but (*que*) in 1694 that one removed the obstacles, at the great displeasure of the king and of his ministers who not seeing nowhere under (any = *aucun*) government, either in the present or in the past an example of a liberty so illimited, doubted of its effect salutary and thought probably that it was impossible that any book or writing (*écrit*) (might = *pût*) ever raise the judgment of the men enough for that one might without danger to them permit à pleasure of which one abuses so easily.

26. SINCERITY.

A Corsican who had been made prisoner by the Genoese was thrown into a dark prison where he was chained to the soil. During that he was in that dismal posi-

dismal situation, the Genoese sent a message to him,
that if he would accept of a commission in their service,
he might have it. "No," said he, "were I to accept
your offer, it would be with a determined purpose to
take the first opportunity of returning to the service of
my country. I would not have my countrymen even
suspect that I could be one moment unfaithful."

27. THE DUKE OF GRAFTON.

The late Duke of Grafton, when hunting, was thrown
into a ditch. At this moment a young curate called out,
"Lie still, my lord"; and leaping over him, pursued his
sport. Such an apparent want of feeling might have
been supposed to offend his Grace; but on the contrary,
he knew the enthusiastic ardour which the chase excites,
and on being helped out by his attendant, enquired the
name of the curate, saying: "He shall have the first

t.?

---

tion the Genoese to him sent a message, saying that
if he (would = *voulait*) to accept a commission in their
service he might it have. No, said he for if I accepted
your offer it would be with the plan well determined
of me to save and to reenter at the service of my
country at the first opportunity. I (not would = *ne
voudrais pas*) that my countrymen, might (*pussent*) suspect for one moment that I am without faith.

27. THE DUKE OF GRAFTON.

(The late = *feu le*) duke of Grafton one day that
he was hunting was thrown into a ditch. At that moment a young curate cried, (Lie still = *ne bougez
pas*) my lord and jumping over (*par dessus*) him pursued his hunting. One might have (*aurait pu*) to suppose that a such want apparent of feeling had offended
his lordship, but (on the = *au*) contrary, he knew the
ardour enthusiastic which the hunt excites and as his servant him helped to get out of the ditch he (inquired =
s'informa) of the name of the curate in saying, He

good living that falls to my disposal for his sportsman-
like courage; but had he stopped to have taken care of
me, I would never have thought of noticing him."

28. HOW TO PROCURE A DINNER.

Doctor Arne, a celebrated English musician, when
once travelling, stopped at an inn where, in consequence
of the house being full, he found great difficulty in procuring a dinner. The only joint remaining had just
been taken off the spit, and was about to be served to
a party of gentlemen. On learning this, Arne took a
fiddle-string from his pocket, cut it into small pieces
and strewed it over the meat, so that it had the appearance of being covered with maggots. When it was
served, the gentlemen scolded the waiter for daring to
offer them such meat, and ordered him to take it away.
Arne expected this result, and requested the waiter to

---

will‿have the first good benefice which will‿be at my
disposal for his courage of sportsman, but if (he had ==
s'était) stopped, for to‿take care of‿me, I not would‿have
ever dreamt (to reward him == *à le récompenser*).

28. HOW ONE (PROCURES == *SE PROCURER*) TO DINE.

As the Dr. Arne, celebrated musician English, was‿tra-
velling once he (stopped == *s'arrêta*) at an inn. As it
was full he had a great difficulty (to procure == *à se
procurer*) to dine. The only joint that it remained (had
just been == *venait d'être*) taken‿off of the spit, and
(was going to be served == *allait être servi*) to a society
of gentlemen. In learning this Arne drew from his
pocket a fiddle-string, it cut in small pieces and it strewed
over the meat for to‿it give the appearance of to‿be
covered with maggots. When it was served, the gentlemen scolded the waiter for to‿dare to‿them to‿offer
of such meat and to‿him commanded (to == *de*) it
take‿away. Arne (expected == *s'attendait à*) that and
requested the waiter of it to‿him to‿serve in saying

serve it to him, saying that he would endeavour to make
a dinner of it. Having eaten heartily, he told the trick
he had played, made himself known, and had a hearty
laugh at the expense of the hungry gentlemen.

29. "ORDERS."

A French author, who had produced a very doubtful
production, was very liberal in the distribution of orders
on the first night of its performance. However the play
was so bad, that all his friends deserted him, except
one, who faithful to his promise, was reduced at last
to hiss and cheer at the same time. "Is it possible",
said a spectator, "that you can approve and disapprove
at the same time?" "No, no," said he, "that is not the
case: I know this play is the most execrable thing
that ever was performed, but I came in with an order,
and have a great regard for the author, and so that I

---

that he would strive of of it to make his dinner. Having well eaten, he related the trick which he had played,
(made himself known == *se fit connaître*) and laughed
(heartily == *de bon cœur*) at the expense of the gentlemen hungry.

29. "ORDERS" ("*BILLETS DE FAVEUR*").

An author French who had written a piece of (little
== *peu de*) value distributed very generously some tickets
of favour for the first representation. However the
piece was so bad that all his friends him abandoned
except one who faithful to his promise was at last reduced to whistle and to applaud in same time. Is it
possible, said a spectator, that you (can == *puissiez*)
praise and condemn in same time. No, no, said he,
(it is not thus == *il n'en est pas ainsi*) I know that this
piece is the most detestable which one (has == *ait*) ever
represented, but I am come with an order and I respect
much the author and in order (not to harm == *de ne*

may neither wrong him nor my own judgment, I have
abused the play out of justice to myself until I am
hoarse; and I have clapped it to oblige him until my
hands are sore."

30. LORD BYRON'S IDEA OF HIS OWN SUPERIORITY.

A dialogue which Lord Byron himself used to mention as having taken place between him and Polidori,
an Italian physician and an exceedingly vain young man.
"It was during their journey on the Rhine, and is amu-
singly characteristic of both the persons concerned. "After all," said the physician, "what is there you can do,
that I cannot?" "Why, since you force me to say,"
answered the other, "I think there are three things I
can do which you cannot." Polidori defied him to name
them. "I can," said Lord Byron, "swim across this
river. — I can snuff out that candle with a pistol-shot

---

faire tort) neither to to him nor to my judgment, I condemn the piece by justice for myself (until I am hoarse
= *jusqu'à en être enroué*) and I it have applauded for
him to oblige (until my hands are sore = *jusqu'à ce
que les mains m'en fassent mal*).

30. IDEA OF LORD BYRON ON HIS OWN SUPERIORITY.

Dialogue that Lord Byron himself had the habit of
to relate as having (taken place = *eu lieu*) between
him and Polidori physician italian young and excessively
vain. "It took place during their voyage upon the Rhine
and characterizes of a fashion amusing the two persons
in question.

After all said the physician, what can you do that
I not may do. Now, since you me force to it to say,
replied the other, I believe that (there are = *il y a*)
three things which I can do and that you not can
do. Polidori him defied of them to name. I can,
said Lord Byron, cross this river (by swimming = *à la
nage*). I can snuff this candle of a (pistol-shot = *coup*

at the distance of twenty paces — and I have written
a poem (the Corsair) of which 14,000 copies were sold
in one day."

31. GOLDSMITH'S FIRST ARRIVAL IN LONDON.

After having fruitlessly applied to several apothecaries, in hopes of being received in the capacity of a journeyman, Goldsmith was at length taken into the laboratory
of a chemist who was struck with his forlorn condition
and the simplicity of his manners. Here he continued
till he discovered that his old friend Dr. Sleigh was in
London. "It was Sunday," said Goldsmith, "when I paid
him a visit; and it is to be supposed, in my best clothes.
Sleigh scarcely knew me; such is the tax the unfortunate pay to poverty. However, when he did recollect
me, I found his heart as warm as ever! and he shared
his purse and his friendship with me during his conti-
nuance in London."

---

de pistolet) at 20 paces and I have written a poem (the
Corsair) of which one has sold 14 000 (copies = *exemplaires*) in one day.

31. FIRST ARRIVAL OF GOLDSMITH AT LONDON.

After (having applied = *s'être adressé*) in vain at
several apothecaries in the hope of to be admitted in
quality of (journeyman = *homme de peine*) Goldsmith was
at last accepted in the laboratory of a chemist who was
struck of his condition forlorn and of the simplicity of
his manners. He there remained until that he discovered
that his old friend the Dr. Sleigh was at London. It
was a sunday, says Goldsmith, when I to him made a
visit and as one can it to suppose clad of my best clothes. Sleigh me recognized hardly, such is the tax which
the unfortunate pay to the poverty. However when (he
had remembered me = *il se fut souvenu de moi*) I found
that his heart was as warm as ever and he shared with
me his purse and his friendship during his stay at London.

32. EXTRACT FROM A LEISURELY GENTLEMAN'S DIARY.

Monday, 8 o'clock. I put on my clothes and walked into the parlour.

9 o'clock. Tied my knee-strings and washed my hands. Hours 10, 11 and 12. Smoked three cigars. Read the "Times" and "Morning Chronicle". Things go ill in the North. Mr. Nisby's opinion on them.

One o'clock in the afternoon. Scolded Frank for mislaying my cigar-case.

2 o'clock. Sat down to dinner. Too many plums, and no suet. Wine excellent.

From three to four. Took my afternoon's nap.

From four to six. Walked in St. James's Park. Wind S. S. E. (South South East).

From six to ten. At the coffee-house. Mr. Nisby's opinion about the peace.

Ten o'clock. Went to bed, slept soundly.

---

32. EXTRACT FROM THE JOURNAL OF A MAN OF LEISURE.

Monday, 8 o'clock. (I put on my clothes = *je me suis habillé*) and am entered at the parlour.

9 o'clock. I have attached my cords of breeches and me am washed the hands.

10 o'clock, 11 o'clock and noon. I have smoked 3 cigars. I have read the "Times" and the "Morning Chronicle". The affairs go badly in the North. Opinion of Mr. Nisby upon these affairs.

1 o'clock of the afternoon. Have reprimanded Frank for to have mislaid my cigar-case.

2 o'clock. I me am put to table for to dine. Too many plums and not enough of suet. Wine excellent.

From three to four. Have made my nap of the afternoon.

From four to six. Me am walked in the Park of St. James. Wind S. S. E.

From six to ten. At the coffee house. Opinion of Mr. Nisby upon the peace.

10 o'clock. Am gone me to lie down. Have slept profoundly.

33. SIR RICHARD STEELE.

Sir Richard Steele, the founder and principal conductor of the "Tatler", the "Spectator" and the "Guardian",
and at the same time, a dramatic writer of considerable
merit, having one day invited to his house a great many
persons, they were surprised at the number of liveries which
surrounded the table; and after dinner, when wine and
mirth had set them free from the observation of rigid
ceremony, one of them inquired of Sir Richard, how
such an expensive train of domestics could be consistent
with his fortune. Sir Richard very frankly confessed,
that they were fellows of whom he would willingly be
rid: and being then asked why he did not discharge
them, declared that they were bailiffs, who had introduced themselves with an execution, and whom, since
he could not send them away, he had thought it con-

---

33. SIR RICHARD STEELE.

Sir Richard Steele, founder and principal (manager
= *gérant*) of the Tatler, of the Spectator and of the
Guardian and in same time author dramatic of a merit
considerable, having one day invited (at his house =
chez lui) a great number of persons, they were surprised
of to see the number of persons in livery around of the
table, and after dinner when the wine and the mirth
(them = *les*) had delivered of the observance of the
strict ceremony, the one of them asked to Sir Richard
Steele how he could (*pouvait*) have (such an expensive train
of domestics = *un domestique aussi couteux*) with his fortune. Sir Richard confessed very frankly that they were
some people of whom (he would willingly be rid = *il
serait content d'être debarrassé*): and to him having asked
why he not they had (discharged = *congédiés*) he declared that they were some (bailiffs = *recors*) (who had
introduced themselves with an execution = *qui s'étaient
présentés avec un jugement de saisie*) and whom, as he
not could them send away, (he had thought convenient

venient to embellish with liveries, that they might do
him credit while they staid.

His friends were diverted with the expedient, and
by paying the debt, discharged their attendance, having
obliged Sir Richard to promise that they should never
again find him graced with a retinue of the same kind.

34. SHERIDAN'S INATTENTION TO BUSINESS.

Sheridan, going one day to the banking-house where
he was accustomed to receive his salary as Receiver of
Cornwall, and where they sometimes accommodated him
with small sums before the regular time of payment,
asked, with all due humility whether they could oblige
him with the loan of twenty pounds, "Certainly, Sir,"
said the clerk, "would you like any more, fifty or a
hundred?" Sheridan all smiles and gratitude, answered
that a hundred pounds would suit him much better.

== *il avait cru commode d'*) to dress in livery for that
they to him (should make == *fassent*) (credit == *hon-
neur*) as long as that they should stay. His friends (were
diverted with == *s'amusèrent de*) the expedient and in
paying the debt, paid their attendance having obliged
Sir Richard to promise that they not him (find again ==
retrouveraient pas) graced of a retinue of the same kind.

34. SHERIDAN, HIS WANT OF ATTENTION (TO BUSINESS == *AUX AFFAIRES*).

One day that Sheridan was going to the Bank
where he had custom of to receive his (salary == *appoin-
tements pl.*) of Receiver of Cornwall and where one to him
advanced sometimes (small sums == *de petites sommes*)
before the epoch regular of the payment, asked with all
the humility suitable if one could him to oblige in to him
lending 20 pounds. Certainly Sir, said the clerk, (would
you like any more == *en voudriez-vous davantage*), fifty
or hundred? Sheridan, smiling and full of gratitude replied
that 100 pounds (would suit him much better == *feraient*

"Perhaps you would like to take two hundred, or three?" said the clerk. At every increase of the sum, the surprise of the borrower increased. "Have you not then received our letter?" said the clerk; on which it turned out that, in consequence of the falling in of some fine, a sum of twelve hundred pounds had been lately placed to the credit of the Receiver-general, and that, from not having opened the letter written to apprize him, he had been left in ignorance of his good luck.

35. RUSTIC POLITENESS.

The father of Lord Abingdon, who was remarkable for the stateliness of his manners, one day riding through a village in the vicinity of Oxford, met a lad dragging a calf along the road, who, when his lordship came up to him, made a stop, and stared him full in the face. His lordship asked the boy if he knew him. He replied,

---

bien mieux son affaire). You (of them = *en*) (would like = *voudriez*) perhaps 200 or 300, said the clerk. The surprise of the borrower increased at each augmentation of the sum. (Have you not then = *n'avez-vous donc pas*) received our letter, said the clerk. Then (it turned out = *il se trouva que*) in consequence of (the falling in = *la rentrée*) of some fines, a sum of 1200 pounds had been placed to the (credit = *avoir*) of the Receiver general and that not having opened the letter which one to him had written for to him to learn this fact he ignored his good luck.

35. POLITENESS RUSTIC.

One day that the father of Lord Abingdon, man remarkable by the stateliness of his manners, crossed (on horseback = *à cheval*) a village in the vicinity of Oxford he met a lad who dragged a calf (along = *le long*) of the road and who, when his lordship came to to him (stopped = *s'arrêta*) and him looked fixedly in full face. His lordship asked to the boy if he him knew. Yes,

"Yes." "What is my name?" said his lordship. "Why, Lord Abingdon," replied the lad. "Then why don't you take off your hat!" "So I will, Sir," said the boy, "if ye'll hold the calf."

36. LE BRUN.

Le Brun is one of the instances of that early designation of talent which sometimes takes place in the minds of children. From the age of four, he began to draw with a piece of charcoal upon the walls of his father's house. M. Seguier seeing him thus employed at a very early age, and observing something marked and peculiar in his countenance, took him under his protection, and offered him means to go on regularly with the art of painting.

Le Brun possessed much of that enthusiasm which animates the efforts and increases the rapture of the artist. Some one said before him, of his well-known

---

replied he. What is my name, said his lordship. (Why == *bien súr*) Lord Abingdon, replied the lad. Then why (don't you take off your hat == *n'ôtez-vous pas votre chapeau*). (So I will == *je veux bien*), said the boy, if you will to͜hold the calf.

36. LE BRUN.

Le Brun is one of͜the examples of that designation early of͜the talent which has sometimes taken͜place in the mind of͜the children. From the age of four years he began to draw with a piece of charcoal upon the walls of the house of his father. M. Seguier him seeing thus occupied at a age so tender and remarking that there was something of striking and of peculiar in his countenance him took under his protection and to͜him offered the means of to͜study regularly the art of to͜paint.

Le Brun had much of that enthusiasm which animates the efforts and increases the rapture of the artist. One said one day before him in speaking of his picture

picture of the Magdalen, "that the contrite beautiful penitent was really weeping." "That," said he, "is perhaps all that you can see; I hear her sigh."

37. BOY AND HIGHWAYMAN.

A boy who had sold a cow, at the fair at Hereford, in the year 1766, was way-laid by a highwayman, who at a convenient place demanded the money; thereupon the boy took to his heels and ran away; but being overtaken by the highwayman, who dismounted, he pulled the money out of his pocket and strewed it about, and while the highwayman was picking it up, the boy jumped upon the horse and rode home. Upon searching the saddle bags, there were found twelve pounds in cash, and two loaded pistols.

38. MAN IS THE BOOK OF NATURE.

What is the whole creation but one great library?

---

well known of the Magdalen, that the beautiful penitent contrite was‿weeping really. It is perhaps all that that you see said he, I, I her hear to‿sigh.

37. THE BOY AND THE HIGHWAYMAN.

A boy who had sold a cow at the fair of Hereford in the year 1766 was way-laid by a highwayman, who at a place convenient to‿him asked his money; (thereupon = *sur ce*) the boy (took to his heels = *prit ses jambes à son cou*) and (ran away = *se sauva*) but being overtaken by the thief who (dismounted = *descendit de cheval*) he drew the money of his pocket, it scattered‿about and while that the highwayman it picked‿up, he jumped upon the horse and returned (home = *à la maison*). In searching in the saddle‿bags, one found 12 pounds in (cash = *argent comptant*) and two pistols loaded.

38. THE MAN IS THE BOOK OF THE NATURE.

(What is = *qu'est-ce qu'est*) the creation entire, (but

every volume of which, and every page in each volume is impressed with radiant characters of infinite Wisdom; and all the perfections of the universe are contracted with such inimitable art in man, that he needs no other book but himself, to make him a complete philosopher.

39. HONOUR IS NOT HEREDITARY.

Though an honourable title may be conveyed to posterity, yet the ennobling qualities which are the soul of greatness are a sort of incommunicable perfection, and cannot be transferred. Indeed, if a man could bequeath his virtues by will, and settle his sense and learning upon his heirs, as certainly as he can his lands, a brave ancestor would be a mighty privilege.

Honour and shame from no condition rise.
Act well your part—there all the honour lies.

== *si ce n'est*) one great library, of which the wisdom infinite has marked in characters radiant, each volume and each page of each volume; and all the perfections of the Universe are contracted with an art so inimitable in the man that he not has need of other book (but == *que*) himself for to become a philosopher complete.

39. THE HONOUR IS NOT HEREDITARY.

Although a title honourable (may == *puisse*) descend to the posterity, the qualities which ennoble are the soul of the greatness and a sort of perfection (which cannot be communicated == *qui ne peut se communiquer*) and which one cannot pass to some body. Indeed if a man could bequeath to his heirs, besides his virtues, his sense and his learning of the same manner as he can bequeath his lands, a brave ancestor would be a mighty privilege.

The honour and the shame not come out of (any == *aucune*) condition.

(Act == *jouez*) well your (part == *rôle*) (that is == *c'est là qu'e* all the honour.

40. BRAVERY OF GENERAL DAUMESNIL.

General Daumesnil, who had lost a leg in Napoleon's campaign in Russia, commanded the fortress of Vincennes near Paris at the time of the invasion of the allied armies in 1814. When he was summoned by the Russians to surrender the fortress, he replied: "Not till you restore my leg."

41. CAUSES AND EFFECTS.

A counsellor dying much in debt, his creditors seized his goods for the purpose of paying themselves. The property however not being sufficient to satisfy their demands, one of them expressed great surprise that a lawyer should leave so few effects. "It could not be otherwise," replied another, "seeing he had so few causes."

---

40. BRAVERY OF THE GENERAL DAUMESNIL.

The General Daumesnil who had lost a leg in the campaign of Russia under Napoleon was commanding the fortress of Vincennes, near Paris at the epoch of the invasion of the (allied armies = *alliés*) in 1814. When the Russians him summoned of to surrender the fortress he replied: Not before (you have restored = *que vous ne m'ayez rendu*) my leg.

41. CAUSES AND EFFECTS.

A (counsellor = *avocat*) dying (much in debt = *très endetté*) his creditors seized his (goods = *meubles*) for (to pay themselves = *se payer*). However, the property not being sufficient for to satisfy to their demands, the one of them expressed a great surprise that a (lawyer = *homme de loi*) (should leave = *laissât*) so few of effects. It (could not be = *Il n'en pouvait être*) otherwise, replied another: "seeing that he had so few of causes."

42. DESTRUCTION OF BOOKS.

The Caliph Omar proclaimed throughout the kingdom, at the taking of Alexandria, that the Koran contained every thing that was useful to believe and to know: he therefore ordered all the books in the Alexandrian library, which had been founded by Ptolemy Philadelphos nearly two centuries before Christ, to be distributed to the owners of the baths, amounting to 4000, to be used in heating their stoves during a period of six months. Omar was assassinated by a Persian slave at Jerusalem in 644.

43. A SINGULAR METHOD OF DUELLING.

An apothecary having had a dispute with a military officer, received a challenge to meet him the next morning. Æsculapius was punctual to the minute; but on arriving at the spot he observed to the officer, that not being accustomed either to sword or pistol, it would be a very

---

42. DESTRUCTION OF BOOKS.

When the Caliph Omar took possession of Alexandria he made to proclaim everywhere the kingdom that the Koran contained all that which it was necessary of to believe and of to know, therefore, he commanded that all the books of the library of Alexandria, which had been founded by (Ptolemy Philadelphos = *Ptolemée Philadelphe*) two centuries before the era christian (should be = *fussent*) distributed to the owners of baths, at the number of 4000, for (to be used = *s'en servir*) for to heat their stoves during six months. Omar was assassinated by a slave persian at Jerusalem in 644.

43. SINGULAR MANNER OF (FIGHTING = *SE BATTRE*) IN DUEL.

An apothecary (having had a dispute = *s'étant disputé*) with an officer (of him = *en*) received a challenge for the next day. Æsculapius arrived at the minute but in arriving at the (place = *endroit*) he observed to the officer that not being accustomed neither to the

unequal combat between him and a military man. "I
have no doubt, sir," added he, "that you are a man of
too much honour to wish to avail yourself of any undue
advantage; therefore I have a proposal to make. In
this box are two pills; one of them is composed of the
most deadly poison, the other is perfectly harmless;
choose which of the two you will swallow, and I will
immediately swallow the other. The officer was struck
with the singularity of the proposal, and not being disposed to run the risk of poisoning himself, he declined
swallowing the pill, and the affair was amicably adjusted.

44. ERRATUM.

A printer's wife, in Germany, it is said, while a new
edition of the Bible was printing at her house, one night
took an opportunity of going into the office, to alter
that sentence of subjection to her husband, pronounced

---

sword nor to the pistol, the fight between him and a
military man would be very unequal. I do not doubt,
Sir, that you not (may be = *soyez*) a man of too much
of honour for to desire of to take advantage of a
advantage undue, therefore I have a proposal to you
make. In this box there are two pills of which the
one contains a poison of the most mortal and of which
the other is perfectly (harmless = *inoffensive*) chose this
of the two that you will to swallow and I will swallow
the other immediately. The officer was struck of the
singularity of the proposal and not being disposed to run
the risk of (poisoning himself = *s'empoisonner*) he refused
of to swallow the pill and the affair (was amicably adjusted
= *s'arrangeu à l'amiable*).

44. ERRATUM.

One says that the wife of a printer german, who
reprinted an edition of the Bible (took an opportunity
= *s'arrangea de façon*) to go one night in the printing office for to change the phrase of subjection to her

against Eve in Genesis, chap. III, v. 16. She took out
the first two letters of the word Herr, which signifies
lord or master, or ruler, and substituted Na, which made
Narr, fool; thus altering the sentence from "and he shall
be thy Lord," into "and he shall be thy Fool." It is
said that her life paid for this intentional erratum; and
that some secreted copies of this edition have been
bought up at enormous prices. Such is the passion of
some persons for useless curiosities.

45. PERSEVERANCE AND MISFORTUNE.

About the year 1700, Hudde, an opulent Dutch
burgomaster, animated solely by literary curiosity, devoted
himself and his fortune to the acquisition of knowledge.
He went to China to instruct himself in the language,
and in whatever was remarkable among this singular
people. He acquired the skill of a mandarin in that

---

husband pronounced by the Genesis, chapter III, v. 16.
She (took out $=$ *enleva*) the two first letters of the
word Herr which signifies lord or master or ruler, and
that she (for it $=$ *y*) substituted Na, that which made
Narr, fool, changing thus the (sentence $=$ *phrase*) "and
he will be thy Lord" in "and he will be thy fool."
One says that she paid this erratum intentional of her
life and that some (copies $=$ *exemplaires*) of that edition,
kept in secret, have been bought at some prices enormous. Such is the passion of some persons for some
curiosities useless.

45. PERSEVERANCE AND MISFORTUNE.

Towards the year 1700, Hudde, rich burgomaster
dutch, animated solely by the curiosity literary, employed
his fortune and (devoted himself $=$ *s'adonna*) to the acquisition of the knowledge. He went in China for to learn
the language and all that which was remarkable (among
$=$ *chez*) this people singular. He acquired the skill
of a Mandarin in this language difficult, and the form

difficult tongue, nor did the form of his Dutch face undeceive the physiognomists of China. He succeeded to the dignity of mandarin; he travelled through the provinces under this character, and returned to Europe with a collection of observations, the cherished labour of thirty years, but lost them all by shipwreck on the coast. He died in 1764, leaving some excellent treatises on mathematics and other branches of science.

> All human projects are so faintly framed
> That mutable and mortal are the same.

46. THE COSSACKS.

Rude as the Cossacks are, they are by no means insensible to the charms of music, for which they manifest a strong predilection. During the time that the Russians were at Dresden, in 1813, a party of them, attracted by the solemn peal of the organ entered a church, and while it was playing they continued fixed in silent at-

---

of his face dutch (did not undeceive $=$ *ne détrompa pas*) the physiognomists of China. He arrived at the title of Mandarin and in that character travelled in all the provinces and returned in Europe with a collection of observations, the labour cherished of 30 years, but lost all in a wreck, on the coast. He died in 1764 leaving some treatises excellent on the mathematics and other branches of the sciences.

All the human projects are so faintly framed
That the mutable and the mortal (are the same $=$ *ne sont qu'un*).

46. THE COSSACKS.

(Rude as the Cossacks are $=$ *tout grossiers que soient les Cosaques*) they are not (by no means $=$ *nullement*) insensible to the charms of the music for which they have a strong predilection. During that the Russians were at Dresden in 1813, a party (of them $=$ *d'entre eux*) attracted by the peal solemn of the organ entered at the church, and all the time that one (of it $=$ *en*) played they remained fixed in a attention silent. The

tention. Its tones ceased, and the officiating clergyman commenced his sermon. This address, in an unknown language, soon began to excite symptoms of impatience in the strangers, one of whom, stealing softly up the steps of the pulpit unobserved by the minister, startled him not a little by tapping him on the shoulder, in the midst of his harangue, and inviting him, as well as he could by signs, accompanied with all sorts of grotesque gestures, to descend, and no longer interrupt the gratification which the organist afforded to himself and his companions.

47. ON BUSY IDLERS.

There is no kind of idleness by which we are so easily seduced, as that which dignifies itself by the appearance of business, and which, by making the loiterer imagine that he has something to do, keeps him in perpetual agitation and hurries him from place to place.

---

sounds ceased and the clergyman who was officiating commenced his sermon. This (address = *discours*) in a language foreign excited soon some symptoms of impatience (among = *chez*) the foreigners and the one of them stealing softly the steps of the pulpit, without to be observed by the minister not him frightened little in to him tapping gently upon the shoulder at the middle of his harangue and in him inviting (as well as he could = *du mieux qu'il pouvait*) by some signs accompanied of all sorts of gestures grotesque to descend and to not to interrupt longer the pleasure that the organist caused to his companions and (to him = *à lui même*).

47. IDLERS BUSY.

(There is no = *il n'y a pas de*) kind of idleness which us seduces as easily as that which (itself = *se*) dignifies of the appearance of the work and which in making to imagine to the idler that he has something to do, him agitates constantly and him (hurries = *pousse*)

It is only by contemplating what we have done that
we can see how we have spent our time.

He that sits still, no more deceives himself than he
deceives others; he knows that he is doing nothing,
and he has no other solace for his insignificance than
the resolution which the lazy often make, of changing
their mode of life.

To do nothing every man is ashamed, and to do
much almost every man is unwilling or afraid. Innumerable expedients have therefore been invented to produce motion without labour, and employment without
solicitude.

"Idleness is the mother of vice."

48. JUDGE NOT HASTILY.

He that enters a town at night, surveys it in the
morning, and then hastens away to another place, and

---

from place in place. (It is only ═ *ce n'est qu'*) in contemplating that which we have done that we can see
how we have employed our time. (He who ═ *celui
qui*) (sits ═ *s'assied*) without nothing to_do (no more
deceive himself ═ *ne se trompe pas plus*) than he (deceives ═ *ne trompe*) the others. He knows that he not
does nothing and he has not of other consolation for his
insignificance that the resolution that takes often the
idler of changing his manner of to_live. All the men
have shame of not nothing to_do and almost all the
men (will not ═ *ne veulent pas*) or have fear of to_make
much. Therefore one has invented innumerable plans
for to produce the motion without labour and the work
without solicitude.

The idleness is the mother of_the vice.

48. JUDGE NOT HASTILY ═ *NE JUGEZ PAS À LA HÁTE*.

He who enters in a town at midnight who it visits
the morning and who then (hastens ═ *s'empresse*) of
to_go in one other place and who describes the man-

guesses at the manners of the inhabitants by the entertainment which his inn afforded him, may please himself for a time with a hasty change of scenes, and a
confused remembrance of palaces and churches; he may
gratify his eye with a variety of landscapes, and regale
his palate with the wines of a succession of vintages:
but let him be contented to please himself, without
endeavouring to disturb others. Why should he record,
in useless publications, excursions by which nothing
could be learned, or wish to make a show of knowledge,
which, without some power of intuition unknown to
other mortals, he never could attain?

He that would travel for the entertainment of others,
should remember that the great object of remark is
human life. Every nation has something peculiar in
its manufactures, its works of genius, its medicines, its

---

ners of the inhabitants by the treatment which he has
received in his hostelry, can (please himself = *se diver-
tir*) during some time by a prompt change of scenes
and by a remembrance confused of palaces and of churches. He can (gratify his eye = *se repaître la vue d'*)
a variety of landscapes and (regale = *se régaler*) the
palate of the wines of different (vintages = *crus*) but
(let him be contented to please himself = *qu'il soit
satisfait de se plaire à lui même*), without (to strive =
s'efforcer) of to trouble the others. Why to us (should
he give = *donnerait-il*) in some publications useless, a
description which not to us teaches nothing; why (should
he display = *étalerait-il*) some knowledge (pl.) (which,
without some power of intuition unknown to other mortals, he never could attain = *qu'il ne pourrait jamais
atteindre, sans une puissance intuitive inconnue aux autres
mortels*). He who will to travel for the amusement
of others (should remember = *devrait se rappeler*) that
the great object of remark is the life human. Each
nation has something of peculiar in its manufactures,
in the works of the intelligence, in the medicine, in the

agriculture, its customs, and its policy. He only is a
useful traveller, who brings home something by which
his country may be benefited; who procures some supply
of want, or some mitigation of evil, which may enable
his readers to compare their condition with that of
others, to improve it whenever it is worse, and, whenever it is better, to enjoy it.

49. JUVENILE PRUDENCE.

The address with which the young Papirius eluded
his fond mother's pressing solicitations to communicate
to her a secret which he possessed, has often been a
subject of praise. This was the circumstance.

His father, who was a senator of Rome, one day
took him to the senate, when they were deliberating
on some subjects of importance. On his return his
mother asked him what had passed at the senate.

---

agriculture, in the customs and in the politics. (He
alone = *celui-là seul*) is a traveller useful, who
brings_back something of_which his country can to_pro-
fit, who gives the means of (supply a want = *suppléer à
un besoin*) or of to_diminish an evil which can to_per-
mit to his readers of to_compare their condition to that
of_the others, of it_to improve, when it is worse and
(to enjoy it = *d'en jouir*) when it is better.

49. PRUDENCE JUVENILE.

The address with which the young Papirius eluded
the solicitations pressing of his mother who (was fond
of him = *raffolait de lui*) of to_her to_communicate
a secret which he possessed has often been a subject of
praise. Here_is the circumstance.

His father who was senator Roman him (took =
emmena) with him when they were_deliberating on
some subjects of importance. At his return his mother
to_him asked (what had passed = *ce qui s'était passé*)
at_the senate.

The young Papirius answered that he was ordered
not to speak of it. This answer, as we may readily
conceive, only increased his mother's curiosity. She
became more solicitous, and employed every means in
her power to obtain the information she wished. Her
son, to avoid any further inquiries, and to satisfy his
mother's anxiety, told her that they had been deliberating whether it would be better for the republic to suffer the men to have two wives, or the women two
husbands.

The senator's wife, much vexed at this pretended
deliberation, went immediately and communicated her
fears to some other Roman ladies. The next morning
a large body of them presented themselves at the door
of the senatehouse, and in a loud voice declared it would
be better to permit the women to have two husbands,

The young Papirius answered that one to him had
commanded (not to speak of it = *de n'en pas parler*).
As we can to us it to imagine, this answer (only increased = *ne fit qu'augmenter*) the curiosity of his mother. She became more solicitous, and employed all the
means in her power for to obtain the information that
she desired. Her son for to avoid of other inquiries
and for to satisfy the anxiety of his mother to her
told that one had deliberated for to know if (it would
be better = *il vaudrait mieux*) for the republic of to permit that the men (have = *aient*) two wives, or the
women two husbands. Very vexed of this pretended
deliberation, the wife of the senator went immediately
to communicate her fears to some other ladies Roman.
The next morning a great number (of them = *d'entre
elles*) (themselves = *se*) presented at the door of the
Senate and declared (in a loud voice = *hautement*) that
it would be better to permit to the women of to have
two husbands, and expressed their surprise that one

4

and expressed their surprise that a matter of such importance to them should be discussed without hearing what they had to say.

The senate not understanding the women's requests, the young Papirius arose, and related in what manner he had eluded his mother's curiosity. The senators applauded his prudence; but it was resolved that in future no young man, except Papirius, should be admitted into the senate.

50. INCREDULITY.

A sailor who had been many years absent from his mother, who lived in an inland county, returned to his native village, after a variety of voyages to different parts of the globe, and was heartily welcomed by the good old woman, who had long considered him as lost.

Soon after his arrival, the old lady became inquisitive, and desirous to learn what strange sights her son

---

(should discuss = *discutât*) a (matter = *affaire*) of a such importance without to‿hear that which they had to say.

The Senate not understanding the request of‿the women, the young Papirius (arose = *se leva*) and related of what manner he had eluded the curiosity of his mother. The senators applauded to his prudence but one resolved that (in future = *à l'avenir*) one should not admit any young man at‿the Senate (except = *si ce n'est*) Papirius.

50. INCREDULITY.

A sailor who, during several years, had been distant from his mother who lived in a county of the Interior returned in his village after a series of voyages in different parts of‿the globe and was received (with open arms = *à bras ouverts*) by the good old woman who him had regarded during a‿long‿time as lost. Soon after his arrival the old woman became inquisitive and wished to‿know what strange sight her son John had seen

John had seen upon the mighty deep. Amongst a variety
of things that Jack recollected, he mentioned his having
frequently seen flying fish. "Stop, Johnny," said his
mother, "don't try to impose such monstrous impossibilities on me, child; for in good truth I could as soon
believe you had seen flying cows; for cows, you know,
John, can live out of water, but fish cannot. Therefore
tell me honestly what you have seen, but no more
falsehoods, Johnny."

Jack felt himself affronted; and turning his quid in
his mouth he said, "Mayhap, mother, you won't believe
me when I tell you that having cast anchor once in
the Red Sea, it was with difficulty we hove it up
again; which was occasioned, do you see, mother, by a
large wheel hanging on one of the flukes of the anchor.

---

upon the mighty deep. Among a variety of things
of which John (remembered = *se souvenait*) he related
that he had often seen some flying-fish (*poissons volants*).
Ah, No, little John, said his mother, do not try (*the
words spoken by the mother to be throughout in the
second person singular*) of me to make to swallow some
impossibilities as monstrous, for in truth, I (might =
pourrais) as easily to believe that thou hast seen some
(flying cows = *vaches volantes*) for the cows can live
outside of the water, but the fishes never. Therefore,
tell me honestly that which thou hast seen, but not
me tell more of falsehoods, little John.

John (felt himself affronted = *se sentit piqué*) and
turning his (quid = *chique*) in his mouth he said: Perhaps, mother, that (you won't believe me = *vous n'allez
pas me croire*) when I you shall tell that once having
cast the anchor in the Sea Red we had some trouble
to it raise that being caused, (do you see = *voyez-vous*),
mother, by a great wheel suspended to one of the (flukes = *pattes*) of the anchor. That had the air of a

It appeared a strange old Grecian to look at, so we
hoisted it in; and our captain, do you mind me, being
a scholar, overhauled it and discovered it was one of
Pharaoh's chariot-wheels when he was capsized in the
Red Sea." This suited the old lady's understanding.
"Ay, ay, Johnny," cried she, "I can believe this, for we
read of this in the Bible; but never talk to me of flying fish, no, no, never, never."

---

funny (thing = *de chose*) grecian when we it drew
(on board = *à bord*), and our captain, remark well, being
a (scholar = *savant*) it examined and discovered that
it was one of the wheels of a chariot of Pharaoh when
he capsized in the Sea Red. Ah, Ah, John, cried she,
I can believe that for one to͜us speaks of that in the
Bible, but not to͜me speak never of flying-fish, no, no,
never, never.

FRENCH COMPOSITION PART II.

51. ARABIAN HOSPITALITY AND GENEROSITY.

The same hospitality which was practised by Abraham and celebrated by Homer, is still renewed in the camps of the Arabs. The ferocious Bedoweens, the terror of the desert, embrace without inquiry or hesitation, the stranger who dares to confide in their honour and to enter their tent. The treatment he receives is kind and respectful; he shares the wealth or the poverty of his host: and after a needful repose, *he is dismissed on his way*[1], with thanks, with blessings, and perhaps with gifts. *The heart and hand are more largely expanded by the wants of a brother or a friend*[2]: but the heroic acts that could deserve the public applause, must have passed the narrow measure of discretion and experience. A dispute *had arisen*[3], *who*[4], among the citizens of Mecca, was entitled to the prize of generosity, *and a successive application was made*[5] to the three who were deemed

---

51. ARABIAN HOSPITALITY AND GENEROSITY.

[1] he is dismissed on his way = *on le congédie.*

[2] The heart and hand are more largely expanded by the wants of a brother or a friend = the wants of a brother or a friend expand still more the heart and open still more the hand. still more, *encore plus.*

[3] had arisen, *s'était élevée.*

[4] who, (*pour savoir*) *qui.*

[5] and a successive application was made, *et on s'adressa successivement.*

most worthy of the trial. Abdallah, the son of Abbas,
had undertaken a distant journey, and his foot was in
the stirrup when he heard the voice of a suppliant. —
"O son of the uncle of the apostle of God, *I am a traveller and in distress!*"[6] He instantly dismounted *to
present the pilgrim with his camel, her rich caparison,
and a purse of four thousand pieces of gold*[7], excepting
only the sword, either for its intrinsic value, or as the
gift of an honoured kinsman. The servant of Kais informed the second suppliant that his master was asleep;
but he immediately added: "Here is a purse of seven
thousand pieces of gold (it is all we have in the house),
and here is an order *that will entitle you*[8] to a camel
and a slave." The master, as soon as he awoke, praised
and enfranchised his faithful steward with a gentle re-
proof that by respecting his slumbers, he had stinted
his bounty. The third of these heroes, the blind Arabah,
at the hour of prayer, was supporting his steps on the
shoulders of two slaves. "Alas!" he replied, "my coffers
are empty! but these you may sell; if you refuse, I
renounce them." At these words, pushing away the
youths, he groped along the wall with his staff. The
character of Hatem is the perfect model of Arabian virtue; he was brave and *liberal*[9], an eloquent poet and a
successful robber: forty camels were roasted at his hospitable feast; and at the prayer of a suppliant enemy,
he restored both the captives and the spoil. The freedom of his countrymen disdained the laws of justice:
they proudly indulged the spontaneous impulse[10] of pity
and benevolence.

---

[6] I am a traveller and in distress, *je suis un voyageur dans la
détresse.*

[7] to present . . . of gold = *to present to the pilgrim his camel,
her rich caparison &c.*

[8] that will entitle you, *qui vous donnera droit.*

[9] liberal = *généreux.*

[10] they proudly indulged the spontaneous impulse &c. *ils s'aban-
donnaient avec orgueil à l'impulsion spontanée &c.*

52. RICHARD SAVAGE.

This meritorious though unhappy writer[1] *had, in the world, besides fortune, but*[2] one indefatigable and un-relenting enemy, *her whom*[3] God assigns every living creature for its natural protector, a mother. Though born with a legal claim to honour and to affluence (being the son of Lady Macclesfield and Earl Rivers), he was disowned by his mother; and soon after, deprived of a considerable paternal inheritance by an atrocious false-hood of that same parent. Although she could not *transport*[4] her son to the plantations, bury him in the shop of a mechanic, or hasten the hand of the public exe-cutioner (*all which she endeavoured*)[5], yet she had the satisfaction of embittering all his hours and of forcing him into exigences that hurried on his death.

Savage, in a midnight broil, slew a gentleman *by the name of*[6] Sinclair, was tried, found guilty, condemned to death, and in spite of his mother's efforts to have the extreme penalty of the law carried into execution, he obtained the king's pardon. Some time after his release, he met in the street a woman that had sworn with much malignity against him. She informed him *that she was in distress*[7], and with a degree of confidence not easily attainable, desired him to relieve her. He, instead of insulting her misery and taking pleasure in the calami-ties of one *who had brought his life into danger*[8], re-

---

52. RICHARD SAVAGE.

[1] This meritorious though unhappy writer = *This writer meri-torious though unhappy.*

[2] had, in the world, besides fortune, but, *n'eut dans ce monde, outre la fortune qu'.*

[3] her whom, *'celle que'.*

[4] transport, *faire déporter.*

[5] all which she endeavoured, *'toutes choses qu'elle s'efforça de faire'.*

[6] by the name of, *'du nom de'.*

[7] that she was in distress, *'qu'elle était dans le besoin'.*

[8] who had brought his life into danger, *'qui avait mis sa vie en danger'.*

proved her gently for her perjury; and changing the
only guinea he had, divided it equally between her and
himself.

This action is an instance of uncommon generosity,
an act of complicated virtue: by which *he at once relieved*[9] the poor, corrected the vicious, and forgave an
enemy; by which he at once remitted the strongest pro-
vocations and exercised the most ardent charity.

53. COLUMBUS'S FIRST RETURN TO EUROPE.

The voyage was prosperous *to*[1] the fourteenth of February, and *he had advanced*[2] near five hundred leagues
across the Atlantic ocean, when the wind began to rise,
and continued to blow with increasing rage which terminated in a furious hurricane. Every thing that the
naval skill and experience of Columbus could devise was
employed in order to save the ships. But it was impossible to withstand the violence of the storm, and, as
they were still *far from any land*[3], destruction seemed
inevitable. The sailors had recourse to prayers to Al-
migthy God, to the invocation of saints, to vows and
charms, to every thing that religion dictates or super-
stition suggests to the affrighted mind of man. No prospect of deliverance appearing, they abandoned themselves
to despair, and *expected every moment*[4] *to be swallowed
up in*[5] the waves. Besides the passions which naturally
agitate and alarm the human mind in such awful situa-
tions, when certain death, in one of his most terrible
forms, is before it, Columbus had to endure feelings of

---

[9] he at once relieved = *he relieved at once.*

53. COLUMBUS'S FIRST RETURN TO EUROPE.

[1] to = *until.*
[2] he had advanced = *il s'était avancé de.*
[3] far from any land, *loin d'aucune terre.*
[4] expected every moment, *s'attendaient à tout moment.*
[5] to be swallowed up in, *à être engloutis par.*

distress *peculiar to himself*[6]. He dreaded that all knowledge of the amazing discoveries which he had made,
was now to perish[7] and that mankind *were to be deprived*[8]
of every benefit that might have been derived from the
happy success of his schemes, and his own name would
descend to posterity as that of a rash deluded adventurer,
instead of being transmitted with the honour due to the
author and conductor of the most noble enterprise *that
had ever been undertaken*[9]. These reflections extinguished
all sense of his own personal danger. Less affected with
the loss of life, than solicitous to preserve the memory
of what he had attempted and achieved, he retired to
his cabin, and wrote, upon parchment, a short account
of the voyage which he had made, *of the course which
he had taken*[10], of the situation and riches of the countries
which he had discovered and of the colony that he had
left there. Having wrapped up this in an oiled cloth,
which he inclosed in a cake of wax, he put it into a
cask *carefully stopped up*[11] and threw it into the sea, *in
hopes*[12] that some fortunate accident might preserve a
deposite of so much importance to the world. At length
Providence interposed to save a life reserved for other
services. The wind *abated*[13], the sea became calm, and
on the evening of the fifteenth, Columbus and his companions discovered land. *They found it to be*[14] St.-Mary,
one of the Azores.

---

[6] peculiar to himself = *que lui seul connaissait.*
[7] was now to perish, *n'allât maintenant perir.*
[8] were to be deprived, *ne fut privé.*
[9] that had ever been undertaken = *qu'on eût jamais tentée.*
[10] of the course which he had taken, *de la route qu'il avait suivie.*
[11] carefully stopped up = *soigneusement fermé.*
[12] in hopes, *espérant,* or *dans l'espoir.*
[13] abated, *tomba.*
[14] They found it to be, *ils virent que c'était.*

54. SHERIDAN'S GOOD-HUMOURED TRICKERY.

The disputatious humour of Richardson (*not the author of Clarissa Harlow, Pamela and Sir Charles Grandison*) *was once turned to account by Sheridan in a very characteristic manner*[1]. Having had a hackney-coach in employ for five or six hours, and not being provided with the means of paying for it, *he happened to espy*[2] Richardson in the street, and proposed to take him in the coach *some part of his way*[3]. The offer being accepted, Sheridan lost no time *in starting*[4] a subject of conversation, in which he knew his companion was sure to become argumentative and animated. Having, by well managed contradiction, brought him to the proper *pitch*[5] of excitement, he affected to grow impatient and angry himself, and saying that *"he could not think of remaining*[6] in the same coach with a person *that would use such language*[7]," pulled the *check-string*[8], and desired the coachman to let him out. Richardson, wholly occupied with the argument, and regarding the retreat of his opponent as an acknowledgment of defeat, still *pressed his point*[9], and even hollowed "more last words" through the *coach-window*[10] after Sheridan, who, *walking quietly home*[11], left the poor disputant responsible for the heavy fare of the coach.

---

54. SHERIDAN'S GOOD-HUMOURED TRICKERY.

[1] The disputatious humour of Richardson, not (*ne pas*) the author &c. ... characteristic manner, *to be turned:* Once Sheridan (turned to account = *mit à profit*) in a characteristic manner, the disputatious humour of Richardson &c. &e.

[2] he happened to espy, *il lui arriva* (*par hasard*) *d'apercevoir,* ...

[3] some part of his way, *pendant un bout de chemin.*

[4] in starting, *en faisant naître.*

[5] pitch, *point.*

[6] he could not think of remaining, *il ne saurait rester.*

[7] that would use such language, *qui se servait d'un tel language.*

[8] check-string, *cordon.*

[9] pressed his point, *hâta la conclusion.*

[10] coach-window, *portière.*

[11] walking quietly home, *s'en allant tranquillement chez lui.*

55. THE DERVISES OF CONSTANTINOPLE.

They have permission *to marry*[1], but are confined to an old habit which is only a piece of coarse white cloth wrapped about them with their legs and arms naked. Their order has few rules, except that of performing their fantastic rites every Tuesday and Friday, *which is done in this manner*[2]. *They meet together*[3] in a large hall, where they all stand with their eyes fixed on the ground and their arms across while the Imaum or preacher reads part of the Koran from a pulpit placed in the midst; and when he has done, eight or ten of them make a melancholy concert with their pipes, *which are no unmusical instruments*[4]. Then he reads again and makes a short exposition on what he has read; after which they sing and play, till their superior (the only one of them dressed in green) rises and begins a sort of solemn dance. They all stand still about him *in a regular figure*[5], and while some play, the others *tie their robe* (which is very wide) *fast*[6] round their waist, and begin to turn round with amazing swiftness, *and yet with regard to the music*[7], moving faster or more slowly as the tune is played. This lasts above an hour, *without any of them shewing*[8] the least appearance of giddiness, which is not to be wondered at, when it is considered, they are all used to it from their infancy; most of them being devoted to this way of life from their birth. There

---

55. THE DERVISES OF CONSTANTINOPLE.

[1] to marry = *de se marier.*

[2] which is done in this manner = *ce qu'ils font de cette manière.*

[3] they meet together, *ils s'assemblent.*

[4] which are no unmusical instruments, *instruments qui ne sont pas dépourvus d'harmonie.*

[5] in a regular figure, *en formaut une figure régulière.*

[6] tie their robe fast, *serrent fortement leur robe.*

[7] and yet with regard to the music, *tous en suivant la musique.*

[8] without any of them showing, *sans qu'aucun d'eux montre.*

turned amongst them some little Dervises of six or seven
years old, who seemed no more disordered by that exercise than the others. At the end of the ceremony they
shout out: "There is no other God but God, and Maho-
met is his Prophet," *after which*[9] they kiss the Superior's
hand and retire. The whole is performed with the most
solemn gravity. Nothing can be more austere than the
form of these people; they never raise their eyes and
seem devoted to contemplation. And *as ridiculous as
this is in description*[10] , there is something touching in
the air of submission and mortification they assume.

56.   THE STEAM-ENGINE.

In the present perfect state of the steam-engine, in
which the fertile genius of Watt contrived miracles of
simplicity and usefulness, it appears a thing almost endowed
with intelligence.   It regulates with perfect accuracy
and uniformity the number of its *strokes*[1] in a given
time, *and counts and records them moreover*[2], to tell how
much work it has done, as a clock records the beats of
its pendulum; it regulates the quantity of steam admitted
to work, the briskness of the fire, the supply of water
to the *boiler*[3] , the supply of coal to the fire; it opens
and shuts its valves with absolute precision *as to*[4] time
and manner; it oils its joints; it takes out any air which
may accidentally enter into parts *that should be vacuous*[5] ;
and when anything goes wrong which it cannot of itself

---

[9] after which, *après quoi.*
[10] And as ridiculous as this is in description, *et quelque ridicule
qu'en soit la description.*

56.   THE STEAM ENGINE.

[1] stroke == *coup de piston.*
[2] and counts and records them moreover, *et de plus, les compte
et les enregistre.*
[3] boiler == *chaudière.*
[4] as to, *quant au.*
[5] that should be vacuous, *où il doit y avoir un vide.*

rectify[6], it warns its attendants *by*[7] ringing a bell: yet with all these talents and qualities, and even when possessing the power of six hundred horses, *it is obedient*[8] to the hand of a child; its aliment is coal, wood, charcoal, or other combustible; it consumes none *while idle*[9]; it never tires and wants no sleep; it is not subject to malady when originally well made; and only refuses to work *when worn out with age*[10]; it is equally active in all climates, and will do work *of any kind*[11]; it is a water-pumper, a miner, a sailor, a cotton-spinner, a weaver, a blacksmith, a miller, etc.; and a small engine *in the character of a steam-pony*[12] may be seen dragging after it on a rail-road a hundred tons of merchandise, or a regiment of soldiers with greater speed than that of our fleetest coaches. It is the king of machines, and a permanent realization of the genii *of Eastern fable*[13], whose supernatural powers were occasionally at the command of man.

57. SHORTNESS OF LIFE.

We all of us complain[1] of the shortness of time, says Seneca, and yet *have much more than we know what to do with*[2]. *Our lives, says he, are spent either in*

---

[6] and when anything goes wrong which it cannot of itself rectify, *et quand quelque chose va mal, et qu'elle ne peut le rectifier par elle-même.*

[7] by, *en.*

[8] it is obedient, *elle obéit.*

[9] while idle, *pendant qu'elle est au repos.*

[10] when worn out witn age, *lorsqu'elle est usée par l'âge.*

[11] of any kind, *de n'importe quel genre.*

[12] in the character of a steam pony, *qui joue le rôle d'un pony à vapeur.*

[13] of Eastern fable, *des fables de l'Orient.*

57. SHORTNESS OF LIFE.

[1] We all of us complain, *nous nous plaignons tous.*

[2] have much more than we know what to do with, *nous en avons bien plus que nous ne savons en employer.*

doing nothing at all[3], or in doing nothing to the purpose, or in doing nothing *that we ought to do*[4]. We
are always complaining our days *are few*[5], and acting
as though there would be no end of them[6]. That noble
philosopher has described our inconsistency with ourselves *in this particular*[7], by all those various turns of
expression and thought which are peculiar to his writings.

I often consider mankind as wholly inconsistent with
itself in a point that bears some affinity to the former.
Though we seem grieved at the shortness of life in
general, we are wishing every period of it at an end.
The minor longs *to be of age*[8], then to be a man of
business, then to make up an estate, then to arrive at
honours, then to retire. *Thus although the whole life
is allowed by every one to be short*[9], *the several divisions
of it*[10] appear long and tedious. We are for lengthening
our span in general, but would fain contract the parts
of which it is composed. The usurer would be very
well satisfied to have all the time annihilated that lies
between the present moment *and next quarter-day*[11]. The
politician would be contented to lose three years in his
life, could he place things in the posture which he fan-
cies they will stand in after such a revolution of time.
The lover would be glad to strike out of his existence
all the moments that are to pass away before the happy
meeting. Thus, as fast as our time runs, we should be

---

[3] Our lives, says he, are spent either in doing nothing at all,
notre vie se passe, dit-il, soit à ne rien faire du tout.
  [4] that we ought to do, *de ce que nous devrions faire.*
  [5] are few = *sont peu nombreux.*
  [6] as though there would be no end of them, *comme s'ils ne
devaient pas avoir de fin.*
  [7] in this particular, *à cet égard.*
  [8] to be of age, *être majeur.*
  [9] Thus although the whole life is allowed by everyone to be
short, *ainsi quoique tout le monde admette que la vie entière soit courte.*
  [10] the several divisions of it, *les diverses portions en.*
  [11] and next quarter-day, *et la prochaine échéance trimestrielle.*

very glad in most parts of our lives that it ran much faster than it does. *Several hours of the day hang upon our hands*[12]; nay *we wish away whole years*[13], and travel through time as through a country filled with many wild and empty wastes, *which we would fain hurry over, that we may arrive*[14] at those several little settlements or imaginary points of rest which are dispersed up and down in it.

58. THE DEAD ASS.

And this, said he, putting the remains of a crust into his wallet—and this should have been thy portion, said he, hadst thou been alive to share it with me. I thought, by the accent, it had been an apostrophe to his child; but it was to his ass. The man seemed to lament it much; and it instantly *brought to my mind*[1] Sancho's lamentations for his: but he did it *with more touches of nature*[2].

The mourner was sitting upon a stone bench at the door, with the ass's pannel and its bridle on one side, which he took up from time to time—then laid them down—looked at them, and shook his head. He then took his crust of bread out of his wallet again, as if to eat it, held it some time in his hand—then laid it upon the bit of his ass's bridle—looking wistfully at the little arrangement he had made—and then *gave*[3] a sigh.

---

[12] Several hours of the day hang upon our hands, *plusieurs heures du jour nous sont à charge*, or *il y a dans la journée plusieurs heures dont nous ne savons que faire.*

[13] we wish away whole years, *nous desirons que les années s'envolent.*

[14] which we would fain hurry over, that we may arrive, *que nous voudrions volontiers passer rapidement pour arriver.*

58. THE DEAD ASS.

[1] brought to my mind, *me mit en l'esprit.*

[2] with more touches of nature, *avec plus de naturel.*

[3] gave, *poussa.*

The simplicity of his grief drew *numbers*[4] about him, and La Fleur *among the rest*[5] , *while the horses were getting ready*[6] : *as I continued sitting in*[7] the postchaise, I could see over their heads and hear.

He said he had come last from Spain, *where he had been from the farthest borders of*[8] Franconia; and had got so far on his return home, when the ass died. Every one seemed desirous to know *what business could have taken so old and poor a man so far a journey from his own home*[9].

It had pleased Heaven, he said, to bless him with three sons, the finest lads in all Germany; but having in one week lost two of them *by*[10] the small-pox, and the youngest falling ill of the same distemper, he was afraid of being bereft of them all, and made a vow, *if Heaven would not take him from him also*[11], he would go in gratitude to Saint-Iago in Spain.

When the mourner *got thus far in his story*[12], he stopped to pay nature her tribute—and wept bitterly.

He said Heaven had accepted the conditions; and that he had set out from his cottage with this poor creature, who had been a patient partner of his journey—that it had eaten the same bread with him all the way, *and was unto him as a friend*[13].

---

[4] numbers, *nombre de personnes.*

[5] among the rest, *parmi eux.*

[6] while the horses were getting ready, *pendant qu'on apprêtait les chevaux.*

[7] as I continued sitting in, *comme j'étais toujours assis dans.*

[8] where he had been from the farthest borders of, *des frontières les plus reculées de* &c.

[9] what business could have taken so old and poor a man so far a journey from his own home, *ce qui avait pu faire entreprendre un voyage si lointain à un homme si vieux et si pauvre.*

[10] by = of.

[11] if heaven would not take him from him also, *que si le ciel voulait ne pas le lui enlever comme les autres.*

[12] got thus far of his story, *en arriva là de son histoire.*

[13] and was unto him as a friend, *et était pour lui comme un ami.*

Every body who stood about heard the poor fellow
with concern—La Fleur offered him money—the mourner said he did not want it—it was not the value of
the ass—but the loss of him—The ass, he said, *he was
assured*[14], loved him—and *upon this*[15], he told them a
long story of a mischance, which, upon their passage
over the Pyrenean mountains, had separated them from
each other three days; during which time the ass had
sought him as much as he had sought the ass, and that
neither had scarce eaten or drunk *till they met*[16].

Thou hast one comfort, friend, said I, at least, in
the loss of thy poor beast; I am sure thou hast been
a merciful master to him—Alas! said the mourner, I
thought so, when he was alive—but now he is dead I
think otherwise—I fear the weight of myself, and my
afflictions together, have been too much for him—they
have shortened the poor creature's days, and *I fear I
have them to answer for*[17].—Shame on the world! said I
to myself—*did we but love each other as*[18] this poor soul
loved his ass—it would be something.

59. DESCARTES.

*If the distractions of business or professional duties
are to be deemed*[1] an insurmountable *bar*[2] to the *cultivation*[3] of science or literature, what annoyances or
interruptions of this description shall seem more unfa-

---

14 he was assured, *il en était sûr.*

15 upon this, *sur ce.*

16 till they met, *jusqu'à ce qu'ils se rencontrassent.*

17 I fear I have them to answer for, *je crains que je n'aie
à en répondre.*

18 did we but love each other as, *si nous nous aimions seulement
comme.*

59. DESCARTES.

1 If the distractions . . . are to be deemed == if one deems
the distractions of business or of professional duties.

2 bar, *barrière.*

3 cultivation == *culture.*

vourable for such an attempt than those which beset
the rude and unsettled life of a seaman or a soldier!
Yet it has been in the midst of these that some of
the persons whose names are most distinguished in the
annals of literature and philosophy have begun their
career. The great Descartes *entered*[4] the army, *in obedience to the wishes of his family*[5], at the age of twenty,
and served first with the troops of the prince of Orange,
and afterwards with those of Maximilian of Bavaria.
With the latter prince he was present at the battle of
Prague, in 1620, when Maximilian acting *in concert*[6]
with the emperor Ferdinand II, obtained a signal victory over the elector palatine, Frederick. During his
military life, *however*[7], Descartes never neglected his
philosophical studies, *of which*[8] he gave a striking proof
on one occasion while he was in the service of the
prince of Orange. *He happened to be*[9] in garrison with
his regiment at the town of Breda in the Netherlands,
when walking out one morning, he observed a crowd
of people assembled around a placard or advertisement
which was *stuck up*[10] on the wall. *Finding*[11] that it was
written in *the Dutch language*[12], which he did not understand (*he was a native of Touraine*[13]), *he inquired of
a person*[14] whom he saw reading it, what it meant.
The individual to whom he addressed his inquiries *happened to be*[15] the principal of the university of Dort,

---

   [4] entered, *entra dans.*
   [5] in obedience to the wishes of his family, *pour obéir aux désirs
de sa famille.*
   [6] in concert = *de concert.*
   [7] however, must begin the sentence.
   [8] of which, *ce dont.*
   [9] He happened to be, *il se trouvait par hasard.*
   [10] stuck up, *affiché.*
   [11] finding = seeing.
   [12] the Dutch language = *Hollandais.*
   [13] he was a native of Touraine, *il était natif de la Touraine.*
   [14] he inquired of a person, *il s'informa auprès d'une personne.*
   [15] happened to be, *se trouva être.*

a man of distinguished mathematical attainments[16]; and it was *with something*[17] of a sneer that he informed the young officer, in reply to his question, that the paper contained the announcement of a difficult geometrical problem, of which the proposer challenged the most able men of the city to attempt the solution. *Not repulsed, however*[18] by the tone and manner of the learned professor, Descartes *requested to be favoured with a translation*[19] of the placard, *which he had no sooner received*[20] than he calmly remarked that he thought he should be able to answer the challenge. Accordingly, next day, he presented himself again before Beckman (that was the name of the professor), with a complete solution of the problem, *greatly to the astonishment*[21] of the distinguished person, who had probably never before dreamed of the possibility of so much learning being found *beyond the walls*[22] of a university.

It was at this period of his life, that this illustrious person laid the foundation of most of those mathematical discoveries which subsequently obtained for him so much celebrity. He wrote a Latin treatise on music, and projected several of his other works, during the time he was stationed at Breda.

60. TRUTH ABOVE ALL THINGS.

Abdool-Radir, a Persian *boy*[1], the son of a widow,

---

[16] a man of distinguished mathematical attainments, *mathematicien distingué.*

[17] with something, *avec une sorte.*

[18] not repulsed, however = however, not repulsed "however", *quoi qu'il en soit.*

[19] requested to be favoured with a translation, *demanda qu'on lui fît la faveur de traduire.*

[20] which he had no sooner received, *qu'il n'eut pas plus tôt reçue.*

[21] greatly to the astonishment, *au grand étonnement.*

[22] beyond the walls, *en dehors des murs.*

60. TRUTH ABOVE ALL THINGS.

[1] boy, *jeune homme.*

desired leave of his mother to take[2] a journey to Bagdad to seek *his*[3] fortune; she wept *at the thoughts of the parting*[4]; *then*[5], taking out forty of the gold coins called dinars, she gave them to him, telling him that was *the whole of*[6] his inheritance. After this, she made him swear never to tell a lie; then *she bade him farewell*[7].

The boy *set out upon his journey*[8]. On the road, the party with which he travelled was suddenly attacked by a *great*[9] troop of robbers. One of them asked Ab-dool-Radir what money he had got. "Forty dinars," he answered, "are sewed up in my garments." The robber took this for a jest, and laughed. Another asked him the same question, and he made the same reply. When they began to divide the plunder among them, *he was called to the chief*[10], who was standing on an eminence, *and he too asked him*[11] what he had got. "*I have told two of your men already,*"[12] said he, "that I have forty dinars carefully sewed up in my clothes." The chief immediately *ordered*[13] the clothes *to be*[14] ripped up, and the gold was found. He was astonished. "How came you," said he, "to discover what had been so carefully hidden?" — "Because," replied Abdool-Ra-dir, "*I will not be false*[15] to my mother, to whom I

---

[2] desired leave of his mother to take, *demanda à sa mère la permission de faire.*

[3] his, not to be translated.

[4] at the thoughts of the parting, *à la pensée de se séparer.*

[5] then, *puis.*

[6] the whole of, *tout.*

[7] she bade him farewell, *elle lui dit adieu.*

[8] set out upon his journey, *se mit en route.*

[9] great, *nombreuse.*

[10] he was called to the chief, *on l'appela devant le chef.*

[11] and he too asked him, *et lui aussi lui demanda.*

[12] I have told two of your men already = I have already told to two of your men.

[13] ordered = ordered that.

[14] to be, must be in the subjunctive.

[15] I will not be false, *je ne manquerai pas de parole.*

have promised never to tell a lie!" — *"What*[16], child!"
said the chief, "hast thou, at thy age, such a sense of
thy duty *to*[17] thy mother, and have I, at mine, so little
sense of my duty *to*[17] my God, *as to lead*[18] the life
of a robber? Give me *thy*[19] hand, innocent boy, that
I may swear upon it to forsake my evil ways."

And he swore it; and his followers, all struck like
him with sudden repentance, made the same vow; *and
as the first fruits of it*[20], returned to the travellers
whatever they had taken from them.

61. A SENSE OF DUTY.

The Arabs have so great a regard for the rights of
hospitality, that if any one, even an animal, takes shelter under the shade of their tents, they think it base
to give him up. And *it is astonishing*[1] what wealth has
been spent, and what blood has been shed among them,
in[2] maintaining this principle of duty.

Bahram Gor, *when a young man*[3], passed *much*[4] of
his time in Arabia, and was fond of hunting over those
extensive deserts. *As he was out one day*[5], *he fell in*[6]

---

[16] what, *comment.*
[17, 17] to, *envers.*
[18] as to lead, *que je mène.*
[19] thy, *la.*
[20] and as the first fruits of it, *et comme premiers fruits de cette
repentance.*

61. A SENSE OF DUTY.

[1] it is astonishing, *il est étonnant,* must nearly always be followed
by *de* and a verb in the infinitive: generally *voir, penser* &c. and
in the portions of the sentence where "it is astonishing" is understood, the same thing also takes place, as, for instance, before
"what blood".

[2] in, *pour.*

[3] when a young man, *lorsqu'il était jeune.*

[4] much, *une grande partie.*

[5] as he was out one day, *un jour qu'il était dehors, qu'il était
à la chasse.*

[6] he fell in, *il rencontra.*

with a doe so remarkably swift, that though mounted
on one of the fleetest horses, *he could never get within
shot of her*[7]. When the chase had now lasted some
hours, the poor creature, faint with heat, fled, in despair, to an encampment of Arabs, and took refuge in
one of the tents. Bahram followed at full speed, and
pulling up at the door of the tent, called to the man
to give up the deer. "The arrow that is now *set*[8] in
your bow, *must first go through my heart*[9]," said the
man, "and even then, you will not escape the vengeance of my people. Take my horse, if you will, which
stands at the door; but not a *hair*[10] of this doe shall
you touch. *When did an Arab ever betray*[11] his guest?"

Bahram, recollecting the habits of the people, turned
away without saying another word: and when he afterwards succeeded to the throne of Persia, he took care
that the hospitable Arab should be placed in a wealthy
and honourable condition.

62. THE KING AND THE HAWK.

The Persians relate of one of their kings, that being
one day *on a hunting party*[1] with his hawk upon his
hand[2], a deer *started up*[3] before him; he let the hawk
fly, and followed it with great eagerness, till at length
the deer was taken. The courtiers were all left behind
in the chase. The king thirsty, rode about in quest of

---

[7] he could never get within shot of her, *il ne put jamais s'en
approcher assez pour la tirer.*
[8] set, *ajustée.*
[9] must first go through my heart, *me percera d'abord le cœur.*
[10] hair, *poil.*
[11] when did an Arab ever betray, *quand un Arabe a-t-il jamais
trahi.*

62. THE KING AND THE HAWK.

[1] On a hunting party, *à une partie de chasse.*
[2] hand, here to be translated, *"poing".*
[3] started up, *se leva.*

water, till having reached the foot of a mountain, *he discovered some*[4] *trickling down*[5] in drops from a rock. He took a little cup out of his quiver, and held it to catch the water. *Just when*[6] the cup was filled, and as he was going to drink, the hawk shook his pinions, and overset the cup. The king was vexed at the accident, and again applied the cup to the crevice in the rock. When the cup was replenished, *and he was lifting it*[7] to his mouth, the hawk clapped his wings, and threw it down a second time. The king *enraged*[8], flung the bird with such force against the ground, that it expired.

At this moment, the table-decker came up. The king having still a great mind to taste the water that trickled down the rock, but being too impatient to wait till it was again collected by drops, ordered the table-decker to go to the top of the rock, and fill the cup *at the fountain head*[9]. The table-decker on reaching the top of the rock, found an immense serpent *lying dead*[10], and his poisonous foam mixing with the water that fell over. He descended, related the fact to the king, and presented him with a cup of cold water out of his own flagon.

As the king lifted the cup to his lips, the tears gushed from his eyes. He related to the table-decker the adventure of the hawk, and reproached himself deeply *for*[11] the fatal consequences of his anger and precipitancy. During the remainder of his life, say the Persians in their figurative style, "the arrow of regret continually rankled in his breast."

---

[4] he discovered some, *il en découvrit.*
[5] trickling down = which was trickling down.
[6] just when, *au moment où.*
[7] and he was lifting it, *et qu'il la portait.*
[8] enraged, *transporté de fureur.*
[9] at the fountain head, *à la source même.*
[10] lying dead, *qui gisait mort.*
[11] for, *not to be translated.*

63. THE PEARL OF PRICE.
(AN¹ EASTERN TALE.)

In the days of old² a wild goose made her nest on
the shore of the Caspian Sea, among the sedges, under-
neath a shelving bank. And she brooded certain days
over her eggs, and many *young ones³* came forth. But
behold *there arose a mighty tempest⁴*, and the waves
were lifted up, and dashed upon the bank, and it crum-
bled and fell down upon the nest, so that her mate was
crushed to death⁵, and all the young, except one, which
dived under the waters and escaped away, *and in like
manner the mother bird escaped also⁶*.

And the mother loved the young one, that was left
to her a widow, with exceeding love: and she fed him,
and watched him day and night; and he was now well-
nigh fledged. But the fowler *spread⁷* his net, cunningly
he spread it, and the young bird was taken, and fell
into the hands of the fowler. And the mother bird
followed, and cried to the fowler to have pity and mercy
upon her which had but one young one, and to spare
and set him free. And the fowler answered and said,
"Why should I set him free for thee? What gift wilt
thou give me, if I set him free?" And the bird made
reply, „Behold, I would give my life for his ransom,
say what is it that thou wouldst have of me." And
the fowler said, *"Stretch thy wing to⁸* the South, and
after many days thou wilt behold the city where dwel-

---

63. THE PEARL OF PRICE.

¹ An, to be left out.
² in the days of old, *dans le temps jadis*.
³ young ones, *oisons*.
⁴ there arose a mighty tempest = *a mighty tempest arose*.
⁵ was crushed to death, *fut écrasé*.
⁶ and in like manner the mother bird escaped also = *and the
mother bird escaped also in like manner*, *"In like manner"*, *de la
même manière*.
⁷ spread, *tendit*.
⁸ stretch thy wing to, *tire de l'aile vers*.

leth the great king, *even the king of Persia*[9]. And thou
wilt see him go forth in the morning, and call to him
his beautiful steed that he loveth, and give him barley
out of a golden dish. In all the world there is no barley *like unto that*[10] for goodness, bring me one grain
thereof in thy bill, that I may sow it, and it may bring
forth abundantly; then will I restore unto thee thy
young one."

And the bird stretched her wing to the South many
days, and at last she stood before the Great King, even
the king of Persia, when he went forth with barley in
a golden dish; and she besought him that he would
give her one barley-corn to redeem her young one from
the death. But the great king frowned terribly, and
he said, "What gift hast thou brought? Darest thou
advance thy prayer unto the king without bringing with
thee thy gift? Stretch now thy wing towards the setting sun, and after many days thou shalt behold the
orchards of the West; bring to me in thy bill the fairest
pomegranate of all those orchards, then will I give thee
a barley-corn to redeem thy young one."

And the bird stretched her wing toward the setting
sun, and behold, the planter *was walking*[11] in his orchard, and she said, "Give me the fairest pomegranate
of thy orchard to give to the Great King, *so shall he
give unto me*[12] the barley-corn to give unto the fowler
to redeem my young one from the death." But he answered, "Bring me a gift. Seek thou the herdsman of
the plain, bid him bring hither unto me an ox to turn
the wheel of the cistern which watereth my orchard,
then will I give unto thee my fairest pomegranate."
And *she sought out*[13] the herdsman, the master of a

---

9 even the king of Persia, *le roi de Perse lui-même.*
10 like unto that, *comme celui là.*
11 was walking, *se promenait.*
12 so shall he give me, *qui ainsi me donnera.*
13 she sought out, *elle se mit à la recherche.*

hundred herds, and she entreated him to be merciful
unto her, and to give the ox to the gardener. But he
answered *even as the rest*[14], "Bring me a gift. Go thou
to the chief who dwelleth on the borders of the desert,
let him send unto me one of his steeds of noble blood,
and let him be bridled and saddled for the course, —
then shall the ox be thine."

And the bird went, and besought the chief who
dwelt on the borders of the desert to bestow upon her
one of his steeds of noble blood, bridled and saddled
for the course. But he mocked at her, and he said,
"Give thou first unto me the Pearl of Price to adorn
the forehead of my bride, *even the pearl*[15] of the princess Zobeid, the greatest pearl of the whole earth." The
poor bird answered and said, "Alas! *as easily might I
give thee the earth itself*[16] !" But it was for the life of
her young one, and there was no other help for him,
and nothing had she to lose; she spread therefore her
wings and *away*[17] to the dwelling of the princess Zobeid. And the princess was in a fair garden, adorned
with great trees and with bushes, and with all sweet
smelling flowers; and she was sitting beside a fountain
of clear water, and she held her young son in her arms.
And she said, "What aileth thee, poor bird, why droo-
pest thou thy wings, and wherefore bowest thou thy
head unto the earth? Rest thyself on the fresh herbage,
and drink of the fountain of clear water; afterwards tell
unto me thy grief." And the bird did as she had said,
and she told her her grief. And the princess answered
and said, "Didst thou all this, poor creature! And stretch-
edst thou thy wings hither even from the Caspian

---

[14] even as the rest, *tout comme les autres.*
[15] even the pearl, *la perle même.*
[16] as easily might I give thee the earth itself = *I might as
easily give thee* &c.
[17] away, *se dirigea vers.*

Sea, *on the further side of all the land of Persia*[18], only
to seek for pity and for help, for thee and for thy little
one, and foundest nothing in the heart of man, *from
high to low*[19], from the Great King to the humble pea-
sant, but cruelty and covetousness! But I, that am a
mother, *even as thyself*[20], of an only dear little one,
shall I not pity thee[21]? Take my pearl, — a pearl of
price is light as a barley-corn weighed in the balance
against kindness and mercy. Take thou my pearl, and
speed thee on thy way to redeem thy little one whom
thou lovest, lest he perish."

And the bird took the pearl in her bill, rejoicing
that she had found favour at the last. *And she returned on her way*[22], and sought out the chief of the borders of the desert, and she said unto him, "Behold the
Pearl of Price, even the great pearl of the princess
Zobeid; give now unto the herdsman thy steed of noble
blood ready bridled and saddled, that he may give me
his ox, and so I may redeem my young one." Then
the chief beat his breast and gnashed his teeth, and
he said, "Thou hast brought the Pearl of Price; but it
is not for me! Two terrible lions have been here, they
have slain *my noble horses every one*[23], — *would I had
given the best of them rather unto thee*[24], at thine en-
treaty!" The bird answered him never a word. She
spread her wings, and soared up over the plain, seeking
far and near to find the master of a hundred herds.
But behold the robbers had come down from the moun-

---

[18] on the further side of all the land of Persia, *de l'extrémité
de la Perse.*

[19] from high to low, *de haut en bas.*

[20] even as thyself, *tout comme toi.*

[21] shall I not pity thee, *n'aurais-je pas pitié de toi.*

[22] and she returned on her way, *et elle s'en retourna.*

[23] my noble horses every one = *everyone of my noble horses.*

[24] would I had given the best of them rather unto thee, *que
ne t'ai-je plutôt donné le meilleur d'entre eux.*

tains, and they had seized upon the herdsman, and
bound him, and carried him away into captivity, him
and all his household; and his herds and his flocks they
had driven away, and over the whole plain there was
nought but loneliness and the stillness of death. "The
Pearl of Price is not for the herdsman" (so said the
bird in the musings of her heart); "behold, I will deliver it unto the planter, *so*²⁵ shall he yield unto me the
fairest pomegranate of his orchard. And she went: but
lo, the earthquake had been there, and the earth *had
opened*²⁶ and swallowed up that orchard, with its trees,
and its fruits, and all its deliciousness; the planter also
lay there bruised and bleeding unto death. The bird
saw all that had befallen, and she said, "Let then the
Pearl of Price be for the Great King, in exchange for
one barley-corn to redeem the life *that is dear unto
me*²⁷." But *woe unto the proud*²⁸ who are hard of heart,
and the mighty who know not mercy! A king greater
and more powerful than he *hath come up against him*²⁹,
he hath routed his hosts, and slain his captains, *the
king himself also he hath smitten with the edge of the
sword*³⁰, and he hath put on his crown, and reigneth
in his stead.

And the bird saith, "Shall I not then give the Pearl
of Price to the fowler, instead of the barley-corn, for
redemption of my young one?" So she stretcheth her
wing northward for many days. And when she dra-
weth near the margin of the Caspian Sea, another bird
cometh to meet her, and behold, it is her own nestling,

---

²⁵ so, *et ainsi.*
²⁶ had opened, *s'était ouverte.*
²⁷ that is dear unto me, *qui m'est chère.*
²⁸ woe unto the proud, *malheur aux orgueilleux.*
²⁹ hath come up against him, *a marché contre lui.*
³⁰ the king himself also he hath smitten with the edge of the
sword = *he hath also smitten the king himself* (*with the edge of the
sword = du tranchant de son épée*).

and they kiss one another with their bills a hundred
times. "But where is the fowler?" saith the mother
bird; "and how hast thou escaped out of his hands?"
"The officers have taken him," saith the young bird,
"and the judge has judged him, because he laid wait
for the traveller to slay him, and his body now hangeth
on a tree. And I took my flight, for there was none
to stay me." "Then", saith the mother, "let us bear
back to the princess Zobeid her Pearl of Price, for only
she took pity on us". And they did as she had said.
But lo! the prince her husband was grown a great king,
and Zobeid was a queen and sat on a throne, and all
men *did her homage*[31]. And when the bird had showed
her all that had come to pass, *she caused it to be written
in a book*[32], *that men*[33] might remember mercy, and
help the poor and miserable, and not look for a gift
again[34].

64. THE ASS AND THE TREASURE.

Rajeb was a young man of Cairo, *who had been left
by his father with a fortune* of about two thousand piastres. *Had he*[1] embarked this little fortune in trade, and
been industrious, he might have lived very comfortably;
but *he fell in love*[2] soon after his father died, and could
think of nothing but the fair object of his passion. She
was a young girl, whose countenance he had first seen
for a moment, when by chance she put aside her veil
to drink at the fountain of a mosque. She was very

---

[31] did her homage, *lui rendaient hommage*.

[32] she caused it to be written in a book, *elle le fit écrire dans
un livre*.

[33] that men, *pour que les hommes*.

[34] again, *en retour*.

64. THE ASS AND THE TREASURE.

[1] Had he = *if he had*.

[2] he fell in love, *il devint amoureux*.

plainly dressed, and appeared to belong *to some humble, but decent family*[3]. But she was rich in beauty, at least, and in modesty, *for she hastily replaced her veil on seeing a young man looking at her*[4], and walked away without turning to the right or the left, or looking back *as coquettes do*[5]. Rajeb followed her, and saw her enter a plain house, of the kind inhabited by the middle orders. *From this time forward*[6], Rajeb was consumed by the passion which had sprung up in his breast. *Of the object of it he could learn no more than that she was as virtuous and well-behaved as she was beautiful*[7]. At length he *went to*[8] the parents of his mistress, and asked her hand *in marriage*[9]. They received him very kindly; but when he came to speak of the dowry *which they expected to be given by their daughter's husband*[10], they demanded the sum of five thousand piastres. This was above the lover's means, and *he exclaimed loudly*[11] against the enormity of the sum; but they were obstinate, and Rajeb could only prevail on them to give him a few days to reflect, and to look about him for means. If he did not appear at the end of the stated time, *they*

---

[3] to some humble, but decent family = *to some family humble, but decent.*

[4] for she hastily replaced her veil, on seeing a young man looking at her = *for, on seeing a young man looking at her, she hastily replaced her veil.*

[5] as coquettes do, *comme le font les coquettes.*

[6] from this time forward, *à partir de cette époque.*

[7] Of the object of it he could learn no more than that she was as virtuous and well behaved as she was beautiful, *Tout ce qu'il put apprendre sur cette jeune fille, c'est qu'elle était aussi vertueuse et d'aussi bonne conduite que belle.*

[8] he went to, *il alla trouver.*

[9] in marriage, not to be translated.

[10] which they expected to be given by their daughter's husband, *qu'ils attendaient du mari de leur fille.*

[11] he exclaimed loudly, *il se récria.*

would hold themselves at liberty[12], *they told him*[13], to accept of other offers.

Rajeb returned home, lamenting and reproaching himself with having idled away his past time. "Ah! if I had worked hard," said he, "I might have increased my fortune, and might now have been happy!" He took out his money, and counted it several times, *but he could not thus make it more than it was*[14] — two thousand piastres. He lay down on his bed, and tried to sleep, but his mind was too much occupied with projects for procuring the required dowry to permit him to rest. At last *he bethought him*[15] of a maternal uncle at Tantah, whom he had not seen *for*[16] eighteen years, *and who was said to be rich*[17]. Rajeb had no sooner thought of this person than he resolved to visit him. He would borrow the three thousand piastres; a rich relation could not refuse such a sum. The young man longed for the coming of day to set out on this hopeful errand.

Morning at length dawned, and Rajeb *started on his journey*[18]. In order to save money he went on foot, hoping, also, to interest his uncle the more by this economy. When he reached the first houses of Tantah, he inquired for his uncle Yousoff, "the rich Yousoff," of several boys whom he met. "The rich Yousoff!" cried they, "say rather the old beggarly miser Yousoff, who regrets to throw away a bone when he has picked *it white*[19]!" One of the boys, however, conducted Rajeb

---

[12] they would hold themselves at liberty, *ils se considéreraient libres.*

[13] they told him, *lui dirent-ils.*

[14] but he could not thus make it more than it was, *mais il ne pouvait l'augmenter ainsi.*

[15] he bethought him, *il se souvint d'un.*

[16] for, *depuis.*

[17] and who was said to be rich, *et qu'on disait être riche.*

[18] started on his journey, *se mit en route.*

[19] white, *à fond; complètement.*

to his uncle's house. The young man entered it trembling, for the description which he had heard was by no means encouraging. When his uncle came to him, Rajeb saw an old, withered, ragged, dirty being, who cried, "What do you want?" in a rough voice. "Ah, my dear uncle!" cried Rajeb, throwing his arms about the old man, "do you not remember me? I am Rajeb, the son of your sister—little Rajeb, whom you loved *when a boy*[20]; I am come, dear uncle, to see if you are well." "Very well," said Yousoff, "I am very well, but very poor. I shall not be able to show you very splendid hospitality." "What then?" said Rajeb, cheerfully; "riches and poverty come from God." At these words, they entered the old man's apartment, dark and dingy, without any other furniture than an old mat, and a jar of water; *neither pipes nor coffee were to be seen*[21]. Rajeb, however, was patient, and showed no ill humour. That evening they feasted upon a crust of wretched cheese, and some crumbs of black, detestable bread. The cheese, such as it was, was a novelty in that place, and the neighbours who saw the old man buy it, could scarcely believe their eyes.

Rajeb was not accustomed to rich fare, but after his journey *he stood really in need*[22] of soup and roast, or something else that was good. But he ate the bread and cheese, and said nothing. When they had done, he tried *to lead the conversation by degrees*[23] to the object of his journey. The old man, however, anticipated his purpose, and cried, "I am poor, a beggar; no der-

---

[20] when a boy, *quand il était enfant.*

[21] neither pipes nor coffee were to be seen = *one saw there neither pipes nor coffee.*

[22] he stood really in need, *il avait réellement besoin.*

[23] to lead the conversation by degrees, *d'amener peu à peu la conversation.*

vish is poorer than I am; I am ruined; all the world
robs me; I have spent my last para upon a dinner for
you." Rajeb perceived that he had to deal with a heart
of marble; so, after trying in vain to soften the old
man by descriptions of his mistress's beauty and his
own passion, the youth rose, and under pretence of taking the air, went out to conceal his bitter disappointment and vexation.

Troubled as he was with his own matters, Rajeb
could not look without pity on a poor ass which he
saw *on going out of doors*[24], and which was lying in a
little shed, munching some morsels of straw that lay
within its reach. Rajeb, who loved animals, approached
to caress the poor lean, starved creature, *which was all
hide-sore*[25]; and the ass seemed sensible of the affection
shown to it. Prompted by his natural benevolence,
Rajeb then went away, and bought a measure of barley,
and almost forgot his own griefs in the pleasure of
seeing the ass *fall to its food*[26] with the liveliest marks
of joy. After bringing it water to complete its meal,
the youth went back to his uncle. It is needless to
say that Rajeb passed an unhappy night; he lay on the
floor, and the vermin infesting the place were sufficient
of themselves to banish sleep. In the morning, the two
relations breakfasted on the relics of yesterday's meal,
and then the nephew *was about to take his leave*[27].
But his uncle stopt him, and said, "I have an ass which
is of no use to me. It is all that remains to me of
my substance, and if you wish" — Rajeb thought his
uncle was about to make him a present of the ass, but
he was in error, for the old man proceeded — "if you
wish, you may go with me to the market, and see me

---

[24] on going out of doors, *en allant dehors.*
[25] which was all hide-sore, *qui avait des ulcères plein la peau.*
[26] fall to its food, *tomber sur sa nourriture.*
[27] was about to take his leave, *était sur le point de prendre
congé.*

sell him." Rajeb consented, and when they went to
the stall of the ass, the young man again caressed the
poor animal. In return, it looked at him with eyes
full of intelligence, and struck the ground several times
with its foot. Rajeb even thought he heard it say,
"Buy me." *Its looks at least, he thought, said so*[28].

On the way to the market, Rajeb reflected on the
subject, and felt himself impelled to purchase the ass
by some involuntary feeling, which most people would
have been disposed merely to call good-nature or pity.
As the ass was young, *and had no faults but those arising from starvation*[29], several purchasers *came forward*[30].
One offered two hundred piastres, another three hundred, and at last the price *mounted*[31] to five hundred.
When Rajeb saw that his uncle was willing to take
this, he offered a few piastres more, assured that he
would get the ass. *"What do you want with the ass?"*[32]
said the old man. "I am resolved *upon having it*[33]," was
all that the nephew answered. "Ah, well!" said Yousoff,
with a smile of greedy pleasure, "you must give me a
thousand piastres, and then it shall be yours." Rajeb
was shocked at the miser's demand; but the old man,
seeing his nephew's anxiety, would not abate of his ex-
orbitant request, and the youth at last agreed, and a
bargain *was struck*[34].

As Rajeb had left all his money at Cairo, it was
agreed that Yousoff should go back with his nephew to
that city, and there receive the purchase-money. Ac-

---

[28] Its looks, at least he thought, said so, *du moins, pensait-il,
ses regards le disaient.*

[29] and had no faults but those arising from starvation, *et n'avait
d'autres défauts que ceux qui provenaient du manque de nourriture.*

[30] came forward, *se présentèrent.*

[31] mounted, *s'éleva.*

[32] what do you want with the ass, *que voulez-vous faire de l'âne.*

[33] upon having it, *à l'avoir.*

[34] was struck, *fut conclu.*

cordingly, they set out, and the ass with them. By the
way, the creature seemed to be inspired with fresh life,
and gambolled and danced *as if to please*[35] its new master.
Arrived at Cairo, Rajeb gave his uncle the promised
sum, and entertained him handsomely. After a few days
Yousoff departed, and left his nephew alone. The latter
occupied himself in making a good stall for his ass, and
in tending and cleaning it, *by which means*[36] it soon became
quite a new creature. As for the mistress of his heart,
Rajeb had almost given up all hope of her. The interval
allowed him by the parents had expired, and the youth,
now poorer than before, did not dare to present himself
before them. *Whilst matters stood thus*[37], information
was brought to him that his uncle had been found dead
by the road-side[38], having been plundered and killed by
robbers. The young man shed a tear for the sudden
end of the miser, and then made preparations to go to
Tantah *to take up*[39] the deceased's inheritance, though
there seemed little hope of its proving great, notwithstanding the reputation which Yousoff had once acquired
for being rich.

Mounting his ass, Rajeb proceeded to Tantah. He
put up the ass in its old stall, and went into the house
to search it. As he had almost expected, not a para
was to be found; not a vestige of any thing valuable
was visible in any corner of the wretched abode. While
Rajeb was prosecuting his examination, he was surprised by the continued whining and braying of his ass.
Thinking he had neglected its wants, he went out
several times, and put barley, straw, and water before it;
but the animal would not touch them, and continued

---

[35] as if to please, *comme pour plaire.*
[36] by which means, *par ce moyen.*
[37] whilst matters stood thus, *pendant que les affaires en étaient
à ce point.*
[38] by the road-side, *sur la route.*
[39] to take up, *pour prendre possession.*

to stamp on the floor of its stall with its foot. Rajeb's attention was at length attracted to this movement, and the ass, seeing this, repeated it with increased vehemence. Its master, seizing a bar of rusty iron which stood by, then commenced to turn up the ground where the ass sruck. As he did this, the animal looked on with eyes glistening with eager pleasure, and seemed as if it would fain say, "Go on, go on; it is there". At last, Rajeb came to a coffer. He turned it out, and behold! it was filled to overflowing with doubloons, sequins, and all sorts of precious coins. The youth hugged his treasure, but the ass would not yet let him rest. It struck the ground in another spot with his feet, and Rajeb, on digging anew, found a second coffer, filled with pearls, rubies, emeralds, and other valuable gems.

The ass stamped no more, and Rajeb hastened to secure his treasures, and to get them transported to Cairo. He put them into two panniers, and, although they were very heavy, the ass never slackened its speed, nor gave any signs of weariness, until it brought its burden to its master's door. On the night of his arrival, Rajeb *hastened to the house*[40] of his mistress. He was just *in the nick of time*[41], for an old Turk had seen her, and offered the five thousand piastres to the parents. Rajeb, however, took the father home with him, and showed a part of his treasures, when the marriage was at once agreed on. The young bride proved to be really as virtuous as she was beautiful and made Rajeb happy. He *gave*[42] large donations to the poor *on*[43] the occasion of his wedding. As for the ass, it had the place of honour, during its life, in the stable, and was never doomed to any other toil than that of bear-

[40] hastened to the house of, *se hâta d'aller chez.*
[41] in the nick of time, *à point nommé.*
[42] gave, *fit.*
[43] on, *à.*

ing its mistress and her children. Its master visited the stable every day, and spoke with it as with an old friend.

65. LADY JANE GREY.

This amiable and accomplished lady, who fell a victim *to*[1] ambition *not her own*[2], was daughter of Henry Grey, marquis of Dorset, and granddaughter of Mary, queen-dowager of France, widow of Louis XII. and sister of Henry VIII.: thus, being of royal blood, her hand was sought *by many of*[3] the nobles. Among the most ambitious was the rich and powerful duke of Northumberland, who to maintain and advance the influence of his own family, contrived *to bring about*[4] a marriage between his son lord Guildford Dudley and the lady Jane.

Having succeeded in this preliminary step, his next project was to seat his daughter-in-law, and consequently his son beside her, on the throne of England after the death of Edward VI., whose health was in such a precarious state that it was evident *he was hastening to his fathers*[5]. — Between lady Jane and the crown stood Mary and Elizabeth, daughters of Henry VIII.; but Northumberland flattered himself that he could easily remove those obstacles, as Henry's marriage with their mothers, Catherine of Aragon and Ann Boleyn, had been dissolved and the children declared illegitimate.

Having matured his plan, the ambitious duke availed himself of the weakness of the king, who was almost

---

65. LADY JANE GREY.

[1] to = *of an.*
[2] not her own, *qui n'était pas la sienne.*
[3] by many of, *par un grand nombre de.*
[4] to bring about, *à faire faire.*
[5] he was hastening to his fathers, *qu'il allait à grand pas retrouver ses aïeux.*

at the point of death[6], declaring that, if Mary should succeed to the throne, the kingdom would fall again under
the influence of Rome, and also that the illegitimacy of both
her and her sister rendered their claims invalid, and might
expose the kingdom to the dangers of a disputed succession and civil war. All this, he added, might be avoided
by his majesty's entailing[7] the crown on the descen-
dants of his aunt the queen-dowager of France.

These specious arguments had such an effect on Edward that with his own hand he sketched the draught
of a *deed of settlement*[8], changing the succession, and
ordered his *privy councillors*[9] to give it all the legal
forms. This was done, but not without such opposition
as convinced the duke there would be ulterior difficulties to surmount.

About a fortnight after, on the 6th of July 1553,
the king expired: his death was however kept a secret
till the 10th, when Northumberland and the lords of
his party went to the house of lady Jane, told her that
her cousin Edward was dead, and that he had bequea-
thed her the crown. On hearing the news she trembled,
shrieked, and fell to the ground; but on recovering she
observed[10] that she thought herself a very unfit person
to be a queen; however, if it were her right, she
hoped that "God would enable her to wield the sceptre
to his honour, and for the good of the nation." On the
following day the queen was conveyed to the Tower to
await her coronation, and in the afternoon the heralds
proclaimed her accession with the usual ceremonies.

Northumberland however had miscalculated his resources; the people rose in favour of Mary, the elder

[6] at the point of death, *à l'article de la mort.*
[7] by his majesty's entailing, *si sa majesté substituait.*
[8] deed of settlement, *acte de substitution.*
[9] privy councillors, *membres du conseil privé.*
[10] she observed, *elle fit observer.*

sister of Edward, and after a slight show of resistance
the partisans of lady Jane *laid down their arms*[11], and
dispersed. Mary was proclaimed queen, and thus, in
the short space of eight days, terminated the ephemeral
reign of Jane Grey. Her father-in-law, the duke, and
two of the most active of his adherents, were executed;
but Mary refused to condemn lady Jane and her husband, saying *they had only been puppets*[12] in the hands
of the ambitious Northumberland. But in the following
year a dangerous insurrection alarmed the queen and
threatened the stability of her throne. Her councillors
told her that her lenity had encouraged her enemies,
and that she must not expect[13] to reign in peace while
her adversaries could rally round a person, whose pretended claim to the throne had already rendered her
accession very doubtful.

These persuasions decided her to sacrifice her cousin
to her own safety, and she immediately signed a war-
rant for the execution of lord Guildford Dudley and his
wife, who were already in the Tower. — *On the fatal
morning*[14] permission was granted them *to take a last
farewell of each other*[15]; but Jane declined the indulgence, saying they should soon meet *in*[16] heaven. From
the window of her cell *she saw her husband led to execution*[17], *and beheld his bleeding corpse brought back*[18].
He had been executed on Towerhill in sight of the po-

---

[11] laid down their arms, *mirent bas les armes.*

[12] they had only been puppets, *qu'ils n'avaient été que des jouets.*

[13] and that she must not expect, *et qu'il ne fallait pas qu'elle s'attendît à.*

[14] On the fatal morning, *le matin du jour fatal.*

[15] to take a last farewell of each other, *de se dire un dernier adieu.*

[16] in, *au.*

[17] she saw her husband led to execution, *elle vit conduire son mari à l'échafaud.*

[18] and beheld his bleeding corpse brought back, *et vit ramener son corps sanglant.*

pulace; *but she, in consideration of her royal descent, was spared*[19] the ignominy of a public execution. A scaffold was prepared for her on the parade within the walls of the Tower. She was conducted to it by sir John Gage, the constable; sir John Brydges the lieutenant's brother, who was present, requested her to give him some token of her remembrance; she immediately presented to him *her table-book*[20], in which she had just written three sentences, one in Greek, one in˙Latin and one in English, concerning the execution of her husband. She *mounted*[21] the scaffold *with*[22] a firm step, addressed the spectators, stating that her crime *was having consented*[23] to the treason of Northumberland, and denying all previous knowledge of the conspiracy. *She then, with the assistance of the priest, laid her head upon the block*[24]; it was severed by one blow, and thus perished one of the most accomplished and amiable ladies of the English court, a victim to the inordinate ambition of her intriguing father-in-law, the duke of Northumberland.

66.   HOW *TO BREAK ILL NEWS*[1].

A dialogue.   Scene: The *rooms*[2] of Mr. G—, at Oxford.

(Enter his father's steward.)

Mr. G.   Ha Jervas! how are you *my old boy*[3]? How do things go on at home?

---

[19] but she, in consideration of her royal descent, was spared, *mais, en considération de sa naissance royale, on lui épargna.*

[20] her table-book, *ses tablettes.*

[21] mounted, *monta sur.*

[22] with, *d'un.*

[23] was having consented, *était d'avoir consenti.*

[24] she then ... laid her head = *then, with the assistance of the priest, she laid her head upon the block.*

66.   HOW TO BREAK ILL NEWS.   (HOW ONE BREAKS ILL NEWS.)

[1] to break ill news, *faire part de mauvaises nouvelles.*

[2] rooms, *appartements.*

[3] my old boy, *mon vieux.*

Steward. Bad enough, *your honour*[4], the magpie's dead.

Mr. G. Poor Mag! So he is *gone*[5]. *How came he to die*[6].

Steward. *Overate himself*[7], Sir.

Mr. G. Did he faith! *A greedy dog*[8]! Why, what did he get, that he liked so well?

Steward. Horseflesh, Sir! He died of eating horseflesh.

Mr. G. *How came he to get*[9] so much horseflesh?

Steward. All your father's horses, Sir.

Mr. G. What! Are they dead too?

Steward. Aye, Sir, they died of overwork.

Mr. G. And why were they overworked, pray?

Steward. To carry water, Sir.

Mr. G. To carry water! And what were they carrying water for?

Steward. Sure, Sir, to put out the fire.

Mr. G. *Fire*[10]! What fire?

Steward. Oh Sir, your father's house is burnt down to the ground.

Mr. G. My father's house burnt down; And *how came it set on fire*[11]?

Steward. I think, Sir, it must have been the torches . . . . .

Mr. G. Torches! What torches?

Steward. At your mother's funeral.

Mr. G. My mother dead!

Steward. Ah poor lady! *She never looked up after it*[12].

---

[4] your honour, *mon maître.*
[5] gone = *dead.*
[6] how came he to die, *comment a-t-elle fait pour mourir.*
[7] overate himself, *s'est tuée de trop manger.*
[8] a greedy dog, *gourmand de chien.*
[9] how came he to get, *comment lui est-il arrivé d'avoir.*
[10] fire = *the fire.*
[11] how came it set on fire, *comment en est elle venue à être brûlée.*
[12] she never looked up after it, *elle ne s'en est jamais remise·*

Mr. G. *After what*[13]?

Steward. *The loss of your father*[14].

Mr. G. My father gone too?

Steward. Yes, poor *gentleman*[15]! *He took to his bed*[16] as soon as he *heard of it*[17].

Mr. G. *Heard*[18] of what!

Steward. The bad news, Sir.

Mr. G. What! More miseries! More bad news!

Steward. Yes, Sir, your bank has failed, and *you are not worth*[19] a shilling in the world. *I made bold*[20], Sir, to come to wait on you to tell you about it, for I thought you would like to *hear*[21] the news.

67. A DANGEROUS JOURNEY IN LABRADOR.

Samuel Liebisch was required by the duties of his office to visit Okkak[1], the most northern of the settlements, *and about one hundred and fifty English miles distant*[2] from Nain, the place where he resided. Another European, named Turner, *being appointed*[3] to accompany him, they left Nain on March 11th 1782, *early in the morning*[4], with very clear weather, the stars shining

---

[13] after what? *de quoi?*

[14] the loss of your father = *of the loss* &c.

[15] gentleman, *monsieur*.

[16] he took to his bed, *il prit le lit.*

[17] heard of it, *en entendit parler.*

[18] heard, *entendit parler.*

[19] you are not worth, *vous ne possédez pas.*

[20] I made bold, *je me suis hasardé à.*

[21] to hear, *à apprendre.*

67. A DANGEROUS JOURNEY IN LABRADOR.

[1] Samuel Liebisch was required by the duties of his office to visit Okkah, *les devoirs de sa profession demandaient que Samuel Liebisch visitât Okkah.*

[2] and about 150 English miles distant = *and distant of about* &c. &c.

[3] being appointed = *having been appointed.*

[4] early in the morning, *le matin de bonne heure.*

with uncommon lustre.—The sledge drawn by dogs
in which the brethren travelled, was driven by the bap-
tized Esquimaux Mark, and another sledge carrying some
heathen Esquimaux *joined company*[5].

The two sledges contained five men, one woman and
a child. All were in good spirits, and appearances being
much in their favour, they hoped to reach Okkak in
safety in two or three days. The track over the frozen
sea was in the best possible order, and they went with
ease at the rate of six or seven miles an hour. After
they had passed the islands in the bay of Nain, they
kept at a considerable distance from the coast, both to
gain the smoothest part of the ice, and *to weather*[6] the
high rocky promontory of Kiglapeit. About eight o'clock,
they met a sledge with Esquimaux, *turning in from the
sea*[7]. After the usual salutations, the Esquimaux alight-
ing, held some conversation, as is their general practice,
the result of which was, that some hints were thrown
out by the strange Esquimaux, that it might be as well
to return.—However, as the Missionaries saw no reason
whatever for it, and only suspected that the Esquimaux
wished to enjoy the company of their friends a little
longer, they proceded.—After some time, their own Esquimaux hinted, *that there was a ground swell*[8] under
the ice. It was then hardly perceptible, except on lying
down and applying the ear *close to the ice*[9], *when a
hollow disagreeable grating and roaring noise was heard*[10],
as if ascending[11] from the abyss. The weather remained
clear, except towards the east, where a bank of light

---

5 joined company, *se joignit à eux.*
6 to weather, *pour doubler.*
7 turning in from the sea, *qui venait du côté de la mer.*
8 that there was a ground swell, *qu'il y avait de la houle.*
9 close to the ice, *près de la glace.*
10 when a hollow disagreeable ... was heard = *then one could
hear* &c.
11 as if ascending, *qu'on aurait dit monter.*

clouds appeared, interspersed with some dark streaks. But the wind being strong, from the north west, nothing was less expected than a sudden change of weather.

The sun had now reached *its height*[12], and there was as yet little or no alteration in the appearance of the sky. But the motion of the sea under the ice had grown more perceptible, so as rather to alarm the travellers, and they began to think it prudent to keep closer to the shore. The ice had cracks and large fissures in many places, some of which formed chasms of one or two feet wide; but as they are not uncommon, even in its best state, and the dogs easily leap over them the sledge following without danger, they are only terrible to new comers, inexperienced, in the peculiarities of Labrador travelling.

As soon as the sun declined towards the west, the wind increased and *rose to a storm*[13], the bank of clouds from the east began to ascend, and the dark streaks to put themselves in motion against the wind. The snow was violently driven about by partial whirlwinds both on the ice, and from off the peaks of the high mountains, and filled the air. At the same time the ground swell had increased so much, that its effect upon the ice became very extraordinary and alarming. The sledges instead of gliding along smoothly upon an even surface sometimes ran with violence after the dogs, and shortly after seemed with difficulty to ascend the rising hill, for the elasticity of so vast a body of ice, of many leagues square, supported by a troubled sea, though in some places three or four yards in thickness, would *in some degree*[14] occasion an undulatory motion not unlike that of a sheet of paper, accommodating itself to the surface of a rippling stream. Noises were likewise

---

[12] its height, *son méridien.*
[13] and rose to a storm, *et finit par souffler en tempête.*
[14] in some degree, *jusqu'à un certain point.*

distinctly heard in many directions, like the report of cannon, *owing to*[15] the bursting of the ice at some distance.

The Esquimaux therefore drove with all haste towards the shore, intending to take up their nightquarters on the south side of Uivak. But, as it plainly appeared that the ice would break and disperse in the open sea, Mark advised to push forward to the North of Uivak, from whence he hoped the track to Okkak might still remain entire. To this proposal the company agreed, but when the sledges approached the coast, the prospect before them was truly terrific. The ice having broken loose from the rocks, was forced up and down, grinding and breaking into a thousand pieces against the precipices with a tremendous noise, which, added to the raging of the wind, and the snow driving about in the air, deprived the travellers almost of the power of hearing and seeing anything distinctly. *To make*[16] the land at any risk, was now the only hope left, but it was with the utmost difficulty the frightened dogs could be forced forward, the whole body of ice sinking frequently below the level of the rocks, and then rising above it. As the only moment to land was that, when it gained the level of the coast, the attempt was extremely nice and hazardous. However, providentially it succeeded; both sledges gained the shore and were drawn up the beach with much difficulty.

The travellers had hardly time to reflect with gratitude to God, on their safety, when that part of the ice, *from which they had but just made good their landing*[17], burst asunder and the water forcing itself from below, covered and precipitated it into the sea. In an

---

[15] owing, *dus.*

[16] to make, *pour atteindre.*

[17] from which they had just made good their landing, *d'où ils venaient à peine d'effectuer leur débarquement avec succès.*

instant, as if by a signal given, the whole mass of ice,
extending for several miles from the coast, and as far
as the eye could reach began to burst, and to be overwhelmed by the immense waves. The sight was tremendous and awfully grand, the large fields of ice raising themselves out of the water, striking against each
other and plunging into the deep, with a violence *not
to be described*[18], and a noise like the discharge of innumerable batteries *of heavy guns*[19]. The darkness of
the night, the roaring of the wind and sea, and the
dashing of the waves and ice against the rocks, filled
the travellers with sensations of awe and horror, so as
almost to deprive them of the power of utterance. They
stood overwhelmed with astonishment, at their miraculous
escape, and even the heathen Esquimaux expressed gratitude to God for their deliverance.

68. MASSACRE AT THE CORONATION OF WILLIAM I. IN LONDON.

*William I., duke of Normandy, may be said to have
been crowned*[1] *in the character of*[2] a conqueror. *Having*, by the battle of Hastings, *made himself master*[3] of
England, Christmas-day 1066 was appointed for his coronation, at Westminster. He was surrounded by his Norman barons, *and a full attendance*[4] of the English nobles
and prelates.—Aldred, then archbishop of York, put the

---

[18] not to be described, *qu'on ne peut décrire.*
[19] heavy guns, *canons de gros calibres.*

68. MASSACRE AT THE CORONATION OF WILLIAM I. IN LONDON.

[1] William I, duke of Normandy, may be said to have been
crowned = *one may say that William I, duke of Normandy, was
crowned.*
[2] in the character of, *comme.*
[3] Having made himself master, *s'étant rendu maître.*
[4] and a full attendance, *et une nombreuse suite.*

questions of recognition[5] to his new subjects; and the
bishop of Coutances, who was in his train, put them to
the Normans.

The assent of both nations was given with loud ac-
clamation. So boisterous indeed was their loyalty at
this part of the ceremony, that the Norman soldiers of
William, who were on the outside of the Abbey church,
affected to consider the shouts as the signal of insurrection, and immediately *set fire to*[6] the houses of the
neighbourhood, and began to plunder, to the great mortification of the king. All now became confusion in the
interior of the Abbey: the Norman barons prepared for
battle; the native nobles regarded themselves as victims
selected for slaughter, and the king is said to have been
left alone with the ecclesiastics to conclude the ceremony.

That the shouts were but the pretext[7] for a precon-
certed attack and plunder of the people, *appears but
too clearly*[8] from the subsequent remonstrances of the
king with the barons, *whom he warned against*[9] the
dangerous result of oppressing the English while he
strictly prohibited the soldiers from appearing at taverns,
or molesting the private abodes of the citizens, and appointed a commission to enforce his regulations.

69. CURIOUS ANECDOTE OF OLIVER CROMWELL.

Oliver Cromwell was, perhaps, the most finished hypo-
crite that ever raised himself upon the ruins of a power,
in whose destruction[1] he had taken so active a part;

---

[5] questions of recognition, *questions de confirmation.*
[6] set fire to, *mirent le feu à.*
[7] That the shouts were but the pretext, *que les cris n'étaient qu'un
prétexte.*
[8] appears but too clearly, *n'apparait que trop clairement.*
[9] whom he warned against, *qu'il avertit du.*

69. CURIOUS ANECDOTE OF OLIVER CROMWELL.
[1] in whose destruction = *to the destruction of which.*

and he became, like many popular leaders, far more despotic than his victim Charles I., whose want of firmness caused the ruin of his throne, and enabled his enemies to offer him *as a*[2] sacrifice to popular discontent and excitation.

When Cromwell *had succeeded in placing himself*[3] at the head of the government, his conduct became so arrogant and arbitrary that many who had assisted him, discovering he had only used them as stepping-stones, to reach the object of his ambition, became his greatest enemies. The protector, knowing that there were many who would be glad *to get rid of*[4] him, began to fear assassination. He therefore took the greatest precautions, *such as*[5] *wearing*[6] armour under his clothes, *being*[7] accompanied by a numerous escort, *carrying*[8] loaded pistols in his pockets, and, when he went out, *changing*[9] his road, and *returning*[10] in a contrary direction.

An extraordinary accident, *which had well nigh proved*[11] fatal to Cromwell, discovered to the public *the circumstance of his wearing firearms*[12]. The duke of Oldenburgh had sent him a present of six Friesland coach-horses, and one day after, dining with his secretary Thurloe, Cromwell took a fancy *to try his hand at*[13] driving them. He told Thurloe *to enter*[14] the carriage, while he

---

[2] as a, *en.*
[3] had succeeded in placing himself, *eut réussi à se placer.*
[4] to get rid of, *de se débarrasser.*
[5] such as, *telle que celle de.*
[6] wearing = *to wear.*
[7] being = *to be.*
[8] carrying = *to carry.*
[9] changing = *to change.*
[10] returning = *to return, all these verbs are governed by the "de" of "telle que celle de." Note 5.*
[11] which had well nigh, *qui avait failli être.*
[12] the circumstance of his wearing fire-arms, *le fait qu'il portait des armes à feu.*
[13] to try his hand at, *d'essayer de.*
[14] to enter, *de monter dans.*

himself *mounted the box*[15], and taking the reins in his
hand, began to apply the whip with a prodigal hand to
his new subjects; but he soon discovered that they were
not easily governed, and that he was less adroit *in*[16]
holding the reins on the coach-box, than those of the
government. The horses, frightened by his unskilful
driving, *ran away*[17] with the carriage, *nor could Cromwell, with all his efforts*[18], stop them. At length, by a
sudden jerk, he was thrown from the box, and fell on
the *pole*[19] between the horses. The shock of the fall
caused one of the pistols *to go off*[20] and the explosion
increased the fright and rapidity of the animals, so that
Cromwell *expected nothing less than*[21] to be killed; however, contriving to disengage himself, he fell under the
carriage, which passed over him without *doing him any
injury*[22].

He was taken up by the guards who followed[23], and conveyed to Whitehall, where he was confined during some
time in consequence of the fright and bruises he had
received. Thurloe had leaped from the carriage *while
at full speed*[24], and escaped with a few slight contusions.
The Cavaliers[25] diverted themselves at the expense of
Cromwell, saying his first fall had been from a coach,
but his next would probably be from a cart.

---

[15] mounted the box, *monta sur le siège.*
[16] in = *à*
[17] ran away, *prirent le mors aux dents.*
[18] nor could Cromwell, with all his efforts = *and with all his
efforts, Cromwell could not.*
[19] pole, *flèche.*
[20] caused to go off, *fit partir.*
[21] expected nothing less than, *ne s'attendait à rien moins qu'à.*
[22] without doing him any injury, *sans lui faire aucun mal.*
[23] he was taken up by the guards who followed = *the guards
who followed took him up.* took him up, "*le ramassèrent.*"
[24] while at full speed, *pendant qu'elle allait à toute vitesse.*
[25] cavaliers, *royalistes.*

70. THE DEFENCE OF THE CASTLE OF DUNBAR.
(FROM SCOTT'S "TALES OF A GRANDFATHER".)

Among the warlike exploits in Scotland of 1335[1] we may give an account of the defence of the castle of Dunbar, by the celebrated Countess of March. Her *lord*[2] had embraced *the side*[3] of David Bruce, and *taken the field*[4] with the Regent. The Countess, who from her complexion was termed *Black Agnes*[5], *by which name she is still familiarly remembered*[6], was a highspirited and courageous woman, the daughter of that Thomas Randolph, Earl of Moray, whom I have so often mentioned, and the heiress of his valour and patriotism. The castle of Dunbar *itself was very strong*[7], being built upon a chain of rocks stretching into the sea, having only one passage to the mainland which was well fortified. It was besieged by Montague, Earl of Salisbury, who employed to destroy its walls great military engines, constructed to throw huge stones, with which machines fortifications were attacked before the use of cannon. Black Agnes *set all his attempts at defiance*[8], and showed herself with her maids on the walls of the castle, wiping the places where the huge stones fell with a clean towel, as if they could do no ill to her castle save raising a little dust which a napkin could wipe away.

The Earl of Salisbury then commanded them, to bring forward to the assault an engine of another kind, being a species of wooden shed or house, rolled forwards on

---

70. THE DEFENCE OF THE CASTLE OF DUNBAR.

[1] Among the warlike exploits in Scotland of 1335 = *Among the warlike exploits of the year 1335 in Scotland.*

[2] lord, *époux.*

[3] the side, *le parti.*

[4] taken the field, *s'était mis en campagne.*

[5] Black Agnes = *Agnes the black.*

[6] by which name she is still familiarly remembered, *nom sous lequel on se la rappelle encore familièrement.*

[7] itself was very strong = *was very strong by itself.*

[8] set all his attempts at defiance, *se rit de toutes ses tentatives.*

wheels, with a roof of peculiar strength, *which from resembling the ridge of a hog's back occasioned the machine to be called a Sow*[9]. This, according to the old mode of warfare, was thrust up to the walls of a besieged castle or city and served to protect from the arrows and stones of the besieged a party of soldiers placed within the sow, who were in the meanwhile to undermine the wall, or *break*[10] an entrance through it with pickaxes and mining tools. When the Countess of March saw this engine advanced to the walls of the castle, she called out to the Earl of Salisbury in derision, and making a kind of rhyme, —

"Beware, Montagow,
For farrow shall thy sow."

At the same time she made a signal, and *a huge fragment of rock, which hung prepared for the purpose was dropped*[11] down from the wall upon the sow, whose roof was thus dashed to pieces. As the English soldiers who had been within it were running as fast as they could to get out of the way of arrows and stones from the wall, Black Agnes called out, "Behold the *litter of English pigs*[12]!"

The Earl of Salisbury could jest also on such occasions. One day he rode near the walls with a knight dressed in armour of proof, having three folds of mail over an *acton*[13], or leathern jacket, notwithstanding which one William Spence shot an arrow with such force that it penetrated all these defences, and reached the

---

[9] which from resembling the ridge of a hog's back occasioned the machine to be called a Sow, *qu'à cause de sa ressemblance avec l'échine d'un porc on appella "truie"*. The equivalent French word for the military engine called sow is *Tortue*.

[10] break, *forcer*.

[11] and a huge fragment of rock, which hung prepared for the purpose was dropped, *et on laissa tomber un énorme fragment de rocher qu'on avait suspendu à dessein.*

[12] litter of English pigs, *la cochonnée anglaise.*

[13] acton, *hoqueton.*

7 *

heart of the wearer. "That is one of my lady's love tokens," said the Earl, as he saw the knight fall dead from his horse. "Black Agnes' love shafts pierce to the heart."

71. SINGULAR RECOGNITION.

During the siege of Kuddalore, in 1785, the French commander, M. de Bassy, having received a reinforcement of troops from the fleet of M. de Suffren *determined*[1] to make a sortie, which was successful. *In the*[2] number of the wounded prisoners, which he left *in the*[2] power of the English, there was a young French serjeant who by his interesting manner of expressing himself, and by his conduct, drew so strongly the attention of Colonel Wangenheim, who commanded the Hanoverian troops *in the*[2] service of England, *that he caused him to be brought*[3] to his tent, where he was treated with much kindness and care, until his cure and exchange.

Some years ago when General Bernadotte commanded the French army in Hanover, General Wangenheim, accompanied by many officers, went *to pay him*[4] a visit. When he was presented to the French general, he informed him that he had served in the Indies before Kuddalore. Bernadotte said he had served there also; "and do you not recollect," pursued he, "a wounded serjeant whom you took under your protection during the siege?" The general, after some reflection, said: "Yes, I remember that adventure. He was a young man of fine talents; I have never *heard of him*[5] since. I should be delighted to hear of him." "That young

---

71. SINGULAR RECOGNITION.

[1] determined, *se détermina.*
[2]. [2]. [2] in the, *au.*
[3] that he caused him to be brought, *qu'il le fit porter.*
[4] to pay him, *lui faire.*
[5] heard of him, *entendu parler de lui.*

serjeant," replied Bernadotte, "is the same person who
now has the honour of entertaining you, who esteems
himself happy to acknowledge here publicly all that he
owes to you, and who will suffer no occasion to pass
by of manifesting to General Wangenheim *how grateful
he is to him for* [6] his kindness.

72. WHALE FISHING.

The maternal affection of the whale, *which in other
respects is apparently* [1] a stupid animal, is striking and
interesting. The cub, being insensible to danger is easily
harpooned, when the tender affection of the mother is
so manifested, *as* [2] not unfrequently to bring it within
reach of the whalers. Hence, though a cub is of little
value, yet it is sometimes struck, as a snare for its mother. In this case she joins it at the surface of the
water, *whenever it has occasion to rise for respiration* [3];
encourages it to swim away, assists its flight by taking
it under her fin; and seldom deserts it while life remains.
She is then dangerous to approach, but affords frequent
opportunities for attack. *She loses all regard for her
own safety, in anxiety for the preservation of her young* [4];
dashes through the midst of her enemies; despises the
danger that threatens her, and even voluntarily remains
with her offspring, after various attacks have been made
upon herself. In the whale fishery of 1814 a harpooner

---

[6] how grateful he is to him for, *combien il lui est reconnais-
sant de.*

72. WHALE FISHING (*la pêche à la baleine*).

[1] which in other respects is apparently, *qui sous d'autres rap-
ports paraît être.*

[2] as = *that it.*

[3] whenever it has occasion to rise for respiration, *lorsqu'il lui
arrive de remonter pour respirer.*

[4] She loses all regard for her own safety, in anxiety for the
preservation of her young = *in her anxiety for the preservation of
her young, she loses all regard for her own safety.*

struck a young whale, with the hope of its leading to the mother. Presently, *she arose*[5] and seizing the young one, dragged about a hundred fathoms of line out of the boat, with remarkable force and velocity. Again she rose to the surface: darted furiously to and fro; frequently stopped short, or suddenly changed her direction, and gave every possible intimation of extreme agony. *For a length of time*[6] she continued thus to act, though closely pursued by the boats; and inspired with courage and resolution by her concern for her offspring, seemed regardless of the danger, that surrounded her: Being at length struck with six harpoons, she was killed.

73. LOPE DE VEGA.
ASTONISHING FECUNDITY OF HIS POETIC TALENT.

Lope de Vega is called by Cervantes[1] a prodigy of nature, *and such he really may be reckoned*[2], not that we can ascribe to him a sublime genius, or a mind abounding with fine original thought; but his fertility of invention and readiness of versifying *are beyond competition*[3]. *He required no more than*[4] four and twenty hours to write *a versified drama*[5] of three acts, interspersed with sonnets, and abounding in intrigue. This astonishing facility enabled him to supply the Spanish theatre with more than two thousand original dramas. In gene-

---

[5] she arose, *elle remonta.*
[6] for a length of time, *pendant longtemps.*

73. LOPE DE VEGA.

[1] Lope de Vega is called by Cervantes = *Cervantes calls Lope de Vega.*
[2] and such he really may be reckoned = *and one may reckon him for such.*
[3] are beyond competition, *sont hors concours.*
[4] he required no more than, *il ne lui fallait pas plus de.*
[5] a versified drama = *a drama in verse.*

ral the *theatrical manager*[6] carried away what he wrote
before he had even time to revise it; and immediately
a fresh applicant would arrive, to prevail on him to
commence a new piece. According to his own testimony
he wrote *on an average*[7] five *sheets*[8] a day, so that he
must have written upwards of 21,300,000 verses.

This peculiar gift of rapid composition will appear
more extraordinary when we attend to the nature of
Lope's versification. At every step we meet with acro-
stics, echoes, and compositions *of that perverted and
laborious kind*[9], which, though they require no genius,
exact much time, *that one should think such a voluminous poet could little afford to waste*[10]. But Lope made
a parade of his power over the *vocabulary*[11] : he was not
contented with displaying the various order in which he
could dispose the syllables, and *marshal*[12] the rhymes
of his language; *he also prided himself upon*[13] the celer-
ity with which he brought them to go through the most
whimsical, but the most difficult evolutions. He seems
to have been partial to difficulties for the gratification
of surmounting them.

74. RURAL LIFE IN ENGLAND.

The stranger *who would form*[1] a correct opinion of
the English character, *must not*[2] confine his observations

---

[6] the theatrical manager, *le directeur du théâtre.*
[7] on an average, *l'un dans l'autre.*
[8] sheets, *feuilles (of 16 pages).*
[9] of that perverted and laborious kind, *de ce genre faussé et
pénible.*
[10] that one should think such a voluminous poet could little
afford to waste, *qu'on ne croirait pas qu'un poëte aussi prolixe ait pu
se permettre de gaspiller.*
[11] vocabulary, *dictionnaire.*
[12] and marshal, *et d'aligner.*
[13] he also prided himself upon, *il se faisait aussi gloire de.*

74. RURAL LIFE IN ENGLAND.

[1] who would form, *qui veut se former.*
[2] must not, *ne doit pas.*

to the metropolis. *He must*³ go forth into the country; he must sojourn in villages and hamlets; he must visit castles, villas, farm-houses, cottages; he must wander through parks and gardens; along hedges and green lanes; he must loiter about country churches; attend wakes and fairs, and other rural festivals; and cope with the people in all their conditions, and in all their habits and humours.

In some countries the large cities absorb the wealth and fashion of the nation; they are the only fixed abodes of elegant and intelligent society, and the country is inhabited almost entirely by *boorish peasantry*⁴. In England, on the contrary, the metropolis is *a mere gathering-place*⁵, or general rendezvous of the polite classes, where they devote a small portion of the year to *a hurry of gaiety and dissipation*⁶, and *having indulged*⁷ this kind of carnival, return again to the apparently more congenial habits of rural life. The various *orders*⁸ of society are therefore diffused over the whole surface of the kingdom, and the most retired neighbourhoods *afford*⁹ specimens of the different ranks.

*The English, in fact*¹⁰, are strongly gifted *with the rural feeling*¹¹. They possess *a quick sensibility to the beauties of nature*¹², and a keen relish for the pleasures and employments of the country. This passion *seems inherent in them*¹³. Even the inhabitants of cities, born

---

³ he must, *il faut, with the following verb in the subjunctive.*

⁴ boorish peasantry, *des paysans grossiers.*

⁵ gathering-place, *rendez-vous.*

⁶ to a hurry of gaiety and dissipation, *à un tourbillon de joie et de plaisir.*

⁷ having indulged, *s'étant permis.*

⁸ orders, *classes.*

⁹ afford, *présentent.*

¹⁰ The English, in fact = *in fact, the English; in fact, "de fait".*

¹¹ with the rural feeling, *du sentiment de la campagne.*

¹² a quick sensibility to the beauties of nature, *une vive perception des beautés de la nature.*

¹³ seems inherent in them, *semble leur être inhérente.*

and brought up among brick walls and bustling streets, enter with facility into rural habits, and evince a taste for rural occupation. The merchant has his snug retreat in the vicinity of the metropolis, where he often displays as much pride and zeal *in the cultivation of his flower-garden*[14], and *the maturing of his fruits*[15], *as he does*[16] in the conduct of his business and the success of a commercial enterprise. Even those less fortunate individuals, who are doomed to pass their lives in the midst of din and *traffic*[17], *contrive to have something that shall remind them of the green aspect of nature*[18]. In the most dark and dingy quarters of the city, the drawing-room window resembles frequently a bank of flowers; every spot capable of vegetation has its grass-plot and flower-bed; and every *square*[19] its mimic park, laid out with picturesque taste, and gleaming with refreshing verdure.

Those who see the Englishman only in town, are apt to form an unfavourable opinion of his social character. He is either absorbed in business, or distracted by the thousand engagements that dissipate time, thought, and feeling, in this huge metropolis. *He has, therefore, too commonly a look of hurry and abstraction*[20]. Wherever he happens to be, he is on the point of going somewhere else; *at the moment he is talking on one subject*[21], his mind is wandering to another; and *while*

---

[14] in the cultivation of his flower-garden, *dans la culture de son jardin à fleurs.*

[15] and the maturing of his fruits, *et à faire mûrir ses fruits.*

[16] as he does, *que.*

[17] traffic, *mouvement.*

[18] contrive to have something that shall remind them of the green aspect of nature, *s'arrangent pour avoir quelque chose qui leur rappelle la verdure de la nature.*

[19] square, *the same word is used in French in this sense.*

[20] He has, therefore, too commonly a look of hurry and abstraction, *c'est pourquoi, il a trop communément l'air d'être pressé et absorbé.*

[21] at the moment he is talking on one subject, *au moment où il parle d'un sujet.*

*paying a friendly visit*²², he is calculating how he shall economise time *so as to pay*²³ the other visits allotted in the morning. An immense metropolis, like London, is calculated to make men selfish and uninteresting. In their casual and transient meetings *they can but deal briefly in commonplaces*²⁴. They present but the cold superficies of character; its rich and genial qualities have no time *to be warmed into a glow*²⁵.

It is in the country that the Englishman *gives scope*²⁶ to his natural feelings. He breaks loose gladly from the cold formalities and negative civilities of town; throws off his habits of shy reserve, and becomes joyous and freehearted. *He manages*²⁷ to collect round him all the conveniences and elegances of polite life, and to banish its restraints. His *country-seat*²⁸ abounds with every requisite, either for studious retirement, tasteful gratification, or rural exercise. Books, paintings, music, horses, dogs, and sporting implements of all kinds, *are at hand*²⁹. *He puts no constraint either upon his guests, or himself*³⁰ but in the true spirit of hospitality provides the means of enjoyment, and leaves every one *to partake*³¹ according to his inclination.

Nothing can be more imposing than the magnificence of English park scenery. Vast lawns that extend like sheets of vivid green, with here and there clumps of

---

²² while paying a friendly visit, *pendant qu'il fait une visite d'amitié.*

²³ so as to pay, *de façon à faire.*

²⁴ they can but deal briefly in common-places, *ils ne peuvent que s'occuper brièvement de choses banales.*

²⁵ to be warmed into a glow, *de se développer en chaleur.*

²⁶ gives scope, *donne carrière.*

²⁷ He manages, *il s'arrange pour.*

²⁸ country-seat, *maison de campagne.*

²⁹ are at hand, *sont sous la main.*

³⁰ He puts no constraint either upon his guests or himself, *il ne gêne ni ses invitées ni lui même.*

³¹ to partake, *en prendre.*

gigantic trees, heaping up rich piles of foliage: the solemn
pomp of groves and woodland glades, with the deer troop-
ing in silent herds across them; the hare, bounding away
to the covert; or the pheasant, *suddenly bursting upon
the wing*[32]; the brook, *taught to wind in natural meanderings*[33], *or expand into a*[34] glassy lake; the sequestered
pool, reflecting the quivering trees, with the yellow leaf
sleeping on its bosom, and the trout roaming fearlessly
about its limpid waters, while some rustic temple or
sylvan statue, *grown green and dank with age*[35], gives an
air of classic sanctity to the seclusion.

The great charm, however, of English scenery is the
moral feeling that seems to pervade it. It is associated
in the mind with ideas of order, of quiet, of sober, well-
established principles, of hoary usage and reverend custom.
Everything seems to be the growth of ages of regular
and peaceful existence. The old church of remote archi-
tecture, with its low, massive portal, its Gothic tower,
its windows *rich with tracery and painted glass*[36], its
scrupulous preservation, its stately monuments of warriors
and worthies of the olden time, ancestors of the present
lords of the soil; its tombstones, recording successive gene-
rations of sturdy yeomanry, whose progeny still plough
the same fields, and kneel at the same altar. The par-
sonage, a quaint, irregular pile, partly antiquated, but
repaired and altered *in the tastes of various ages and occupants*[37]. The stile and footpath leading from the
churchyard, across pleasant fields, and along shady hedge-
rows, according to an immemorial right of way—the

---

[32] suddenly bursting upon the wing, *qui tout à coup prend son vol.*
[33] taught to wind in natural meanderings, *que l'on a fait serpen-
ter d'une manière naturelle.*
[34] or expand into a, *ou que l'on a forcé de s'étaler en.*
[35] grown green and dank with age, *verdie et rendue moite par l'âge.*
[36] rich with tracery, and painted glass, *riches de sculptures à
jour et de vitraux.*
[37] in the tastes of various ages and occupants, *selon le goût
de différentes périodes et de différents propriétaires.*

neighbouring village, with its venerable cottages, its public green sheltered by trees, under which the forefathers of the present race have sported. The antique family mansion, standing apart in some little rural domain, but looking down *with a protecting air*[38] on the surrounding scene: all these common features of English landscape evince a calm and settled security, and hereditary transmission of *homebred virtues and local attachments, that speak deeply and touchingly for the moral character of the nation*[39].

75. ASSASSINATION OF ALI PASHA.

The life and death of Ali Pasha, governor of Albania, having excited great interest in Europe, we flatter ourselves that a correct detail of the circumstances will not be unacceptable.

Ali, knowing he had rendered himself very obnoxious to the sultan, and *expecting*[1] a death firman, had placed at Constantinople, a confidential Albanian *who was to give him secret information of all that was going on*[2]. Suspecting however that he betrayed his confidence, he resolved *to get rid of him*[3]. *For this purpose*[4], he employed two men, giving them letters for the *Reis Effendi*[5], and directing them to execute his project on the Albanian *on their return*[6].

---

[38] with a protecting air, *d'un air de protection.*
[39] of homebred virtues and local attachments, that speak deeply and touchingly for the moral character of the nation, *de vertus domestiques et d'attachements au sol qui parlent hautement et pathétiquement en faveur du caractère moral de la nation.*

75. ASSASSINATION OF ALI PASHA.
[1] expecting, *s'attendant à.*
[2] who was to give him secret information of all that was going on, *qui devait l'informer en secret de tout ce qui se passait.*
[3] to get rid of him, *de se débarrasser de lui.*
[4] for this purpose, *à cet effet.*
[5] Reis Effendi, *the title given to one of the state lawyers.*
[6] on their return, *à leur retour.*

They delivered their letters to the Reis Effendi, received the answers, *mounted their horses*[7] to return, and *on the way*[8] *they called at the house of their intended victim*[9], knocked at the gate and asked to see him. Having some suspicion, he did not go to the gate; but looking from a window, asked what communication they had for him. *The only answer was two pistol-balls immediately fired at him*[10], he was severely wounded, but not mortally. The assassins *clapped spurs to their horses*[11], and fled *at full gallop*[12]. They were shortly pursued by the Tartar cavalry, and overtaken at Rodosto, about ninety miles from Constantinople. One of them was seized, brought back, and executed; the other, after a vigorous resistance, escaped.

This was the immediate cause of the deposition of Ali, though he had long merited his fate for other crimes. The Porte expressed horror at the assassination, and immediately issued a firman deposing Ali, and giving his place to one of his enemies. He refused however to obey, and an army was sent against him commanded by an officer named Hourchid.

After *many*[13] vicissitudes, he was so pressed that he was compelled to take refuge in a part of the citadel of Yanina with about fifty men who had remained faithful to him; but he first set fire to the town. The building which he had chosen for his retreat *was three storeys high*[14]; Ali and his suite occupied *the upper one*[15]; in

---

[7] mounted their horses, *montèrent à cheval.*

[8] on the way, *sur leur route.*

[9] they called at the house of their intended victim, *ils passèrent chez la victime désignée.*

[10] The only answer was two pistol-balls, immediately fired at him, *deux balles de pistolet qu'on lui tira immédiatement furent la seule réponse.*

[11] clapped spurs to their horses, *piquèrent des deux.*

[12] at full gallop, *au grand galop.*

[13] many, *bien des.*

[14] was three stories high, *avait trois étages.*

[15] the upper one, *l'étage supérieur.*

the second were deposited his immense treasures, and
the lowest was filled with gun-powder, etc., *ready to be
blown up at a moment's warning*[16] in case of necessity.

Hourchid *summoned*[17] Ali *to surrender*[18], saying that
if he did not, he would come himself and *put the match
to the train*[19]. This determined communication terrified
the old man, who had till then remained inflexible: *he
agreed*[20] to surrender *on*[21] condition *that his life should
be spared*[22]. Hourchid assured him that he would do
all in his power to obtain that condition, *but he must
not hope it unless he immediately submitted*[23].

Lulled by these hopes and promises he yielded, and
was sent with his little troop to the island[24]. Several Pa-
shas visited Ali from time to time, and *pretended great
friendship for him*[25], expressing their hopes to see him
reinstated. *One particularly*[26], Mohammed-Pasha, paid
him a visit on the 5th of February 1823, bearing with
him the death firman; they had a long conversation,
and mutual confidence seemed to be established between
them. Mohammed, after many protestations of attach-
ment and good-will, rose to depart; and as they were
both of the same rank, they both rose at the same mo-

---

[16] ready to be blown up at a moment's warning, *qu'on pouvait
faire sauter d'un moment à l'autre.*

[17] summoned, *somma.*

[18] to surrender, *de se rendre.*

[19] to put the match to the train, *de mettre la mèche à la trainée
de poudre.*

[20] he agreed, *il convint.*

[21] on, *à.*

[22] that his life should be spared, *qu'on lui laisserait la vie.*

[23] but he must not hope it unless he immediately submitted,
*mais qu'il ne fallait pas qu'il espérât qu'il en fût ainsi, s'il ne se
soumettait immédiatement.*

[24] was sent with his little troop to the island, *et on l'envoya
dans l'île, lui et sa petite troupe.*

[25] pretended great friendship for him, *affectèrent une grande
amitié pour lui.*

[26] One particularly, *un, entre autres.*

ment from the divan where they had been sitting. The Pasha Mohammed making *a very low bow*[27], Ali *returned it*[28]; *but before he could rise again*[29]. Mohammed had drawn his yataghan from his girdle, and plunged it with such violence into the back of his victim, that it went completely through his heart, and the point came out at his left breast. Ali fell dead at his feet; the assassin then called in some of his soldiers, who immediately severed the head from the body, according to the orders in the firman.

It was at this time rumoured at Constantinople[30] that Ali *was on his road to*[31] that city, and a superb equipage was sent out to meet him; it brought back however only his head, which was exhibited the next day in the court of the seraglio, in a sort of dish: *a writing was placed over it containing a list of the crimes for which he had been punished*[32].

76. *MAST-HEADING A YOUNG GENTLEMAN*[1].
FROM BASIL HALL'S VOYAGES.

The next morning 24th April, a boat *came alongside from the Boston*[2], *a*[3] frigate *lying near the Leander*[4]. The captain of that ship was then, and is *now*[5], one of

---

[27] a very low bow, *une profonde révérence.*
[28] Ali, returned it, *Ali la lui rendit.*
[29] but before he could rise again, *mais avant qu'il pût se relever.*
[30] It was at this time rumoured at Constantinople, *On faisait alors courir le bruit à Constantinople.*
[31] was on his road to, *qu'il était en route pour.*
[32] a writing was placed over it containing a list of the crimes for which he had been punished, *on plaça au dessus un écrit contenant la liste des crimes pour lesquels il avait été puni.*

76. MAST-HEADING A YOUNG GENTLEMAN.
[1] Mast heading a young gentleman, *un jeune monsieur au haut du mât.*
[2] came along side from the Boston, *vint à notre bord du Boston.*
[3] a, *not to be translated.*
[4] lying near the Leander, *mouillée près du Léandre.*
[5] now, *encore.*

my kindest and steadiest friends. *And right well did he
know how to confer a favour at the fitting season*[6]. The boat
contained one of the most acceptable presents, *I will
answer for it*[7], that ever was made to mortal; it was
truly manna to starved people—being no less than a
famous fat goose, a huge leg of pork, and a bag of potatoes!

Such a present *at any other time and place*[8] would
have been ludicrous; but *at Bermuda*[9], where we had
been famishing and growling, *for many months*[10], *with
hardly a fresh meal*[11]— *it was to us hungry, salt-fed
boys*[12], the "summum bonum" of human happiness.

Next day, after breakfast, the *barge*[13] being sent
with one of the Lieutenants; the Admiral came on board
at eleven o'clock. But while his Excellency was entering the ship on one side, I quitted my appointed station
on the other and without leave slipped out of one of
the *main-deck ports*[14] into the pilot-boat, to secure some
conch shells[15] and corals, I had bespoken and wished
to carry from Bermuda to my friends at Halifax. Having made my purchases, *in the utmost haste and trepidation*[16] *I set about retreating again to my post*[17], when,

---

[6] and right well did he know how to confer a favour at the
fitting season, *et il savait tout à fait bien accorder une faveur en
temps opportun.*

[7] I will answer for it, *j'en réponds.*

[8] at any other time and place, *à tout autre endroit et dans toute
autre circonstance.*

[9] at Bermuda, *aux Bermudes.*

[10] for many months, *pendant bien des mois.*

[11] with hardly a fresh meal, *ayant à peine fait un repas de viande
non salée.*

[12] it was to us hungry, salt-fed boys, *c'était pour nous, gaillards
affamés, nourris de salaisons.*

[13] barge, *challan.*

[14] main deck ports, *les sabords du premier pont.*

[15] conch shells, *des conches.*

[16] in the utmost haste and trepidation, *dans la plus grande hâte
et dans la crainte la plus vive.*

[17] I set about retreating again to my post, *je me disposais à
battre en retraite jusqu'à mon poste.*

as my ill star would have it[18], the first Lieutenant looked *over the gangway*[19]. He saw at a glance, what I was about; and, calling me up, sent me by way of punishment, to the masthead, "for being off deck when the Admiral was coming on board".

Having succeeded, however, in getting hold of my shells and some lumps of coral, I made myself as comfortable as possible, in my elevated position; *and upon the whole rather enjoyed it, as a piece of fun*[20].

We then *hove up the anchor*[21], and as we made sail through the passage I could not only distinguish, from the mast-head, the beautifully coloured reefs under water, but trace with perfect ease, all the different channels between them, through which *we had to thread our winding, and apparently dangerous course*[22]. As the ship passed, the fort saluted the flag *with twelve guns*[23], *which were returned with a like number*[24]: after which *we shaped our course*[25] for Norfolk, in Virginia.

So far all was well[26]. I sat enjoying the view, on one of the finest days that ever was seen. But it almost makes me hungry now, *at this distance of time*[27] to tell what followed.

From the *maintop cross trees*[28], on which I was perched for my misdeeds, I had the cruel mortification

---

[18] as my ill star would have it, *ma mauvaise étoile voulut que.*

[19] over the gangway, *par dessus le passe-avant.*

[20] and upon the whole rather enjoyed it, as a piece of fun, *et somme toute je m'en amusai plutôt comme d'une plaisanterie.*

[21] we then hove up the anchor, *alors nous virâmes au cabestan.*

[22] we had to thread our winding and apparently dangerous course, *il nous fallait suivre notre route, apparemment sinueuse et dangereuse.*

[23] with twelve guns, *de douze coups de canon.*

[24] which were returned with a like number, *auxquels on répondit par un nombre égal.*

[25] we shaped our course, *nous fîmes route.*

[26] So far all was well, *jusque là tout allait bien.*

[27] at this distance of time, *après ce lapse de temps.*

[28] from the maintop cross trees, *des barres traversières de grand hunier.*

of seeing my own beautiful roast goose pass along the *maindeck*[29], *on its way to the cock-pit*[30]. As the scamp of a servant boy, who carried the dish, came abreast of the gang-way, *I observed him cock his eye aloft*[31], to discover how I relished the prospect. No hawk, or eagle, or vulture, ever gazed from the sky more wistfully on its prey beneath, than I did upon the banquet, I was doomed never to taste. What was still more provoking, each of my mess-mates, as he ran down the quarter-deck ladder, on being summoned to dinner, looked up at me and grinned. One malicious dog provoked me a good deal by patting his fat paunch, as much as to say, "What a glorious feast we are going to have! *Should not you like a bit?*"[32]

77. DESCRIPTIVE SKETCH OF A VOYAGE UP THE GANGES.

As the boat glides along, drawn by our boatmen, we perceive the corn in full growth *on both sides*[1] of the river, *proofs of the care of Him on whom all creatures wait*[2]; and, if imagination, could supply a pleasing variety of hill and dale, and some green hawthorn hedges, we might fancy ourselves passing through the open fields of our own country; *and the ascending larks*[3], the reapers *cutting*[4] the corn, and the boy driving the herd to

---

[29] maindeck, *premier pont.*

[30] on its way to the cock-pit, *en route pour le poste des malades.*

[31] I observed him cock his eye aloft, *je le remarquai qui lançait un coup d'œil en l'air.*

[32] Should not you like a bit, *n'en voudriez-vous pas bien un brin.*

77. DESCRIPTIVE SKETCH OF A VOYAGE UP THE GANGES, *ESQUISSE DESCRIPTIVE D'UN VOYAGE EN REMONTANT LE GANGE.*

[1] on both sides, *sur les deux rives.*

[2] proofs of the care of Him on whom all creatures wait, *preuves du soin de Celui que toutes les créatures adorent.*

[3] and the ascending larks, *et les alouettes qui s'élèvent dans les airs.*

[4] cutting, *sciant.*

graze in some corner of the field, *might keep up for a moment, the pleasing illusion*[5]. But a herd of buffaloes at a distance, staring stupidly and wildly, and the lofty *stage*[6] in the middle of the field, erected for the protection of the keeper, *soon remind us of our mistake*[7], and warn us of a danger to which the English husbandman is not exposed.

Even the silent, smooth, and unvarying element on which we now move, is not destitute of its variety of objects: here, *men, women and children*[8] are bathing together, *the men uniting idolatrous rites with their ablutions*[9], the women washing their long hair with mud, and the children gamboling in the water with all the gaiety *of the finny tribes*[10] which surround them; *we next pass by some men*[11] sitting on the bank, with their rods and lines, and others in their boat with their nets, fishing; *and we no sooner pass these*[12], than we are amused by the sight of an open ferry boat, *crowded with passengers till they almost sit one upon another*[13]; the slightest loss of the *balance*[14] would immediately compel them to seek the shore as they might be able; and gliding along the

---

[5] might keep up for a moment the pleasing illusion, *pourraien faire durer cette plaisante illusion pendant un instant.*

[6] stage, *plate-forme.*

[7] soon remind us of our mistake, *nous font bientôt reconnaître notre erreur.*

[8] men, women and children, *des hommes, des femmes et des enfants.*

[9] the men uniting idolatrous rites with their ablutions, *les hommes joignant à leur ablutions des rites idolâtres.*

[10] of the finny tribes, *des habitants de la plaine liquide.*

[11] we next pass by some men, *après cela nous passons à côté d'hommes.*

[12] and we no sooner pass these, *et nous ne les avons pas plustôt laissés derrière nous.*

[13] crowded with passengers till they almost sit one upon another, *tellement encombré de passagers qu'ils sont presque assis les uns sur les autres.*

[14] balance, *équilibre.*

water's edge, comes a man in the trunk of a tree hollowed out *into the form*[15] of a canoe: he sits at his ease, his oar is at the same time his rudder: *and this he*[16] moves with his leg, for both his hands are *engaged in*[17] holding the *hooka*[18] to his head while he smokes. Here an *adjutant*[19] stalks along the side of the river, thrusts his long bill among the weeds in search of fish, while the *paddy birds*[20], in the shallower parts, are silently watching them, and the finely plumed kingfisher is darting on his prey.

At a small distance, several large alligators present the ridges of their backs on the surface, and ere we have proceeded a hundred yards, we hear the shrieks of a boat's crew, and the cries of a man. "An alligator has carried off my son!" As we approach another village, we see a man *washing clothes*[21] by *dipping them*[22] in the river, and beating *them*[23] on a slanting board; a brahmin sits on the brink, *now*[24] washing his *padda*[25], *now*[24] making a clay image for worship, and *now*[24] pouring out libations to his deceased ancestors. Near to the spot where this man sits *on his hams*[26] to worship, lies a greasy pillow, a water pot, the ashes of

---

[15] into the form, *en forme.*

[16] and this he, *qu'il.*

[17] are engaged in, *sont occupées à.*

[18] hooka or hookah, *the Eastern hukkah is a pipe so arranged that the tobacco smoke passes through water before it reaches the mouth of the smoker.*

[19] adjutant, *called in India Arjala, is a large bird very numerous in Calcutta and other parts of India. It is extremely useful in removing offals of all kinds.*

[20] paddy birds, *a species of adjutants.*

[21] washing clothes, *qui lave du linge.*

[22] by dipping them, *en le trempant.*

[23] them = *it.*

[24], [24], [24] now, *tantôt.*

[25] padda, *au outer garment worn by the bhramins.*

[26] on his hams, *sur les fesses.*

a funeral pile, and the bedstead of the man whose body
has just been burnt: in one place we see dogs, crows
and vultures devouring a human body, which had floated
to the shore, and in another, several relations are in the
act of burning a corpse, the smell of which entering the
boat is peculiarly offensive; yet this does not prevent
the people of our boat from eating a very hearty meal
on the grass, in the immediate vicinity of the funeral
pile. In another place, the swallows are seeking their
nests in the holes of the banks while a bird of the heron
species stands on a dead tree, fallen by the side of the
river, and spreading his wings, dries them in the rays
of the sun. From the ascent of a landing place, the
women of a neighbouring village are carrying home water
for their families, *the pans, resting on their sides*[27].

Floats of bamboos *are passing by*[28], carried down by
the current, while the men, in a small boat guide them,
*and prevent their touching the side, or the boats as they
pass*[29]. Long grass, swamps, and *sheets*[30] of water,
with wild ducks and other game, remind us of the perio-
dical rains, which inundate the country. These clusters
of trees indicate that we *approach*[31] a village: the tall
and naked palms *rear*[32] their heads above the branches
of a wide spreading *ficus Indica*[33], under which hundreds
of *people*[34] find a shelter, and in the branches of which
are seen[35] the monkeys, *some*[36] carrying their young

---

[27] the pans resting on their sides, *les pots appuyés sur les hanches.*
[28] are passing by, *passent à côté de nous.*
[29] and prevent their touching the side, or the boats as they
pass, *et les empêchent de toucher en passant soit la rive, soit les
bateaux.*
[30] sheets, *nappes.*
[31] approach, *followed by "de".*
[32] rear, *dressent.*
[33] ficus Indica, *le figuier indien.*
[34] people, *gens.*
[35] are seen, *on voit.*
[36] some, *les uns.*

under their bellies, and others grinning at us, while they
leap from branch *to*[37] branch; *and while nature is drawing the curtains of the evening*[38], in a neighbouring clump
of bamboos, the *minas*[39] make a din like the voices of
a group of women engaged in a fierce quarrel; and the
bats as large as crows, are flying to another clump of
bamboos. Entering the village the next morning, we
overtake a female, who avoids our gaze by drawing her
garment over her face; on one hip sits her child, and
on another she carries a large pan of water; the dogs
half wild[40] *put on*[41] the most threatening aspect, and
bark most savagely; the men come to the doors, and
the women peep at the strangers through the crevices
of the mat walls, manifesting a degree of fear and curiosity; the naked children almost covered with dust, leave
their play and flee at the approach of a Gouru (a white
man).

Before a door near the ficus Indica, where the village
gossips assemble, and under which is placed the village
god, or, *in other words*[42], a round black stone, as large
as a man's head, smeared with oil and red lead, sits a
man cleaning his teeth with the bruised end of a stick;
and we meet another, returning from a neighbouring
field, with a brass water-pot *in his*[43] hand; while the
third person, *that meets our eyes*[44], is the village barber,
sitting on his hams in the street, and shaving one of
his neighbours. One or two women are sticking cakes
of cow dung on the wall, *to dry for fuel*[45], another is

---

[37] to, *en.*
[38] and while nature is drawing the curtains of the evening, *et
pendant que la nature fait tomber le rideau de la nuit.*
[39] minas, *indian birds.*
[40] half wild, *à moitié sauvages.*
[41] put on, *prennent.*
[42] in other words, *en d'autres termes.*
[43] in his, *à la.*
[44] that meets our eyes, *qui frappe nos regards.*
[45] to dry for fuel, *qu'on fait sécher pour brûler.*

washing the door place with water, mud and cowdung,
and two others are *cleaning the rice from the husk*[46],
by pounding it with a pestle. Not far from the ficus
Indica, we see the temple of an idol, and the people
as they pass, raise their hands to their heads in honour
of the abominable image; from thence we go to the
mosque, mouldering to ruins, and see near it a mound
of earth, under a tree raised like a grave, and dedicated
to some Musulman saint.

78. THE DEAN OF SANTIAGO.
FROM THE SPANISH.

It was but a short hour before noon[1], when the Dean
of Santiago alighted from his mule at the door of Don
Julian, the celebrated magician of Toledo. The house,
according to old tradition, stood on the brink of the
perpendicular rock[2], which, now crowned with the Al-
cazar, *rises to a fearful height over the Tagus*[3]. A maid
of Moorish blood led the Dean to a retired apartment,
where Don Julian was reading. The natural politeness
of a Castilian had rather been improved than impaired
by the studies of the Toledan sage, who exhibited nothing either in his *dress*[4] or person that *might induce a
suspicion of his dealing*[5] with the mysterious powers of
darkness.

---

[46] cleaning the rice from the husk, *débarrassent le riz de la
chaffée.*

78. THE DEAN OF SANTIAGO.
[1] It was but a short hour before noon, *Il ne s'en fallait que
d'une petite heure qu'il fût midi.*
[2] perpendicular rock, *roc à pic.*
[3] rises to a fearful height over the Tagus, *s'élève à une hauteur
effrayante au dessus du Tage.*
[4] dress, *habillement.*
[5] that might induce a suspicion of his dealing, *qui pût faire
soupçonner son commerce.*

"*I heartily greet your Reverence*⁶," said Don Julian to the Dean, "and feel highly honoured *by*⁷ this visit. Whatever be the *object of it*⁸, *let me beg you will defer stating it till I have made you quite at home in this house*⁹. I hear my house-keeper making ready the noonday meal. That maid, Sir, will show you the room which has been prepared for you; and when *you have*¹⁰ brushed off the dust of the journey, you shall find a *canonical capon*¹¹ *steaming hot upon the board*¹². " The dinner, which soon followed, was just what a pampered Spanish canon would wish it — abundant, nutritive, and delicate. — "No, no," said Don Julian, when the soup and a bumper of *Tinto*¹³ had recruited the Dean's spirits, *and he saw him making an attempt to break the object of his visit*¹⁴, "no business, *please your Reverence*¹⁵ *while at dinner*¹⁶. Let us enjoy our meal at present; and when we have discussed the *Olla*¹⁷, the capon, and a bottle of *Xeres*¹⁸, it will be time enough to turn to the cares of life." The ecclesiastic's full face had never beamed with more glee at the collation on Christmas eve, when by the indulgence of the church, the fast *is*

---

⁶ I heartily greet your Reverence = *I greet your Reverence heartily.* heartily, *de tout mon cœur.*

⁷ by, *de.*

⁸ whatever be the object of it, *quel qu'en soit le but.*

⁹ let me beg you will defer stating it till I have made you quite at home in this house, *permettez-moi de vous prier d'en remettre l'exposition jusqu'à ce que je vous ai mis tout à fait à l'aise dans cette maison.*

¹⁰ you have, *to be in the future.*

¹¹ a canonical capon, *un chapon de chanoine.*

¹² steaming hot upon the board, *fumant sur la table.*

¹³ Tinto = *red wine.*

¹⁴ and he saw him making an attempt to break the object of his visit, *et qu'il le vit essayer de lui faire part du motif de sa visite.*

¹⁵ please your Reverence, *s'il plait à votre Révérence.*

¹⁶ while at dinner = *while we are at dinner.*

¹⁷ olla, *a kind of stew, ragoût.*

¹⁸ Xeres, *the same word used in French* (Sherry).

broken[19] at sunset, instead of continuing through the night, than it did now under the influence of Don Julian's good humour and *heart-cheering wine*[20]. Still it was evident that some vehement and ungovernable wish had taken possession of his mind, breaking out *now and then*[21] in some hurried motion, some gulping up of a full glass of wine without stopping to relish the flavour, and fifty other symptoms of absence of mind and impatience, which at such a distance from the cathedral could not be attributed to the afternoon bell. The time came at length of rising from table, and in spite of Don Julian's pressing request to *have*[22] another bottle, the Dean, with a certain dignity of manner, led his good-natured host to the recess of an oriel-window, *over looking the river*[23]. — "Allow me, dear Don Julian," he said, "to open my heart to you; for even your hospitality must fail to make me completely happy till I have obtained the boon which I came to ask. I know that no man ever possessed greater power than you over the invisible agents of the universe. I long to become an adept in that wonderful science, and if you will receive me for your pupil, there is nothing I should think of sufficient worth to repay your friendship." — *"Good Sir,"*[24] replied Don Julian, "I should be extremely loath to offend you; but permit me to say, that in spite of the knowledge of causes and effects which I have acquired, all that my experience teaches me of the heart of man is not only vague and indistinct, but for the most part unfavourable. *I only guess*[25], I cannot read their thoughts, nor pry into the recesses of their minds.

---

[19] is broken, *cesse.*
[20] and heart-cheering wine, *et de son vin qui réjouissait le cœur.*
[21] now and then, *de moment à autre.*
[22] to have = *to drink.*
[23] overlooking the river, *qui donnait sur la rivière.*
[24] Good Sir, *mon bon Monsieur.*
[25] I only guess, *je ne fais que deviner.*

As for yourself, I am sure *you are a rising man*[26] and likely to obtain the highest dignities of the church. But whether, when you find yourself in places of high honour and patronage, you will remember the humble personage of whom you now ask a hazardous and important service, it is impossible for me to ascertain." — "Nay, nay," exclaimed the Dean, "but I know myself, if you do not, Don Julian. Generosity and friendship (since you force me to speak in my own praise) have been the delight of my soul even from childhood. Doubt not, my dear friend, (for by that name I wish you would allow me to call you), *doubt not, from this moment to command my services*[27]. Whatever interest I may possess, it will be my highest gratification to see it redound in favour of you and yours." — "My hearty thanks for all, worthy Sir," said Don Julian. "But let us now proceed to business: the sun is set, and, if you please, we will retire to my private study."

Lights being called for[28], Don Julian *led the way to the lower part of the house*[29] : and dismissing the Moorish maid near a small door, of which he held the key in his hand, desired her to get two partridges for supper, but not to dress them till he should order it: then unlocking the door, he began to descend by a winding staircase. The Dean followed with a certain degree of trepidation, which the length of the stairs greatly tended to increase; for, *to all appearance*[30], they reached below the bed of the Tagus. At this depth a comfortable neat room was found, the walls completely covered with shelves, where Don Julian kept his works on Magic; globes, planispheres, and strange drawings occupied the top of the

---

[26] you are a rising man, *vous êtes un homme d'avenir.*

[27] to command my services, *que je suis à votre service.*

[28] lights being called for, *ayant demandé de la lumière.*

[29] led the way to the lower part of the house, *lui montra le chemin qui conduisait à la partie basse de la maison.*

[30] to all appearance, *selon toute apparence.*

book-cases. Fresh air was admitted, though it would be difficult to guess by what means, since the sound of gliding water, such as is heard at the lower part of a ship when sailing with a gentle breeze, indicated but a thin partition between the subterraneous cabinet and the river. — "Here, then," said Don Julian, offering a chair to the Dean, and drawing another for himself towards a small round table, "we have only to choose among the elementary works of the science for which you long. Suppose we begin to read this small volume." The volume was laid on the table, and opened at the first page, containing circles, concentric and eccentric, triangles with unintelligible characters, and the well-known signs of the planets. — "This," said Don Julian, "is the alphabet of the whole science. Hermes, *called*[31] Trismegistus —" The sound of a small bell within the chamber made the Dean almost leap out of his chair. "Be not alarmed," said Don Julian : "it is the bell by which my servants let me know that they want to speak to me." Saying thus, he pulled a silk string, and soon after a servant appeared with a packet of letters. It was addressed to the Dean. A courier had closely followed him on the road, and was that moment arrived at Toledo. *"Good Heaven!"*[32] exclaimed the Dean having read the contents of the letters; "my great uncle, the Archbishop of Santiago, is dangerously ill. This is, however, what the secretary says, from his Lordship's dictation. But here is another letter from the Archdeacon of the diocese, who assures me *that the old man was not expected to live*[33]. I can hardly repeat what he adds — Poor dear uncle! may Heaven lengthen his days! The Chapter seem to have turned their eyes

---

[31] called, *que l'on appelle.*

[32] Good Heaven, *Bon Dieu.*

[33] that the old man was not expected to live, *qu'on ne s'attendait pas à ce que le vieillard survécût.*

towards me[34] and — pugh! it cannot be — but the
Electors, according to the Archdeacon, are quite decided
in my favour." — "Well," said Don Julian, "all I regret
is the interruption of our studies; but I doubt not that
you will soon wear the mitre. In the mean time I
would advise you to pretend that illness does not allow
you to return directly. A few days will surely give a
decided turn to the whole affair: and, at all events,
your absence in case of an election, will be construed
into modesty. Write, therefore, your despatches, my
dear Sir, and we will prosecute our studies *at another
time*"[35].

Two days had elapsed[36] since the arrival of the
messenger, when the Verger of the church of Santiago,
attended by servants, in splendid liveries, alighted at
Don Julian's door with letters for the Dean. The old
prelate was dead, and his nephew had been elected to
the see, by the unanimous vote of the Chapter. The
elected dignitary seemed overcome by contending feelings; but, having wiped away some decent tears, he
assumed an air of gravity, *which almost touched on*[37]
superciliousness. Don Julian addressed his congratulations, and was the first to kiss the new Archbishop's
hand. "I hope," he added, "I may also congratulate
my son, the young man who is now at the University
of Paris; for I flatter myself your Lordship will give
him the Deanery, which is vacant by your promotion." —
"My worthy friend, Don Julian," replied the Archbishop
elect, *"my obligations to you I can never sufficiently
repay*[38]. You have heard my character; I hold a friend
as another self[39]. *But why would you take the lad away*

---

[34] towards me, *sur moi.*
[35] at another time, *une autre fois.*
[36] two days had elapsed, *deux jours s'étaient écoulés.*
[37] which almost touched on, *qui était presque de.*
[38] my obligations to you, I can never sufficiently repay, *je ne
pourrai jamais m'acquitter suffisamment de mes obligations envers vous.*
[39] as another self, *comme un autre moi-même.*

from his studies[40]? An Archbishop of Santiago cannot want preferment at any time. Follow me to my diocese; I will not for all the mitres in Christendom forego the benefit of your instruction. The deanery, to tell you the truth, must be given to my uncle, my father's own brother, who has had but a small *living*[41] for many years; he is much liked in Santiago, and I should lose my character if, to place such a young man as your son at the head of the Chapter, I neglected an exemplary priest, *so nearly related to me.*"[42] — "*Just as you please*[43], my Lord," said Don Julian; *and began to prepare for the journey*[44].

The acclamations which greeted the new Archbishop on his arrival in the capital of Galicia were, *not long after*[45], *succeeded by*[46] a universal regret at his translation to the see of the recently conquered town of Seville. "I will not leave you behind," said the Archbishop to Don Julian, who with more timidity than he showed at Toledo, approached to kiss the sacred ring in the Archbishop's right hand, and to offer his humble congratulations, "but do not fret about your son. He is too young. *I have my mother's relations to provide for*[47], but Seville is a rich see; the blessed King Ferdinand, who rescued it from the Moors, endowed its church *so as to make it rival*[48] the first cathedrals in

---

[40] but why would you take the lad away from his studies, *mais pourquoi enleveriez-vous le jeune homme à ses études.*

[41] living, *cure.*

[42] so nearly related to me, *qui m'est si proche.*

[43] just as you please, *tout comme il vous plaira.*

[44] and began to prepare for the journey, *qui fit ses préparatifs de départ.*

[45] not long after, *peu de temps après.*

[46] succeeded by, *suivies d'.*

[47] I have my mother's relations to provide for, *j'ai à placer les parents de ma mère.*

[48] so as to make it rival the, *de façon à en faire la rivale des.*

Christendom. *Do but follow me*[49], and all *will be*[50] well *in*[51] the end." Don Julian bowed with a suppressed sigh, and was soon after on the bank of the Guadalquivir, in the suite of the new Archbishop.

Scarcely had Don Julian's pupil been at Seville one year[52], when his far extended fame moved the Pope to send him a cardinal's hat, desiring his presence at the Court of Rome. The crowd of visitors who came to congratulate the prelate, kept Don Julian away for many days. He at length obtained a private audience, and, with tears in his eyes, entreated his Eminence not to oblige him to quit Spain. *"I am growing old*[53], my Lord," *he said*[54]. *"I quitted my house at Toledo only for your sake*[55], and in hopes of raising my son to some place of honour and emolument in the church; I even gave up my favourite studies, *except as far as they were of service to your Eminence*[56]. My son —" "No more of that, if you please, Don Julian," interrupted the Cardinal, "Follow me, *you must*[57]; who can tell *what may happen*[58] at Rome? The Pope is old, you know. But do not tease me about preferment. A public man has duties of a description which those in the lower ranks of life cannot either weigh or comprehend. I confess *I am under obligations to you*[59], and feel quite

---

[49] do but follow me, *suivez-moi seulement.*

[50] will be = *will go.*

[51] in, *à.*

[52] scarcely had Don Julian's pupil been at Seville one year, when, *à peine l'élève de Don Julien avait-il été un an à Séville que.*

[53] I am growing old, *je deviens vieux.*

[54] he said = *said he.*

[55] I quitted my house at Toledo only for your sake, *je n'ai quitté ma maison de Tolède que pour vous.*

[56] except as far as they were of service to your Eminence, *excepté en ce qu'elles pouvaient avoir d'utile pour votre Eminence.*

[57] you must, *il le faut.*

[58] what may happen, *ce qui peut arriver.*

[59] I am under obligations to you, *que je vous ai des obligations.*

disposed to reward your services; yet *I must not have*[60] my creditors knocking every day at my door; you understand, Don Julian. In a week we set out for Rome."

With such a strong tide of good fortune as had hitherto buoyed up Don Julian's pupil, the reader cannot be surprised[61] to find him, in a short time, wearing the papal crown. He was now arrived at the highest place of honour on earth; but in the bustle of election *and subsequent coronation*[62], the man to whose wonderful science he owed this rapid ascent, *had completely slipped off his memory*[63]. Fatigued *with the exhibition of himself*[64] through the streets of Rome, which he had been obliged to make in a solemn procession, the new Pope sat alone in one of the chambers of the Vatican. *It was early in the night*[65]. *By the light*[66] of two wax tapers which scarcely illuminated the farthest end of the grand saloon, his Holiness was enjoying that reverie of mixed pain and pleasure which follows the complete attainment of ardent wishes, when Don Julian advanced in visible perturbation, conscious of the intrusion on which he ventured. "Holy Father!" exclaimed the old man, and cast himself at his pupil's feet: "Holy Father, *in pity to these grey hairs*[67] do not consign an old servant — might I not say an old friend? — to utter neglect and forgetfulness. My son —" "By saint Peter!" ejaculated

---

[60] I must not have, *il ne faut pas.*

[61] With such a strong tide of good fortune as had hitherto buoyed up Don Julian's pupil, the reader cannot be surprised &c., *avec un aussi puissant concours de circonstances heureuses que celui qui jusqu'ici avait élévé le disciple de Don Julien, le lecteur ne sera pas surpris* &c.

[62] and subsequent coronation, *et du couronnement qui la suit.*

[63] had completely slipped off his memory, *s'était complètement effacé de sa mémoire.*

[64] with the exhibition of himself, *de se faire voir.*

[65] It was early in the night, *c'était au commencement de la nuit.*

[66] by the light, *à la lumière.*

[67] in pity to these grey hairs, *par pitié pour ces cheveux gris.*

his Holiness, rising from the chair, "your insolence shall be checked — You my friend! A magician the friend of Heaven's vice-regent! — *Away*[68], wretched man! When I pretended to learn of thee, it was only to sound the abyss of crime into which thou hadst plunged; I did it *with a view of bringing thee to condign punishment*[69]. Yet, in compassion to thy age, I will not make an example of thee, provided thou avoidest my eyes. Hide thy crime and shame where thou canst. This moment thou must quit the palace, *or the next*[70] closes the gates of the Inquisition upon thee."

Trembling, and his wrinkled face bedewed with tears, Don Julian *begged to be allowed but one word more*[71]. "I am very poor, Holy Father," said he; "trusting in your patronage *I relinquished my all, and have not left wherewith to pay my journey*[72]." — "Away, I say," answered the Pope; if my excessive bounty has made you neglect your patrimony, I will no farther encourage your waste and improvidence. Poverty is but a slight punishment for your crimes." — "But, Father," rejoined Don Julian, "my wants are instant; I am hungry: give me but a trifle to procure a supper to-night. To-morrow *I shall beg my way out of Rome*[73]." — "Heaven forbid," said the Pope, "that I should be guilty of feeding the ally of the Prince of Darkness. Away, away from my presence, or I instantly call for the guard." — "Well then," replied Don Julian, rising from the ground,

---

[68] away, *retire-toi.*

[69] with a view of bringing thee to condign punishment, *afin de faire tomber sur toi la punition que tu mérites.*

[70] or the next, *ou le moment d'après.*

[71] begged to be allowed but one word more, *demanda qu'il lui fût permis d'ajouter seulement un mot.*

[72] I relinquished my all, and have not left wherewith to pay my journey, *J'ai abandonné tout et je n'ai pas de quoi payer mon voyage.*

[73] I shall beg my way out of Rome, *je mendierai pour sortir de Rome.*

and looking on the Pope with a boldness which began to throw his Holiness into a paroxysm of rage, "if I am to starve in Rome, *I had better return*[74] to the supper which I ordered at Toledo." *Thus saying*[75], he rang a gold bell which *stood*[76] on a table *next*[77] the Pope. The door *opened*[78] without delay, and the Moorish servant came in. The Pope looked round, and found himself in the subterraneous study under the Tagus. "*Desire the cook*[79]," said Don Julian to the maid, "*to put but one partridge to roast*[80]; for I will not throw away the other on the Dean of Santiago."

79. IMPROMPTU REPLY OF LORD CHATHAM TO HORACE WALPOLE, BROTHER OF THE MINISTER, WHO REPROACHED HIM WITH HIS YOUTH.

Sir, — *The atrocious crime of being a young man, which the honourable gentleman has with such spirit and decency charged upon me, I shall neither attempt to palliate nor deny*[1], but content myself *with wishing*[2] that I may be one of those whose follies *may cease with their youth*[3], and not of that number who are ignorant in

---

[74] I had better, *je ferai mieux.*
[75] Thus saying, *en disant ces mots.*
[76] stood = *was.*
[77] next the, *à côté du*
[78] opened, *s'ouvrit.*
[79] Desire the cook, *priez la cuisinière.*
[80] to put but one partridge to roast, *de ne faire rotir qu'une seule perdrix.*

79. IMPROMPTU REPLY OF LORD CHATHAM &c.

[1] The atrocious crime of being a young man, which the honourable gentleman has with such spirit and decency charged upon me, I shall neither attempt to palliate nor deny = *I shall neither attempt to palliate nor deny the atrocious crime (of being a young man = d'être jeune) which (dont) the honourable gentleman (membre) has charged upon me with such spirit and decency.*
[2] with wishing, *de souhaiter.*
[3] may cease with their youth, *cessent avec la jeunesse.*

9

spite of experience. *Whether youth can be imputed to
any man as a reproach, I will not, Sir, assume the province of determining*[4] : but surely age may become justly
contemptible, if the opportunities which it brings have
passed away without improvement, and vice appears to
prevail when the passions have subsided. The wretch
who, after having seen the consequences of a thousand
errors, continues still to blunder, and whose age has
only added obstinacy to stupidity, is surely the object
either of abhorrence or contempt, and deserves not that
his gray hairs should secure him from insult. *Much
more, Sir, is he to be abhorred who, as he has advanced
in age, has receded from virtue, and become more wicked
with less temptation*[5]; who prostitutes himself for money
which he cannot enjoy[6], and spends the remains of his
life in the ruin of his country. But youth, Sir, is not
my only crime; I have been accused *of acting a theatrical part*[7]. A theatrical part may either imply some
peculiarities of gesture, or a dissimulation of my real
sentiments, and an adoption of the opinions and language
of another man.

In the first sense, sir, the charge is too trifling to
be confuted, and deserves only to be mentioned that it
may be despised. I am at liberty, like every other
man, to use my own language; and though, perhaps, 1
may have some ambition to please this gentleman, I

---

[4] Whether youth can be imputed to any man as a reproach,
I will not, sir, assume the province of determining = *I will not, Sir,
(assume the province of determining = prendre sur moi de déterminer)
whether one can impute youth as a reproach to a man.*

[5] Much more, Sir, is he to be abhorred who, as he has advanced in age, has receded from virtue, and become more wicked
with less temptation. *On doit abhorrer encore bien plus, Monsieur,
celui qui s'est éloigné de la vertu à mesure qu'il avançait en âge et
qui est devenu plus mauvais avec moins de tentations.*

[6] which he cannot enjoy, *dont il ne peut jouir.*

[7] of acting a theatrical part, *de jouer la comédie.*

shall not lay myself under any restraint, nor very soli-
citously copy his diction or his mien, *however matured
by age, or modelled by experience*[8]. But if any man
shall, by charging me with theatrical behaviour, imply
that I utter any sentiments but my own, I shall treat
him as a calumniator and a villain; nor shall any protection shelter him from the treatment he deserves. I
shall on such an occasion without scruple, trample upon
those forms with which wealth and dignity entrench
themselves; *nor shall anything but age restrain my resentment*[9]; age which always brings one privilege, that of
being insolent and supercilious without punishment. But
with regard, Sir, to those whom I have offended, I am
of opinion that if I acted *a borrowed part*[10], I should
have avoided their censure, the heat that offended them
is the ardour of conviction, and that zeal for the service of my country which neither hope nor fear shall
influence me to suppress. I will not sit unconcerned
while my liberty is invaded, nor look in silence upon
public robbery. I will exert my endeavours, at whatever hazard, to repel the aggressor, and drag the thief
to justice, whoever may protect him in his villany and
whoever may partake of his plunder.

80. END OF THE SIEGE OF LONDONDERRY.

Among the merchant ships which had come to Lough
Foyle *under Kirke's convoy*[1] was one called the Mount-

---

[8] however matured by age or modelled by experience, *quelque
murie qu'elle puisse être par l'âge ou quelque modélée qu'elle soit par
l'experience.*

[9] nor shall anything but age, restrain my resentment, *rien que
l'âge ne restreindra mon ressentiment.*

[10] a borrowed part, *un rôle d'emprunt.*

80. END OF THE SIEGE OF LONDONDERRY.

[1] under Kirke's convoy, *sous l'escorte de Kirke.*

joy. The *master*[2], Micaiah Browning, *a native*[3] of Londonderry, had brought from England a large cargo of provisions. He had, it is said, repeatedly remonstrated against the inaction of the armament. *He now eagerly volunteered to take the first risk of succouring his fellow citizens*[4]; and his offer was accepted. Andrew Douglas, master of the Phœnix, who had on board a great quantity of meal from Scotland, *was willing*[5] to share the danger and the honour. The two merchantmen were to be escorted by the Dartmouth, a frigate of thirty-six guns, commanded by Captain John Leake, afterwards an admiral of great fame.

It was the twenty-eighth of July. The sun had just set: the evening sermon in the cathedral was over; and the heartbroken congregation had separated; when the sentinels on the tower saw the sails of three vessels *coming up*[6] the Foyle. *Soon there was a stir*[7] in the Irish camp. The besiegers were on the alert *for miles along both shores*[8]. The ships were in extreme peril: for the river was low; and the only navigable *channel*[9] *ran very near*[10] to the left *bank*[11], where the headquarters of the enemy had been fixed, and where the batteries were most numerous. Leake performed his duty with a skill and spirit worthy of his noble profession, exposed his frigate to cover the merchantmen,

---

[2] master, *patron.*

[3] a native, *natif.*

[4] He now eagerly volunteered to take the first risk of succouring his fellow citizens, *il s'était offert avec empressement à risquer d'aller le premier au secours de ses concitoyens.*

[5] was willing, *voulait bien.*

[6] coming up, *qui remontaient.*

[7] Soon there was a stir, *il y eut bientôt du bruit.*

[8] for miles along both shores, *sur une distance de plusieurs milles sur chaque rive.*

[9] channel, *chenal.*

[10] ran very near to, *longeait de près.*

[11] bank, *rive.*

and used his guns with great effect. At length the
little *squadron*[12] came to the place of peril. Then the
Mountjoy *took the lead*[13], and went right at the *boom*[14].
The huge barricade cracked and gave way; but the
shock was such that the Mountjoy rebounded, and stuck
in the mud. A yell of triumph rose from the banks;
the Irish rushed to their boats, and *were preparing to
board*[15]; but the Dartmouth poured on them a well
directed broadside, *which threw them into disorder*[16]. Just
then the Phœnix dashed at the breach which the Mountjoy had made, and was in a moment *within the fence*[17].
Meantime the tide *was rising fast*[18]. The Mountjoy
began to move, and soon passed safe through the broken
stakes and floating spars. But her brave master was
no more. A shot from one of the batteries had struck
him; and he died by the most enviable of all deaths,
in sight of the city which was his *birthplace*[19], *which
was his home*[20], *and which had just been saved by his
courage and self-devotion from the most frightful form of
destruction*[21]. *The night had closed in before the conflict
at the boom began*[22] : *but the flash of the guns was seen,
and the noise heard, by the lean and ghastly multitude*

---

[12] squadron, *escadre.*
[13] took the lead, *se mit en tête.*
[14] boom, *barricade.*
[15] were preparing to board, *se préparaient à l'abordage.*
[16] which threw them into disorder, *qui les mit en désordre.*
[17] within the fence, *dans le bastingage.*
[18] was rising fast, *montait rapidement.*
[19] birthplace, *ville natale.*
[20] which was his home, *qui était sa demeure.*
[21] and which had just been saved by his courage and self-devotion from the most frightful form of destruction == *which had just
been saved from the most frightful form of destruction by his courage
and self-devotion.*
[22] The night had closed in before the conflict at the boom began
la nuit était venue avant que ne commençât le combat de la barricade.

which covered the walls of the city[2 3]. When the Mountjoy grounded, and when the shout of triumph rose from
the Irish on both sides of the river, *the hearts of the
besieged died within them*[2 4]. One who endured the un-
utterable anguish of that moment has told us that they
looked fearfully livid in each other's eyes. Even after
the barricade had been passed, there was a terrible half
hour of suspense. *It was ten o'clock before the ships
arrived at the quay*[2 5]. The whole population was there
to welcome them. A screen made of casks filled with
earth was hastily thrown up to protect the landing place
from the batteries on the other side of the river; and
then the work of unloading began. First were rolled
on shore barrels containing six thousand bushels of meal.
Then came great cheeses, casks of beef, flitches of bacon,
kegs of butter, sacks of pease and biscuit, ankers of
brandy. *Not many hours before, half a pound of tallow
and three quarters of a pound of salted hide had been
weighed out with niggardly care to every fighting man*[2 6].
The ration which each now received was three pounds
of flour, two pounds of beef, and a pint of pease. It
is easy to imagine with what tears grace was said over
the suppers of that evening. There was little sleep on
either side of the wall. The bonfires shone bright along

[2 3] but the flash of the guns was seen, and the noise heard, by
the lean and ghastly multitude which covered the walls of the city,
*mais la multitude maigre et décharnée qui couvrait les murs de la
ville voyait le feu des canons et en entendait le bruit.*

[2 4] the hearts of the besieged died within them, *le cœur des
assiégés leur manqua.*

[2 5] It was ten o'clock before the ships arrived at the quay, *dix
heures sonnèrent avant que les vaisseaux n'arrivassent au quai.*

[2 6] Not many hours before, half a pound of tallow and three
quarters of a pound of salted hide had been weighed out with niggardly care to every fighting man = *peu d'heures auparavant on
avait distribué à chaque soldat et avec un soin parcimonieux une
demi-livre &c.*

the whole circuit of the ramparts. The Irish guns continued to roar all night; and all night the bells of the
rescued city *made answer to the Irish guns with a peal
of joyous defiance*[27]. *Through the three following days*[28]
the batteries of the enemy continued to play. But, on
the third night, flames were seen arising from the camp;
and, when the first of August dawned, a line of smoking
ruins marked the site lately occupied by the huts of
the besiegers; and the citizens saw far off the long
column of spikes and standards *retreating up the left
bank*[29] of the Foyle towards Strabane. So ended this
great siege, the most memorable in the annals of the
British isles. It had lasted a hundred and five days.—
Macaulay.

81. INFLUENCE OF FRANCE DURING THE SECOND HALF OF THE 17TH CENTURY.

France United[1] at that period almost every species of
ascendency. Her military glory *was at the height*[2]. She
had vanquished mighty coalitions; she had dictated treaties;
she had subjugated great cities and provinces; she had
forced the Castilian pride *to yield her the precedence*[3] :
she had summoned Italian princes to prostrate themselves *at her footstool*[4]. Her authority was supreme *in*

---

[27] made answer to the Irish guns, with a peal of joyous defiance,
répondirent aux canons irlandais par une joyeuse volée de défiance.
[28] Through the three following days, *pendant les trois jours
suivants.*
[29] retreating up the left bank, *qui battaient en retraite sur la
rive gauche.*

81. INFLUENCE OF FRANCE DURING THE SECOND HALF OF THE 17TH CENTURY.

[1] united, *réunissait.*
[2] was at the height, *était à son zénith.*
[3] to yield her the precedence, *à lui céder le pas.*
[4] at her footstool, *à ses pieds.*

all matters of good breeding, from a duel to a minuet[5].
...... In literature *she gave law*[6] to the world. The
fame of her great writers filled Europe. No other
country could produce a tragic poet equal to Racine, a
comic poet equal to Molière, a trifler so agreeable as
La Fontaine, a rhetorician so skilful as Bossuet.

The literary glory of Italy and of Spain *had set*[7] ;
that of Germany *had not yet dawned*[8]. The genius, therefore, of the eminent men who adorned Paris shone forth
with a splendour *which was set off to full advantage by
contrast*[9]. France, indeed, had at that time an empire
over mankind, such as even the Roman Republic never
attained. For when Rome was politically dominant, she
was in arts and letters the humble pupil to Greece.
France had, over the surrounding countries, at once the
ascendency which Rome had over Greece, and the ascendency which Greece had over Rome. French was
becoming the universal language—the language *of fashionable society*[10], the language of diplomacy. At several
courts princes and nobles spoke it more accurately and
politely than their mother-tongue.

In our island there was less of this servility than
on the continent. Neither our good nor our bad qualities were those of imitators. Yet even here homage
was paid, awkwardly indeed, and sullenly, to the literary
supremacy of our neighbours. The melodious Tuscan,
so familiar to the gallants and ladies of the court of
Elizabeth, *sank into contempt*[11]. New canons of critic-

---

[5] in all matters of good breeding, from a duel to a minuet,
en tout ce qui touchait à la politesse, d'un duel à un menuet.

[6] she gave law, *elle faisait la loi.*

[7] had set, *avait disparu.*

[8] had not yet dawned, *n'avait pas encore commencé à poindre.*

[9] which was set off to full advantage by contrast, *que le con-
traste faisait pleinement valoir.*

[10] of fashionable society, *du grand monde.*

[11] sank into contempt, *s'engloutit dans le mépris.*

ism, new models of style, *came into fashion*[12]. The quaint ingenuity which had deformed the verses of Donne, and had been a blemish on those of Cowley, disappeared from our poetry. Our prose became less majestic, *less artfully involved*[13], less *variously musical*[14], than that of an earlier age; but more lucid, more easy, and better fitted for controversy and narrative. In these changes it is impossible not to recognise the influence of French precept and of French example.—*Macaulay.*

82. A TALE OF MID-AIR[1].

In a cottage in the valley of Sallanches, near the foot of Mont Blanc, lived old Bernard and his three sons. One morning *he lay in bed sick*[2], and, *burning with fever*[3], watched anxiously for the return of his son, Jehan, who had gone to fetch a *physician*[4]. At length *a horse's tread was heard*[5], and soon afterwards the doctor entered. He examined the *patient*[6] *closely, felt his pulse*[7], *looked at his tongue*[8], and then said, patting the old man's cheek, "It will be nothing, my friend, — nothing!" but he made a sign to three lads, who openmouthed and anxious, stood grouped around the bed. All four withdrew to a distant corner, the doctor shook his head, *thrust out his lower lip*[9], and

---

[12] came into fashion, *vinrent à la mode.*
[13] less artfully involved, *moins finement obscure.*
[14] less variously musical, *moins variée et moins harmonieuse.*

82. A TALE OF MID-AIR.

[1] of mid-air, *d'entre ciel et terre.*
[2] he lay in bed sick, *il était malade au lit.*
[3] burning with fever, *brûlant de la fièvre.*
[4] physician, *médecin.*
[5] a horse's tread was heard, *le pas d'un cheval se fit entendre.*
[6] patient, *malade.*
[7] closely felt his pulse, *lui tâta le pouls avec attention.*
[8] looked at his tongue, *lui regarda la langue.*
[9] thrust out his lower lip, *fit la moue.*

said, "Tis a serious attack—very serious—of fever. He is now *in the height of the fit*[10], and as soon as it abates, *he must have sulphate of quinine*[11]."

"What is that, doctor?".

"Quinine, my friend, is a very expensive medicine, but which you may procure at Sallanches. Between the two fits your father must take at least three francs worth. I will write the prescription. You can read, Guillaume?"

"Yes, *doctor*[12]."

"And you will see that he takes it?"

"Certainly."

When the physician was gone, Guillaume, Pierre, and Jehan looked at each other in silent perplexity. *Their whole stock of money*[13] consisted *of a franc and a half*[14], and *yet the medicine must be procured immediately*[15].

"Listen," said Pierre, "*I know a method of getting from the mountain before night three or four five-franc pieces*[16]."

"From the mountain?"

"I have discovered an eagle's nest in a cleft of a frightful precipice. There is a gentleman at Salanches, *who would gladly purchase*[17] the eaglets; and nothing

---

[10] in the height of the fit, *au plus haut période.*

[11] he must have sulphate of quinine, *il lui faut du sulphate de quinine.*

[12] doctor, *monsieur le docteur.*

[13] Their whole stock of money, *toute leur réserve d'argent.*

[14] of a franc and a half, *un franc cinquante (centimes)* or *trente sous.* (*The latter more colloquial.*)

[15] and yet the medicine must be procured immediately, *et cependant il fallait se procurer le médicament immédiatement.*

[16] I know a method of getting from the mountain before night three or four five-franc pieces, *je connais un moyen d'obtenir de la montagne trois ou quatre pièces de cent sous* (or *trois ou quatre pièces de cinq francs) avant la nuit.*

[17] who would gladly purchase, *qui serait content d'acheter.*

made me hesitate but the terrible risk of taking them; but that's nothing when our father's life is concerned. We may have them now in two hours."

"I will rob the nest," said Guillaume.

"No, no, let me," said Jehan. "I am the youngest and lightest."

"I have the best right to venture," said Pierre, "as it was I who discovered it."

"Come," said Pierre, "let us decide *by drawing lots*[18]. Write three numbers, Guillaume, put them into my hat, and whoever draws number one *will try*[19] the venture."

Guillaume blackened the end of a wooden splinter in the fire; tore an old card into three pieces; wrote on them one, two, three, and threw them into the hat.

How the three hearts beat! Old Bernard lay shivering in the cold fit, and each of his sons *longed*[20] to risk his own life to save that of his father.

The *lot*[21] fell on Pierre, who had discovered the nest; he embraced the sick man.

"We shall not be long absent, father," he said, "and it is needful for us to go together."

"What are you going to do?"

"We will tell you as soon as we come back."

Guillaume took down from the wall an old sabre, which had belonged to Bernard when he served as a soldier; Jehan sought *a thick cord which the mountaineers use when cutting down trees*[22]; and Pierre went towards an old wooden cross, *reared*[23] near the cottage, and knelt before it for some minutes in fervent prayer.

---

[18] by drawing lots, *en tirant au sort* or *à la courte paille*.

[19] will try, *tentera*.

[20] longed, *désirait ardemment*.

[21] lot, *sort*.

[22] a thick cord which the mountaineers use when cutting down trees, *une corde épaisse dont les montagnards se servent quand ils abattent des arbres*.

[23] reared, *qui s'élevait*.

They set out together, and soon reached the brink
of the precipice. The danger consisted not only in the
possibility of falling several hundred feet, but still more
in the probable aggression of the birds of prey, in-
habiting the wild abyss.

Pierre, who was to brave these perils, *was a fine
athletic young man of twenty-two*[24]. Having *measured
with his eye*[25] the distance he would have to descend,
his brothers fastened the cord around his waist, and
began *to let him down*[26]. Holding the sabre in his
hand, *he safely reached*[27] the nook that contained the
nest. In it were four eaglets of a light yellowish-brown
colour, and his heart beat with joy *at the sight of
them*[28]. He grasped the nest firmly in his left hand,
and shouted joyfully to his brothers, "I have them!
Draw me up[29]!"

Already the first upward pull was given to the cord,
when Pierre felt himself attacked by two enormous eagles,
whose furious cries *proved them to be*[30] the parents of
the nestlings.

"Courage, brother! defend thyself! don't fear!"

Pierre pressed the nest to his bosom, and with his
right hand made the sabre play around his head.

Then began a terrible combat. The eagles shrieked,
the little ones cried shrilly, the mountaineer shouted
and brandished his sword. He slashed the birds with
its blade, which flashed like lightning, and only rendered
them still more enraged. He struck the rock, and sent
forth a shower of sparks.

---

[24] was a fine athletic young man of twenty-two, *était un beau
jeune homme robuste de vingt-deux ans.*
[25] measured with his eye, *mesura de l'œil.*
[26] to let him down, *à le faire descendre.*
[27] he safely reached, *il atteint en sûreté.*
[28] at the sight of them, *à leur vue.*
[29] Draw me up, *remontez-moi.*
[30] proved them to be, *prouvaient qu'ils étaient.*

Suddenly he felt a jerk given to the cord that sustained him. Looking up he perceived that, in his evolutions, he had cut it with his sabre, and that half the strands were severed!

Pierre's eyes, dilated widely, remained for a moment immoveable, and then closed with terror. *A cold shudder*[31] passed through his veins, and he thought of letting go both the nest and the sabre.

At that moment one of the eagles pounced on his head, and tried to tear his face. The Savoyard made a last effort, and defended himself bravely. He thought of his old father, and took courage.

Upwards, still upwards mounted the cord: friendly voices eagerly uttered words of encouragement and triumph: but Pierre could not reply to them. When he reached the brink of the precipice, still clasping fast the nest, his hair, which an hour before had been as black as a raven's wing, was become so completely white, that Guillaume and Jehan could scarcely recognise him.

What did that signify[32]? the eaglets were of the rarest and most valuable species. That same afternoon they were carried to the village and sold. Old Bernard had the medicine, *and every needful comfort beside*[33], and *the doctor in a few days pronounced him convalescent*[34].—*Dickens.*

83. MOZART'S REQUIEM.

One evening, the illustrious composer, Mozart, was seated at his piano, *not engaged in playing*[1], but with

---

[31] A cold shudder, *un frisson glacial.*

[32] What did that signify, *mais qu'est-ce que cela faisait.*

[33] and every needful comfort beside, *et en outre toutes les douceurs qu'il lui fallait.*

[34] the doctor in a few days pronounced him convalescent, *au bout de quelques jours le médecin déclara qu'il était convalescent.*

83. MOZART'S REQUIEM.

[1] not engaged in playing, *quoiqu'il n'en touchât pas.*

his head resting upon his hand. *His look was that of one who had just undergone some severe physical exertion, and is left by it weak and exhausted²*. *A hectic flush³* was yet upon his cheek, and an unnatural glow in *his large fine eyes⁴*. "My dear Wolfgang," said the wife of the musician, *entering⁵* the room while he was in this *condition⁶*, *"you have again, I see, made yourself ill⁷—worse⁸* than before. Oh, why, *for my sake⁹*, will you not refrain from this incessant labour?" As she spoke, she kissed his pale brow tenderly, *and a tear rose to her eye¹⁰*.

"It is in vain, my love," answered Mozart; "I cannot avoid my destiny. Were I placed on a barren rock, or in the deserts of Africa, *with neither instrument nor paper within a hundred miles of me¹¹*, my thoughts would be equally intent on my divine art; I should exhaust myself not less than I do here. To follow out the suggestions of fancy, and commit them to paper, is not the weakening or toilsome portion of my occupations. On the contrary, I derive pleasure and refreshment from the fulfilment of my conceptions. The *preliminary workings¹²* of the brain are the causes of ex-

---

² his look was that of one who had just undergone some severe physical exertion, and is left by it weak and exhausted, *son regard était comme celui d'une personne qui vient d'être soumise à un rigoureux effort physique qui l'a laissée faible et exténuée.*

³ A hectic flush, *une rougeur hectique.*

⁴ his large fine eyes, *ses yeux grands et beaux.*

⁵ entering, *en entrant dans.*

⁶ condition, *état.*

⁷ you have again, I see, made yourself ill, *je vois que vous venez encore de vous rendre malade.*

⁸ worse, *plus malade.*

⁹ for my sake, *pour moi; ...or pour l'amour de moi.*

¹⁰ and a tear rose to her eye, *et une larme brilla dans ses yeux.*

¹¹ with neither instrument nor paper within a hundred miles of me, *sans instrument ni papier à cent milles à la ronde.*

¹² preliminary workings, *les travaux préparatoires.*

haustion, *and those I cannot put a stop to*[13]. It is my fate, Constance; it is my fate." The composer seemed so much wearied as he uttered these words, that his attached wife pressed him to lie down upon the sofa, *and endeavour to snatch*[14] some minutes of sleep. Mozart complied with her suggestion, and, having seen him comfortably placed, his wife retired.

The ailing composer—for he had been ill, very ill, for some months—*was not destined, however, to enjoy his repose for any length of time*[15]. He was roused by a servant, who informed him that a stranger desired to speak with him. "*Show him this way*[16]," said the musician, *rising from his recumbent position*[17]. The visitor was immediately introduced. He was a person of very striking appearance, tall and *commanding in stature*[18]. His *countenance*[19] was peculiarly grave, solemn, and *even awe-striking*[20]: and his manners dignified and impressive. *Altogether his aspect was such as to arrest the attention of Mozart in a forcible manner*[21]. "I come," said the stranger, after bowing courteously to the composer's salutation, "to request a peculiar favour from you. A friend, *whose name I am required not to mention*[22], wishes to have a solemn mass composed, as a

---

[13] and those I cannot put a stop to, *et ceux-là je ne puis les empêcher.*

[14] and endeavour to snatch *et de s'efforcer d'arracher.*

[15] was not destined, however, to enjoy his repose for any length of time, *ne devait pas, cependant, jouir de son repos pendant longtemps.*

[16] Show him this way, *faites le entrer par ici.*

[17] rising from his recumbent position, *se levant.*

[18] commanding in stature, *d'une taille imposante.*

[19] countenance, *aspect.*

[20] even awe-striking, *et frappait même d'effroi.*

[21] Altogether his aspect was such as to arrest the attention of Mozart in a forcible manner, *son aspect était tout à fait de nature à fixer l'attention de Mozart d'une manière puissante.*

[22] whose name I am required not to mention, *dont on m'a prié de ne pas dire le nom.*

requiem for the soul of a dear relative, recently lost, *whose memory he is desirous of honouring in*[23] an especial manner. *You alone, he conceives*[24], have the power to execute the task worthily, and I am here to pray you to undertake it." Mozart, though unwell, saw no great difficulty in such a task as this, and *he even felt that to one so interesting in look and deportment as the stranger it would have been difficult for him to refuse a much harder matter*[25]. *"In what time*[26]*,"* said he, after a pause, "must the work be completed?" *"In a month or so*[27]*,"* answered the stranger; *"and expense is not to be considered*[28]. *Make your own term for remuneration*[29].*"* Mozart mentioned a moderate sum. The stranger immediately pulled out a purse, and, taking from it one hundred ducats, a sum exceeding the composer's demand, laid the money on the table. Immediately afterwards *he took his leave*[30].

The concealment[31] of the name of the *party*[32] requiring the requiem, and the remarkable air and appearance of the stranger, *caused*[33] this visit to make a strong impression on the sensitive mind of the great

---

[23] whose memory he is desirous of honouring in, *dont il désire honorer la mémoire d'*.

[24] You alone, he conceives, *il imagine que vous seul*.

[25] he even felt that to one so interesting in look and deportment as the stranger it would have been difficult for him to refuse a much harder matter, *il sentit même qu'il lui aurait été difficile de refuser une chose bien plus importante à une personne aussi intéressante que l'étranger par la mine et par le port*.

[26] In what time, *en combien de temps?*

[27] In a month or so, *dans un mois ou à peu près*.

[28] and expense is not to be considered, *et on ne doit pas regarder à la dépense*.

[29] Make your own term for remuneration, *fixez vous-même vos honoraires*.

[30] he took his leave, *il prit congé de lui*.

[31] The concealment of, *le fait d'avoir caché*.

[32] party, *personne*.

[33] caused, *furent la cause que*.

master. *It was not long after the stranger had left, ere Mozart commenced the work*[34] which he had engaged to perform. He had been brooding over the subject for a time, and suddenly started up, and *called for writing-materials*[35]. For a period he proceeded in his composition with extraordinary ardour, but the excitement of the task *was hurtful to him*[36]. His fainting fits returned, and for some successive days he *was confined to bed*[37].

As soon as he was able he resumed his occupation, but, being too enthusiastic to proceed with only moderate diligence, *he soon brought back his illness*[38]. Thus it was that the work was carried on *by fits and starts*[39]. One day, when his wife was *hanging over him*[40], as he sat at his piano, he abruptly stopped, and said, "*The conviction has seized me*[41] that I am writing my own requiem. This will be my own funeral service!"

At the end of the month, the stranger *made his appearance punctually*[42]. "I have found it impossible to keep my word," said Mozart; "this work has interested me more than I expected, and I have extended it beyond my first design." "Then take a little additional time," answered the stranger. "Another month," said Mozart, "and it shall be ready." "For this added trouble," returned the stranger, "there must be an additional recompense." With these words he drew his purse, and, laying down fifty ducats, took his leave with the promise to return again at the time appointed.

---

[34] It was not long after the stranger had left, ere Mozart commenced the work. *Ce ne fut que peu de temps après le départ de l'étranger que Mozart commença le travail.*

[35] called for writing-materials, *demanda de quoi écrire.*

[36] was hurtful to him, *lui fut détrimental.*

[37] was confined to bed, *il garda le lit.*

[38] he soon brought back his illness, *il retomba bientôt malade.*

[39] by fits and starts, *par foucades.*

[40] hanging over him, *penchée sur lui.*

[41] The conviction has seized me, *la conviction s'est emparée de moi.*

[42] made his appearance punctually, *arriva à l'heure dite.*

Mozart resumed his labours, and the requiem *proceeded*[43]. Every day the composer grew more and more enthusiastic *in the prosecution*[44] of his task, but *every day*[45] *his bodily powers became more and more enfeebled*[46]. The impression which he had communicated to his wife *gained additional strength*[47], *and the more so as*[48] his endeavours *to*[49] discover the name and the character of the interesting and mysterious stranger *proved*[50] unavailing. He had ordered a servant to follow the stranger *on the occasion*[51] of his last visit, but the man had returned with the announcement that the object of his pursuit had suddenly disappeared from before his eyes. Inquiries amongst friends were equally fruitless. These circumstances, as we have said, deepened the conviction of Mozart's mind that he was composing his own requiem, *and composing it at no earthly command*[52]. *This idea so likely to impress the romantic spirit of the great composer, rather favoured than impeded the completion of the requiem*[53]. As his physical powers decayed, the zeal of the composer increased. He finished the task, as far as he considered necessary, and, almost immediately afterwards, the soul of Mozart left its *mortal tenement*[54].

---

[43] proceeded, *s'avançait.*

[44] in the prosecution, *à continuer.*

[45] every day, *de jour en jour.*

[46] his bodily powers became more and more enfeebled, *ses forces s'affaiblissaient de plus en plus.*

[47] gained additional strength, *devenait plus forte.*

[48] and the more so as, *et cela d'autant plus que.*

[49] to = *for.*

[50] proved, *restèrent.*

[51] on the occasion, *lors.*

[52] and composing it at no earthly command, *et qu'il ne le composait pas à la requête d'un mortel.*

[53] This idea so likely to impress the romantic spirit of the great composer, rather favoured than impeded the completion of the requiem, *cette idée si propre à produire une impression sur l'esprit romanesque du grand compositeur favorisa plutôt qu'elle n'empêcha l'achèvement du requiem.*

[54] its mortal tenement, *son enveloppe mortelle,* or *sa demeure terrestre.*

When the stranger returned—for he did return at the appointed day—Mozart was no more. Strange to tell, the visitor showed now no anxiety for the requiem, and it was left to serve as a commemoration of the great master himself. It is still well known *by*[55] the name of Mozart's Requiem.

84. CHIEF-JUSTICE HOLT.

In[1] the time of this eminent judge *a riot happened*[2] in London, *arising*[3] from a wicked practice then very common, *of kidnapping*[4] young persons of both sexes, and sending them to the plantations. *Information having gone abroad*[5], that there was a house in Holborn, which *served as*[6] a lockup place for the persons thus ensnared, till an opportunity could be found *of shipping them off*[7]; the enraged populace assembled in great numbers and were going *to pull it down*[8]. Notice of the tumult being sent to Whitehall, *a party of the guards were commanded to march to the spot*[9]; but an officer was first sent to the *chief-justice*[10], to acquaint him with the state of matters, *and to request that he would send*[11] some of his officers along with the soldiers, in order to give *a countenance to their interference*[12].

---

[55] by, *sous.*

84. CHIEF-JUSTICE HOLT.

[1] In, *du.*
[2] a riot happened, *il y eut une émeûte.*
[3] arising, *causée.*
[4] of kidnapping, *d'enlever.*
[5] Information having gone abroad, *le bruit s'étant répandu.*
[6] served as, *servait de.*
[7] shipping them off, *de les embarquer.*
[8] to pull it down, *la démolir.*
[9] a party of the guards were commanded to march to the spot, *on commanda à un détachement des gardes de se rendre sur les lieux.*
[10] chief-justice, *président.*
[11] and to request that he would send, *et pour le prier d'envoyer.*
[12] to give a countenance to their interference, *afin de donner un appui moral à leur intervention.*

The officer having *delivered*[13] his message, Lord Chief-justice Holt said to him: "suppose the populace should not disperse *at your appearance*[14]; what are you to do then?" "Sir," answered the officer, "we have orders to fire upon them." "*Have you, Sir*[15]?" replied his lordship: "*then take notice of what I say; if there be one man killed and you are tried before me, I will take care that you, and every soldier of your party, shall be hanged*[16]". "Sir," continued he, "go back to those who sent you and acquaint them, that no officer of mine *shall attend*[17] soldiers; and let them know at the same time, that the laws of this kingdom are not to be executed by the sword; these matters belong to the civil power and *you have nothing to do with them*[18]".

The lord chief-justice then went himself in person, accompanied by his tipstaffs and a few constables, to the scene of the disturbance[19]; and by his reasonable expostulations with the mob, succeeded, without the least violence, in making them all disperse quietly.

---

[13] delivered, *fait part de.*

[14] at your appearance, *en vous voyant.*

[15] Have you, Sir? *Vraiment, Monsieur?*

[16] then take notice of what I say; if there be one man killed and you are tried before me, I will take care that you, and every soldier of your party, shall be hanged, *eh bien, prenez note de ce que je vais vous dire: s'il y a un seul homme de tué et que vous soyez jugé par moi, je veillerai à ce que vous et les soldats de votre détachement vous soyez pendus.*

[17] shall attend, *n'accompagnera.*

[18] you have nothing to do with them, *et vous n'avez rien à y voir.*

[19] The lord chief-justice then went himself in person, accompanied by his tipstaffs and a few constables, to the scene of the disturbance = then the lord chief-justice (went himself in person to the scene of the disturbance = *se rendit en personne sur le théâtre de l'émeute*) accompanied by his tipstaffs and a few constables.

85. MOSQUITO HUNT.

In the sleeping apartments of India, *great care is taken*[1] to secure coolness. The beds, which are always large and hard, are generally placed *as nearly as may be in the*[2] very middle of the *apartment*[3], in the line of the freest thorough draught, *which open doors and open windows can command*[4]. I speak now, of course, of the beds of men *who live in single blessedness*[5]. In other cases, a simple contrivance has been devised, which, if it does render the room less airy than that of the free and solitary bachelor, nevertheless accomplishes a good deal, and *secures all the proprieties*[6]. The door, which is shut, has its upper half cut away, so that the air enters freely above; and the windows, also, being high, are always left open.

Round each bed is suspended a gauze curtain, without which sleep would be as effectually murdered *as ever it was by any tragedy king*[7]. For, if even one villainous mosquito contrives to gain admission into your fortress, you may for that night, bid good bye not only to sleep, but to temper, and almost to health. *I defy the most resolute, the most serene, or the most robust person that ever lived between the Tropics, to pass a whole night in a bed, within the curtain of which a single invader has entered, and not to be found, when morning comes, in a*

---

85. MOSQUITO HUNT.

[1] great care is taken, *on prend grand soin.*

[2] as nearly as may be in the, *aussi près possible du.*

[3] apartment, *chambre.*

[4] which open doors and open windows can command, *que l'on puisse obtenir en ouvrant portes et fenêtres.*

[5] who live in single blessedness = *who are not married.*

[6] secure all the proprieties, *et met les convenances à l'abri.*

[7] as ever it was by any tragedy king, *qu'il le fut jamais par un roi de tragédie.*

high fever, with every atom of his patience exhausted[8].
Temper[9], under such circumstances is really out of the
question; the most placid creature on earth, even old
uncle Toby himself *would be driven into a rage*[10].

The process of getting into bed in India is one
requiring great dexterity, and *not a little scientific
engineering*[11]. As the curtains are carefully tucked in
close under the mattress, all round, you must decide at
what part of the bed you choose to make your entry.
Having *surveyed*[12] the ground, and *clearly made up your
mind on this point*[13], you take in your right hand a
kind of brush, or switch, generally made of a horse's
tail: or, if you be tolerably expert, a towel may answer
the purpose. *With*[14] your left hand you then seize that
part of the skirt of the curtain which is *thrust*[15] under
the bedding *at the place you intend to enter*[16], and, *by*

---

[8] I defy the most resolute, the most serene, or the most robust
person that ever lived between the Tropics, to pass a whole night
in a bed, within the curtain of which a single invader has entered,
and not to be found, when morning comes, in a high fever, with
every atom of his patience exhausted = I defy the person the most
resolute, the most serene, or the most robust (that ever lived between
the Tropics = *qui a jamais vécu sous les tropiques*) to pass a whole
night in a bed (within the curtain of which = *sous le moustiquaire
duquel*) a single invader has (*soit*) entered and not to be found,
when comes the morning, in a state of high fever (and with every
atom of his patience exhausted = *sans que toute sa patience ne soit
à bout*).

[9] Temper, *un bon caractère.*

[10] would be driven into a rage, *en arriverait à se mettre en
rage.*

[11] not a little scientific engineering, *et pas peu de science mé-
canique.*

[12] surveyed, *examiné.*

[13] clearly made up your mind on this point, *et vous êtes clairement décidé sur ce point.*

[14] with, *de.*

[15] thrust, *bordé.*

[16] at the place you intend to enter, *à l'endroit où vous avez
l'intention d'entrer.*

the light of the cocoa-nut-oil lamp[17] (which burns on the
floor of every bedroom in Hindustan), *you first drive
away*[18] the mosquitoes from your immediate neighbourhood, by whisking round your horse's tail; and,
before proceeding further[19], you must be sure you have
effectually driven the enemy back. *If you fail in this
matter*[20], your repose is effectually *dashed*[21] for that
night; for the *confounded animals*[22] it is really difficult
to keep from[23] swearing, *even at the recollection of the
villains*[24], though at the distance of ten thousand miles
from them—the well cursed animals, then, appear to
know perfectly well what is going to happen, and
assemble with the vigour and bravery of the flank
companies *appointed to head a storming party*[25], ready
in one instant to rush into the breach, *careless alike*[26]
of horse-tails and towels. Let it be supposed, however,
that you have successfully beaten back the enemy. You
next promptly form an opening, *not a hair's breadth
larger*[27] than your own person, into which you leap,
like harlequin through a hoop, or, to borrow Jack's
phrase, *"as if the devil kicked you on end*[28] *!"* Of course,
with all the speed of intense fear, you close up the

---

[17] by the light of the cocoa-nut-oil lamp, *et à la lumière de la
lampe à huile de coco.*

[18] you first drive away, *vous chassez d'abord.*

[19] and before proceeding further, *et avant d'aller plus loin.*

[20] If you fail in this matter, *si vous ne réussissez pas en cela.*

[21] dashed, *détruit.*

[22] the confounded animals, *ces animaux du diable.*

[23] to keep from, *de s'empêcher de.*

[24] even at the recollection of the villains, *rien qu'en se souvenant
des gredins.*

[25] appointed to head a storming party, *désignées pour marcher à
la tête d'un détachement d'assiégeants.*

[26] careless alike etc., *ne se souciant ni* &c.

[27] not a hair's breadth larger, *pas plus grande de l'épaisseur d'un
cheveu.*

[28] as if the devil kicked you on end, *comme si le diable vous
donnait un coup de pied quelque part.*

gap through which you have shot yourself into your
sleeping quarters.

If all these arrangements have been well managed,
you may amuse yourselves for a while by scoffing at,
and triumphing over the clouds of baffled mosquitoes
outside, who dash themselves against the meshes of the
net, in vain attempts to enter your sanctum. If, however,
for your sins, any one of their number has succeeded in
entering the place along with yourself, *he is not such
an ass*[29] as to betray his presence while you are flushed
with victory, wide awake, and armed with the means
of his destruction. Far from this, the scoundrel allows
you to chuckle over *your fancied great doings*[30], and to
lie down with all the complacency and fallacious security
of your conquest, and under the entire assurance of
enjoying a tranquil night's rest. Alas for such pre-
sumptuous hopes! *Scarcely have you dropped*[31] gradually
from these visions of the day to the yet more blessed
visions of the night, and the last faint effort of your
eyelids has been quite overcome by the gentle pressure
of sleep, *when, in deceitful slumber*[32], you hear something
like the sound of trumpets.

Straightway your imagination is kindled, and you
fancy yourself in the midst of a fierce fight, and
struggling not against petty insects, but against armed
men and thundering cannon! In the excitement of the
mortal conflict of your dream, you awake not displeased
mayhap to find that you are safe and snug in bed.
But in the next instant what is your dismay, when you
are again saluted by the odious notes of a mosquito
close at your ear! The perilous fight of the previous
dream, in which your honour had become pledged, and

---

[29] he is not such an ass, *il n'est pas assez âne pour.*
[30] your fancied great doings, *vos exploits supposés.*
[31] Scarcely have you dropped, *vous êtes à peine tombé.*
[32] when, in deceitful slumber, *lorsque, dans un sommeil trompeur.*

your life at hazard, is all forgotten in the pressing reality of *this waking calamity*[33]. You resolve *to do or die*[34], and not to sleep or even attempt to sleep, till you have finally overcome the enemy. Just as you have made this *manly resolve*[35], and, in order to deceive the foe, have pretended to be fast asleep, the wary mosquito is again heard, *circling*[36] over you at a distance, but gradually coming nearer and nearer in a spiral descent, and at each turn gaining upon you one inch, till, at length, he almost touches your ear, and, as you suppose, *is just about to settle upon it*[37]. With a sudden jerk, and full of wrath, you bring up your hand, *and give yourself such a box on the ear as would have staggered*[38] the best friend you have in the world, and might have crushed twenty thousand mosquitoes, *had they been there congregated*[39]. Being convinced *that you have now done for him*[40], you mutter between your teeth one of those satisfactory little apologies for an oath which indicate gratified revenge, and down you lie again.

In less than ten seconds, however, the very same felon whom you fondly hoped to have executed, is again within hail of you, and you can almost fancy you hear his scorn in the tone of his abominable hum. You, of course, watch his motions still more intently than before, but only by the ear, for you can never see him. We shall suppose that you fancy he is aiming at your left hand, indeed, as you are almost sure of it, you wait till he has ceased his song, and

---

[33] of this waking calamity, *de cette calamité de votre réveil.*
[34] to do or die, *d'agir ou de mourir.*
[35] manly resolve, *résolution mâle.*
[36] circling, *tournoyant.*
[37] is just about to settle upon it, *est sur le point de s'y poser.*
[38] and give yourself such a box on the ear as would have staggered, *et vous vous donnez un soufflet qui aurait fait chanceler* &c.
[39] had they been there congregated, *si ils y avaient été rassemblés.*
[40] that you have now done for him, *que vous l'avez à présent démoli.*

then you give yourself another smack, *which, I need not say, proves*[41] quite as fruitless as the first. About this stage of the action you discover, to your extreme horror, that you have been soundly bit in one ear and in both heels, but when or how, you cannot tell. These wounds, of course, *put you into a fine rage*[42], *partly from*[43] the pain, *and partly*[44] from the insidious manner, in which they have been inflicted. Up you spring on your knees—not to pray, *Heaven knows*[45]! but to fight. You seize your horse's tail with spiteful rage, and after whisking it round and round, and cracking it in every corner of the bed, you feel pretty certain you must at last have demolished your friend.

In this unequal warfare you pass the livelong night, *alternately scratching and cuffing yourself—fretting and fuming to no purpose*[46]—feverish, angry, sleepy, provoked and wounded in twenty different places!

At last, just as the long expected day begins to dawn, you drop off, quite exhausted, into an unsatisfactory, heavy slumber, during which your triumphant enemy banquets upon your carcass at his convenient leisure. As the sun is rising, the barber enters the room to remove your beard before you step into the bath, and you awaken only to discover the bloated and satiated monster clinging to the top of your bed, *an easy, but useless and inglorious prey*[47]!

---

[41] which, I need not say, proves, *qui, je n'ai pas besoin de le dire, est.*

[42] put you into a fine rage, *vous mettent dans une belle fureur.*

[43] partly from, *tant par.*

[44] and partly from, *que par.*

[45] Heaven knows, *Dieu sait.*

[46] alternately scratching and cuffing yourself—fretting and fuming to no purpose—, *en vous grattant et en vous souffletant tour à tour — vous faisant du mauvais sang en vain.*

[47] an easy, but useless and inglorious prey = *prey easy but useless and inglorious. No article to be used before 'prey'.*

86. ACCOUNT OF THE ADJUTANTS IN BENGAL.

Nothing tends more to diversify the scenery of India from that of England, than the number of adjutants (large birds of the stork species, the ardea arjala), which are beheld in all parts of the presidency and military stations. They do not frequent *the native part of Calcutta*[1], nor the dwellings of the natives generally, *so much as they do*[2] the residences of Europeans, *as near the latter (being carnivorous) they find*[3] a greater supply of food *than they possibly can do*[4] around the habitations *of the former*[5], whose diet is principally composed of vegetable productions and milk. Every morning, several of these birds station themselves near the cook-room doors, ready to seize the offal *which may be thrown out by the cooks*[6], and many furious battles take place in the course of the morning, for the possession of bones, and other spoils which may occasionally present themselves to their watchful eyes. *Their beaks are very long and thick, and they possess great strength in them*[7].

When they are fighting, the chopping of the bills and fluttering of their wings are *signals*[8] *to*[9] waiting

---

86. ACCOUNT OF THE ADJUTANTS IN BENGAL.

[1] the native part of Calcutta, *le quartier indigène de Calcutta.*

[2] so much as they do, *autant que.*

[3] as near the latter (being carnivorous) they find = *because, being carnivorous, they find near the latter; near the latter, près de ces dernières.*

[4] than they possibly can do, *qu'ils ne peuvent le faire.*

[5] of the former, *des premières.*

[6] which may be thrown out by the cooks = *which the cooks may throw out.*

[7] Their beaks are very long and thick, and they possess great strength in them = *have a great strength in the beak which is very long and very thick.*

[8] signals, *in the singular.*

[9] to = *for.*

kites and crows, *numbers of which immediately surround them*[10]; and one of these active and vigilant spectators will commonly avail himself of the dispute of the quarelling adjutants to carry of the prize for which they are contending. Sometimes a number of crows will beset an adjutant, and torment him exceedingly. At length the poor bird, quite wearied out by their impertinent attacks, suddenly makes a start, and catching hold of *one of their number*[11], swallows it instantly, when the other crows *set up such a cawing as to disturb*[12] the whole neighbourhood. *This I have witnessed*[13] more than once.

One of the tricks *practised on the adjutants by Europeans*[14] is this:—a large bone is tied to about half a brick or large stone, at the distance of about three feet, *when*[15] the bone and its companion are thrown out to the birds, one of which seizes the bait, and greedily swallows it.—The consequence is that the stone hangs dangling from its beak, until the bird, unable to shake it off, rather than disgorge the bone, gives it a throw upwards, and swallows it also. It is said *that in a few minutes*[16] the powerful chyle of the stomach destroys the string, *when*[17] the stone or brick is cast out again. But I never had patience to watch for this result. Sometimes a bone is tied to a long string, and thrown to a great distance; when the bird having swallowed it, is hauled nearly up to the person who holds the string,

---

[10] numbers of which immediately surround them, *et dont un grand nombre les entoure de suite.*

[11] one of their number = *one of them.*

[12] set up such a cawing as to disturb, *caw in such a fashion that they disturb.*

[13] This I have witnessed = *I have witnessed this.*

[14] practised on the adjutants by Europeans, *que les Européens jouent aux adjutants.*

[15] when, *alors.*

[16] that in a few minutes, *qu'au bout de quelques minutes.*

[17] when, *et qui alors.*

before he will consent to give back the spoil. *I was much grieved at*[18] *one trick I saw played,* and all who witnessed it *joined with me in censuring*[19] the cruelty of him who performed it. A large marrow bone was charged with a cartridge of powder, *and a fusee inserted*[20] which *would*[21] under cover of the bone, keep alight *when swallowed*[22]. This was ignited and thrown out, just after two or three of these birds had been scrambling for other food, and was speedily seized and swallowed by one of them. *No sooner had the poor adjutant thus taken the bait*[23], than feeling the heat of the fusee, it mounted straight upwards and was *in a moment afterwards*[24] literally blown to atoms in the air*.

87. FRANKLIN.

Doctor Franklin, in his memoirs, is particularly anxious to inculcate the duty of industry, in order that his posterity may know the use of a virtue, to which he was so largely indebted. *Throughout the whole*[1] of his long life, his principle was strengthened by an example of the most remarkable industry, of which he furnishes many instances.

---

[18] I was much grieved at one trick I saw played, *je fus très peiné par un tour que je vis jouer.*

[19] joined with me in censuring, *se joignirent à moi pour condamner.*

[20] and a fusee inserted, *and one inserted a fusee.*

[21] would keep, after *bone.*

[22] when swallowed, *quand il serait avalé.*

[23] No sooner had the poor adjutant thus taken the bait = *the poor adjutant had no sooner taken the bait*; had no sooner, *n'eût pas plus tôt.*

[24] in a moment afterwards, *un moment après.*

* The Editor is grieved to say that such acts of wanton cruelty are by no means rare in India even at the present day.

' 87. FRANKLIN.

[1] Throughout the whole, *pendant tout le cours.*

When a printer[2] *he was engaged in a work*[3] of forty sheets, on which he worked exceedingly hard, for the price was low.—"I composed", says he, "a sheet a day, and Meredith *worked it off at press*[4], it was often eleven at night, and sometimes later, before I had finished my *distribution*[5] for the next day's work; for the little jobs sent in by our other friends, now and then put us back. *But so determined was I*[6] to continue *doing a sheet a day of the folio*[7], that one night when having composed *my forms*[8], *and I thought my day's work over*[9], one of them by accident was broken, and two pages *were reduced to pie*[10], I immediately distributed and composed it over again before I went to bed; and this industry, visible to our neighbours, began to give us character and credit; particularly I was told, that mention being made of the new printing office, at the merchant's club every night; the general opinion was, *that it must fail*[11], *there being already*[12] two printers in the place, Keimer and Bradford; but Dr. Baird, a native of St. Andrews, Scotland, gave a contrary opinion."—"For the industry of that Franklin", said he, "is superior to any thing I ever saw; I see him still at work, when I go home from the club, and he is at work again before his

---

[2] when a printer = *when he was printer.*

[3] he was engaged in a work, *il était occupé à un ouvrage.*

[4] worked it off at press, *tirait les épreuves* (technical).

[5] distribution, *distribution*, the separatiug of the types and the apportioning of such types to their proper cases (technical).

[6] But so determined was I = *but I was so determined.*

[7] doing a sheet a day of the folio, *à faire, par jour, une feuille de l'in-folio.*

[8] my forms, *mes formes* (technical).

[9] and I thought my day's work over, *et que je croyais ma journée finie.*

[10] were reduced to pie, *furent réduites en pâte.* (Technical expression meaning that the types have got hopelessly mixed and confused.)

[11] that it must fail, *qu'il était sûr de tomber.*

[12] there being already, *comme il y avait déjà.*

neighbours are out of bed." "This struck the rest, and we soon after had offers from one of them to supply us with stationary; *but as yet we did not choose to engage in shop business*[13]."

88. BRADFORD THE INNKEEPER.

Jonathan Bradford *kept*[1] an inn *in Oxfordshire*[2] on the London road to Oxford, and *bore a respectable character*[3]. Mr. Hayes, *a gentleman of fortune*[4], being on his way to Oxford on a visit to a relation, *put up at*[5] Bradford's. He there *joined*[6] company with two gentlemen, with whom he supped and in conversation unguardedly mentioned that he had then *about him*[7] *a considerable sum of money*[8]. In due time they retired to their respective chambers; the gentlemen to a two-bedded room, leaving *as is customary with many*[9], a candle *burning*[10] in the chimney corner. Some hours after they were in bed, one of the gentlemen being awake, thought he heard a deep groan in an adjoining chamber; and this being repeated, he softly woke his friend. They listened together and the groans increasing, as of one dying and in pain, they both instantly arose and proceeded silently to the door of the next chamber,

---

[13] but as yet we did not choose to engage in shop business, *mais jusqu' alors il ne nous avait pas plu de tenir boutique.*

88. BRADFORD THE INNKEEPER.

[1] kept, *tenait.*
[2] in Oxfordshire = *in the county of Oxford.*
[3] and bore a respectable character, *et avait bonne réputation.*
[4] a gentleman of fortune = *a rich man.*
[5] to put up (at an inn), *descendre à.*
[6] joined, *entra en.*
[7] about him = *upon him.*
[8] a considerable sum of money = *une somme considérable.*
[9] as is customary with many, *comme beaucoup de personnes en ont l'habitude.*
[10] burning, *allumée.*

from which the groans had seemed to come. The door being ajar, they saw a light in the room. They entered, but it is impossible to paint their consternation on perceiving a person weltering in his blood in the bed, and a man standing over him with a dark lantern in one hand and a knife in the other! The man seemed as much petrified as themselves, but his terror *carried with it*[11] all the appearance of guilt. The gentlemen soon discovered that the murdered person was the stranger, with whom they had that night supped, and that the man who was standing over him was their host. They seized Bradford directly, *disarmed him of his knife*[12], and charged him with being the murderer. *He assumed by this time*[13] the air of innocence, positively denied the crime and asserted that he came there with the same humane intentions as themselves; *for that*[14], *hearing*[15] a noise which was succeeded by a groaning, he got out of bed, *struck a light*[16], armed himself with a knife for his defence, *and had but that minute entered the room before them*[17]. These assertions were of little avail: he was kept in close custody till the morning, and then taken before a neighbouring justice of the peace. Bradford still denied the murder, but with such apparent indications of guilt, that the justice hesitated not to make use of this extraordinary expression, on writing his *mittimus*[18], "Mr. Bradford, either you or myself committed this murder."

---

[11] carried with it, *avait.*
[12] disarmed him of his knife, *lui otèrent son couteau.*
[13] he assumed by this time = *but by this time he had assumed;* "by this time", *alors.*
[14] for that = *because.*
[15] hearing = *having heard.*
[16] struck a light, *se procura de la lumière.*
[17] and had but that minute entered the room before them, *et n'était entré dans la chambre qu'un instant avant eux.*
[18] mittimus = *committal.*

This remarkable affair became a topic of conversation to the whole country. Bradford was condemned by the general voice of every company. In the midst of all this predetermination, came on the assizes at Oxford. Bradford *was brought to trial*[19] *: he pleaded not guilty*[20]. Nothing could be stronger than the evidence of the two gentlemen. *They testified to the finding Mr. Hayes murdered*[21] in his bed and that knife and the hand which held it, bloody. They stated that, on their entering the room, he betrayed all the signs of a guilty man; and that but a few minutes preceding, they had heard the groans of the deceased.

Bradford's defence on his trial was the same as before: he had heard a noise, he suspected *that some villany was transacting*[22]*;* he struck a light, snatched up the knife, the only weapon at hand to defend himself, and entered the room of the deceased. He averred that the terrors he betrayed were merely the feelings natural to innocence as well as guilt, on beholding so horrid a scene. The defence however, could not but be considered as weak, contrasted with the several powerful circumstances against him. Never was circumstantial evidence so strong, so far as it went. There was little need for comment from the judge *in summing up the evidence*[23], *no room appeared for extenuation*[24] *;* and the prisoner was declared guilty by the jury without their even leaving the box.

---

[19] was brought to trial, *fut mis en jugement.*

[20] he pleaded not guilty, *et nia sa culpabilité.* To plead not guilty is an untranslatable term into French: a French and an English criminal trial being totally different things.

[21] They testified to the finding Mr. Hayes = *ils affirmèrent avoir trouvé Monsieur Hayes.*

[22] that some villany was transacting, *qu'il se perpétrait quelque scélératesse.*

[23] in summing up the evidence, *en résumant les débats.*

[24] no room appeared for extenuation, *il ne semblait pas y avoir de circonstances atténuantes.*

Bradford was executed shortly after, still declaring *that he was not the murderer, nor privy to the murder*[25] of Mr. Hayes; but he died disbelieved by all.

Yet these assertions were not untrue! The murder was actually committed by the footman of Mr. Hayes; and the assassin, *immediately on stabbing*[26] his master, rifled his pockets of his money, gold watch and snuff box, and then escaped back to his own room. This could scarcely have been effected, as after-circumstances showed, more than two seconds before Bradford's entering the unfortunate gentleman's chamber. The world owed this information to remorse of conscience on the part of the footman (eighteen months after the execution of Bradford) when laid on a bed of sickness. It was *a deathbed repentance*[27] and by that death, the law lost its victim.

It were to be wished[28] that this account could close here, *but there is more*[29] to be told. Bradford though innocent of the murder and not even privy to it, was nevertheless a murderer in design. He had heard, as well as the footman, what Mr. Hayes had declared at supper, of having a sum of money about him, and he went to the chamber of the deceased with the same intentions as the servant. He was struck with amazement on beholding himself anticipated in the crime. He could not believe his senses; and in turning back the bed clothes to assure himself of the fact, he in his agitation dropped his knife on the bleeding body, *by which means*[30] both his hands and the weapon became bloody. *These*

---

[25] that he was not the murderer, nor privy to the murder of Mr. Hayes, *qu'il n'était pas l'assassin de Mr. Hayes et qu'il n'avait pas eu connaissance du crime.*

[26] immediately on stabbing, *immédiatement après avoir poignardé.*

[27] a deathbed repentance, *une repentance au lit de mort.*

[28] It were to be wished, *il serait à désirer.*

[29] but there is more, *mais il y a encore quelque chose.*

[30] by which means, *et ainsi.*

circumstances Bradford acknowledged[31] to the clergyman who attended him after sentence, but who, it is extremely probable, would not believe them at the time.

89. ROBERT BRUCE.

The celebrated Robert Bruce was crowned king of Scotland March 19th 1306. On the 28th of May he was excommunicated by the Pope, a sentence which excluded him from all the benefits of religion and authorised any one to kill him. Finally, on the 19th June, the new king was completely defeated near Methven by the English Earl of Pembroke. Robert's horse was killed under him in the action and he was for a moment a prisoner. But he had fallen into the power of a Scottish knight, who though he served in the English army, *did not choose to be*[1] the instrument of putting Bruce into their hands, and *allowed him to escape*[2].

Bruce with a few brave adherents, among whom was the young Lord Douglas, who was afterwards called the Good Lord James, retired into the Highland mountains, where they were chased from one place of refuge to another, placed in great danger, and underwent many hardships. Bruce's wife, now Queen of Scotland, with several other ladies, accompanied her husband and his few followers during their wanderings. There was no other way of providing for them save by hunting and fishing. It was remarked, that Douglas was the most active and successful in procuring for the unfortunate ladies, such supplies as his dexterity in fishing, or in killing deer could furnish to them.

---

[31] These circumstances Bradford acknowledged = *Bradford acknowledged these circumstances.*

89. ROBERT BRUCE.

[1] did not choose to be, *ne voulut pas être.*
[2] allowed him to escape, *le laissa s'échapper.*

Driven from one place in the Highlands to another, Bruce *endeavoured to force his way*[3] into Lorn, but he found enemies everywhere. The M'Dougal, a powerful family, then called the Lords of Lorn, were friendly to the English, and putting their men *in arms*[4], attacked Bruce and his wandering companions, as soon as they attempted to enter their country. The chief of these M'Dougal, called John of Lorn, hated Bruce *on account of his having slain*[5] in the church at Dumfries the Red Comyn *to whom this M'Dougal was nearly related*[6]. Bruce was again defeated by this chief, through force of numbers at a place called Dalry, but he showed amidst his misfortunes the greatness of his strength and courage. He directed his men to retreat through a narrow pass, and placing himself last of the party *he fought with and slew such of the enemy*[7] as attempted to press hard on them. Three followers of M'Dougal, a father and two sons, called M'Androsser, all very strong men, when they saw Bruce thus protecting the retreat of his followers, made a vow, that they would either kill him or make him prisoner. The whole then rushed on the king at once. The king was on horseback, in the strait pass we have described, betwixt a steep hill and a deep lake. *He struck the first man*, who came up and seized his bridle, *such a blow with his sword as cut off his hand*[8] and freed his bridle. The man bled to death. The other brother had seized him in the mean time by the

---

[3] endeavoured to force his way, *s'éfforça de se frayer un chemin.*
[4] in arms, *sous les armes.*
[5] on account of his having slain = *because he had slain.*
[6] to whom this M'Dougal was nearly related, *qui était proche parent de ce M'Dougal.*
[7] he fought with and slew such of the enemy, see introduction. page XV § 25.
[8] He struck the first man who . . . . such a blow with his sword as cut off his hand, *il porta un tel coup d'épée, au premier qui . . . . qu'il lui coupa la main.*

leg, and was attempting *to throw him from horseback*[9].
The king, setting spurs to his horse, made the animal
suddenly spring forward, so that the Highlander fell
under the horse's feet, and as he was endeavouring to
rise again, the king cleft his head in two with his sword.
The father seeing his two sons thus slain, flew at Robert
Bruce, and grasped him by the mantle so close to his
body, that he could not have room to wield his long
sword; but with the heavy pommel, or as others say
with an iron hammer, which hung at his saddle bow,
the king struck this third assailant so dreadful a blow,
that he dashed out his brains. Still however, the Highlander kept his dying grasp on the king's mantle, so
that to be free of the dead body Bruce was obliged to
undo the brooch or clasp by which it was fastened, and
leave that and the mantle itself behind him. The brooch,
which fell thus into the possession of M'Dougal of Lorn,
is still preserved in that ancient family as a memorial,
that the celebrated Robert Bruce once narrowly escaped
falling into the hands of their ancestor. Robert greatly
resented this attack upon him; and when he was in
happier circumstances, did not fail to take his revenge
on M'Dougal, or as he is usually called, John of Lorn.

At last dangers increased so much around the brave
King Robert, that he was obliged to separate himself
from the ladies and his queen, for the winter was coming
on, and it would be impossible for the women to endure
this wandering sort of life[10], when the frost and the snow
should arrive. So he left his queen, with the countess
of Buchan and others, in the only castle which remained
to him, which was called Kildrummie, and is situated
near the head of the river Don in Aberdeenshire. The
king also left his youngest brother Nigel Bruce, to defend
the castle against the English; and he himself with his

---

[9] to throw him from horseback, *de le démonter*.
[10] this wandering sort of life, *ce genre de vie errante*.

second brother Edward, who was a very brave man, but
still more rash and passionate than Robert himself,
went over to an Island called Rachrin, on the coast of
Ireland, where Bruce and the few men that followed his
fortunes passed the winter of 1306. In the meantime
ill luck seemed to pursue all his friends in Scotland.
The castle of Kildrummie was taken by the English,
and Nigel Bruce, a beautiful and brave youth, was cruelly
put to death by the victors. The ladies who had attended
on Robert's queen, as well as the queen herself and the
countess of Buchan, were thrown into strict confinement,
and treated with the utmost severity. This news reached
Bruce while he was residing in a miserable dwelling at
Rachrin, and reduced him to the point of despair.

It was probably about this time that an incident
took place which although it rests only on tradition in
the family of the name of Bruce, is rendered probable by
the manners of the times. After receiving the last un-
pleasing intelligence from Scotland, Bruce was lying one
morning on his wretched bed and deliberating with himself,
whether he had not better[11] resign all thoughts of again
attempting *to make good his right*[12] to the Scottish crown,
and dismissing his followers, transport himself and his
brothers to the Holy Land and spend the rest of his
life in fighting against the Saracens; by which he thought,
perhaps he might deserve the forgiveness of Heaven
for the great sin of stabbing Comyn in the church at
Dumfries.

But then on the other hand, he thought it would
be both criminal and cowardly to give up his attempts
to restore freedom to Scotland, while there yet remained
the least chance of his being successful in an undertaking,
which rightly considered, was much more his duty, than
to drive the infidels out of Palestine, though the super-
stition of his age might think otherwise.

---

[11] whether he had not better, *s'il ne ferait pas mieux.*
[12] to make good his right, *de prouver son droit.*

While he was divided betwixt these reflections, and doubtful of what he should do, Bruce was looking upward to the roof of the cabin in which he lay, and his eye was attracted by a spider, which hanging at the end of a long thread *of its own spinning*[13] was endeavouring, as is the fashion of that creature, to swing himself from one beam in the roof to another; for the purpose of fixing the line on which he meant to stretch his web. The insect *made the attempt again and again*[14] without success, and at length Bruce counted that it had tried to carry its point six times, and been as often unable to do so. It came into his head, that *he had* himself *fought*[15] just six battles against the English and their allies, and that the poor persevering spider was exactly in the same situation *with himself*[16], having made as many trials, and been as often disappointed in what it aimed at. "Now", thought Bruce, "as I have no means of knowing what is best to be done, I will be guided by the luck that shall attend this spider. If the insect shall make another attempt to fix its thread, *and shall be successful*[17], I will venture a seventh time to try my fortune in Scotland; but if the spider shall fail, I will go to the wars in Palestine and never return to my native country again".

While Bruce was forming this resolution, the spider made another exertion with all the force it could muster, and fairly succeeded in fastening its thread on the beam which it had so often in vain attempted to reach. Bruce seeing the success of the spider, resolved to try his own fortune, and as he never before gained a victory, so he never afterwards sustained any considerable check or defeat. I have often met with people of the name of

---

13 of its own spinning, *qu'elle avait filé elle-même.*
14 made the attempt again and again, *essaya mille et mille fois.*
15 he had fought, *il avait livré.*
16 with himself, *que lui.*
17 and shall be successful, *et qu'il réussisse.*

Bruce, *so completely persuaded*[18] of the truth of this story, that they would not *on any account*[19] kill a spider, because it was such an insect which had shown the example of perseverance, and given a signal of good luck to their namesake.

90. MOUNT VESUVIUS.

Early in the spring[1] I was about to leave Naples, in order to go to Rome. I had just returned to the hotel where I lodged, about eleven o'clock at night, when the people in the house came into my room to inform me, that Vesuvius was beginning to throw up volumes of smoke, and the flames which proceeded from it announced an approaching eruption. The air was hot as in the month of July and as calm as on a fine summer day.

I immediately went out on a terrace before the house. The air was filled with a shower of ashes. *You*[2] might feel them falling but *you*[2] could not see them. They descended gently and imperceptibly, and gradually covered the surface of the ground. They silenced the noise of the carriages and covered the whole country around with a dark tint, as if it had been attired in mourning. The darkness was from time to time illumined by the flames, which darted in long flashes from the crater. Suddenly a luminous point appeared on the side of the mountain, *about*[3] two hundred yards from the summit. It was a new crater, through which the red hot lava *had just forced its way*[4]. At the same time a general exclamation

---

[18] so completely persuaded, *tellement persuadés.*
[19] on any account, *pour rien au monde.*

90. MOUNT VESUVIUS.

[1] Early in the spring, *au commencement du printemps.*
[2] you, *on.*
[3] about = *at about.*
[4] had just forced its way, *venait de se frayer un chemin.*

burst from thousands of people: "There is the lava! There is the new crater! It has opened on this side! We are all lost!"

I went into the city to mingle with the crowd and share in their alarm and their curiosity. The spectacle was extremely grand, I looked upon it with a mixture of awe and astonishment. Anxiety was depicted in every countenance, and all eyes were turned towards the luminous point which was visibly enlarging every instant.

The showers of ashes ceased towards daybreak, and the first rays of the morning sun destroyed the brilliancy of the flames which had appeared so vivid during the night. The return of daylight lessened the fears of the people, they retired to their own homes, forgetting that the same grand scene would be renewed the succeeding evening.

I also retired to rest; for it is only in darkness, that the full magnificence of a volcano is displayed, and I was desirous of taking a nearer view of it the following night.

I set out towards Vesuvius about seven o'clock in the evening, in company with my young friend Louis. As the day *declined*[5], the flames of the volcano resumed their splendour; and, on reaching Portici, we were able to judge of the progress the lava had made during the day. It was no longer a bright luminous point, as on the preceding evening, but a broad stream, flowing slowly along like a very slow river.

We took guides at Portici, where we left our carriage or cabriolet, and mounted mules. We were provided with torches, *but we stood in little need of them*[6], for the sky was sufficiently illuminated by the flames. We ascended ;through vineyards to the hermitage of San Salvador, a long and rugged path bestrewn with stones

---

[5] declined, *baissait.*

[6] but we stood in little need of them, *mais nous n'en avions pas grand besoin.*

and cinders; but our mules *being used to it*[7], pursued their way without difficulty, and left us at liberty to enjoy the grand and majestic scene around us.

The little hermitage stood in a cleft; it consisted of two chapels, (one of which was hewn out of the lava, from a former eruption) also a little refectory, a kitchen and a chamber; the furniture was as simple as the habitation; in the latter was a straw bed, two chairs and a table, with a crucifix on it. The hermit placed before us dates and oranges, brought from the valleys below. Here we sent back our mules to Portici, *for they could no longer be of any use to us*[8]. Two of the guides alone remained, to direct us to the part of the mountain, where the lava *had taken its course*[9]. *Before we set off*[10], we remained for some time on a sort of terrace before the hermitage, contemplating the fiery clouds, which the volcano was spreading around it. At length we continued our way towards the torrent of lava which threatened the unfortunate town of Torre del Greco.

The fire made rapid progress, and we proceeded, through cinders and scoria, along obstructed paths; they at first led us across a wide valley, which separates the hermitage from the upper part of Vesuvius. This valley, *where neither grass, tree, nor shrub was to be seen*[11], extended along the side of the mountain, opposite the eruption. It was dark and still, except that a lucid light was reflected upon it from the clouds. It was the vale of death and eternal silence; but on this night its tranquility was broken by the numerous parties whom curiosity had brought thither, and who were going and coming from the little hermitage to the crater.

---

[7] being used to it, *y étant habituées.*

[8] for they could no longer be of any use to us, *car elles en pouvaient plus nous être d'aucune utilité.*

[9] had taken its course, *s'était dirigée.*

[10] Before we set off, *avant de partir.*

[11] where neither grass, tree, nor shrub was to be seen, *où on ne voyait ni herbe, ni arbres, ni arbustes.*

After marching an hour, we began to climb with difficulty over heaps of scoria. We were obliged to grope our way through passages unknown to the guides, for at each eruption the lava alters its course. We soon found ourselves in a region where every thing bore the marks of fire. The air began to be scorching: the very stones were warm; and we beheld fiery clouds rolling over our heads, and leaving a track of awful red in the sky. We were within half a mile of the end of our journey, when, to our astonishment, we met with a lady, attended by two guides, who had been left behind on the mountain by her party. She was sitting on a rock, wrapped in a shawl, and was talking with great earnestness to her guides. By her accent I was convinced that she was an English woman, I went up to her, to offer her my assistance, and to ask her the cause of her agitation. She replied in French with an eloquence, inspired by the darkness and solemnity of the surrounding scene. She informed me that her husband and a party of friends had accompanied her as far as this place, but that the guides *had persuaded him tha: it would be dangerous for her to proceed any farther*[12]. She had made many entreaties to be allowed to go on, but ineffectually; *and had since used her best endeavours to prevail on her guides to take her forward*[13], but without success. She was mortified, she said, *to the last degree*[14], at being thus prevented from witnessing a scene to which she had looked forward with so much earnestness.

I ventured to offer her the assistance of my arm for the short distance which remained. She accepted it with

---

[12] had persuaded him that it would be dangerous for her to proceed any farther, *l'avait convaincu qu'il serait dangereux pour elle d'aller plus loin.*

[13] and had since used her best endeavours to prevail on her guides to take her forward, *et depuis avait fait tous ses efforts pour engager ses guides à la conduire plus avant.*

[14] to the last degree, *au suprême degré.*

a readiness, arising merely from her anxious desire of being present, at the magnificient spectacle displayed by Vesuvius, and we set off, notwithstanding the remonstrances of her guides.

She leaned on my arm and we proceeded slowly, because we sunk into the ashes, and the scoria wounded her tender feet. Nevertheless, we were drawing nearer the torrent of lava and the glare which it produced gave me an opportunity of observing my courageous companion. She was young and beautiful, but pale with emotion, and seemed to share in the agitation and disorder of the scene. The ground and the air became hot as we drew nearer the mouth of the volcano, and gusts of smoke came rolling towards us. We endeavoured to avoid them by getting out of the current of the wind; but here the blast was so violent, that we were twice enveloped in these fiery clouds and were near being suffocated. The soil gave way under our feet, and the fire appeared beneath the scoria, as it rolled down the precipices.

At length, with some difficulty, we reached *the end*[15] of our journey. The friends of my young *female companion*[16] had already arrived, but their attention was so fully engaged by the sublimity of the objects around them, *that they had not perceived our approach*[17]. We were therefore obliged to introduce ourselves to them, and I was not without some uneasiness as to the reception we might meet with, but success ensured our welcome. We had proceeded safely thither; our imprudence was forgiven; *we had only to enjoy in silence the grand scene before us*[18].

---

[15] the end, *le terme.*

[16] female companion, *compagne.*

[17] that they had not perceived our approach, *qu'ils ne s'étaient pas aperçus de notre approche.*

[18] we had only to enjoy in silence the grand scene before us, *nous n'eûmes qu'à jouir en silence du grand spectacle qui était devant nos yeux.*

The lady's husband called her Florinda, the only name by which I have ever known her; *should she ever read these letters*[19], she will recollect this nocturnal scene upon the mountain, and know *who the stranger was*[20] that conducted her to that ocean of fire.

We gazed in silence upon the burning torrent, as it rolled its waves before us. The red hot liquid lava flowed over a high rock into a valley, and continued to flow increasing in breadth, because as it went on, it rekindled the old scoria, so that the whole mountain *seemed on fire*[21].

The stream of lava, which was now some hundred feet broad, was gradually approaching the brink of another precipice, down which it threatened to fall before morning and we determined to await the event. *It kept slowly but continually drawing nearer*[22]; the scoria taking fire before it, and preparing its way. At length the ignited torrent reached the edge of the rocks, and precipitated itself down them, with a dreadful and tremendous noise; clouds of smoke arose from the abyss, and *were driven*[23] by the wind in all directions, while the lava continued to fall into the *gulf*[24].

The dawn now appeared on the horizon; the sun darted his morning beams: and the splendour of the night faded and disappeared before the radiance of day. The fire grew pale; the vapours became white; and there remained nothing but the singular appearance of a mountain, moving by its own efforts. It was time to retire, for the presence of the ignited matter when veiled by the

---

[19] should she ever read these letters, *si elle lit jamais ces lettres.*

[20] who the stranger was = *who was the stranger.*

[21] seemed on fire, *paraissait être en feu.*

[22] It kept slowly but continually drawing nearer, *il s'en approchait doucement mais continuellement.*

[23] were driven, *furent emportés.*

[24] gulf, *abîme.*

sun, is highly dangerous. The spectator may be consumed before he is aware of its approach.

We therefore returned by the same course to the little hermitage of San Salvadore, where the venerable father again regaled us with pomegranates, grapes and oranges. Thence we proceeded to the town of Portici, where our cabriolets were waiting for us. *Here*[2 5] I bade adieu to the young and lovely Florinda whom I have never since seen.

91. AN AERIAL VOYAGE.

Seventy-two years ago, Montgolfier, a paper maker of Paris, was ascending one of the hills in the neighbourhood of that City, when, looking at the large clouds sailing majestically above his head, *the thought occurred to him*[1],—"What if I could harness one of these clouds to a car, or clothe it with a garment, *and make it lift me with it*[2] into that blue ocean?" Thinking erroneously, but naturally enough, that the cloud was but condensed smoke, he and his brother set about accomplishing the feat; and with the hot gases *given off*[3] from burnt straw, filled a huge paper bag, and there arose through the unresisting air the first fire-balloon.

The idea of the brothers Montgolfier was soon extended and improved upon. Animals were first sent up, and then adventurous mortals *suffered themselves to be lifted into the air*[4] by the imprisoned cloud. Even in the same year hydrogen, the lightest of all gases, was *substituted for*[5] the hot smoke. Presently the French took up

---

[2 5] here, *là*.

91. AN AERIAL VOYAGE.

[1] the thought occurred to him, *la pensée lui vint.*
[2] and make it lift me with it, *et faire qu'il m'enlève.*
[3] given off, *dégagés.*
[4] suffered themselves to be lifted into the air, *se laissèrent enlever dans les airs.*
[5] substituted for, *substitué à.*

ballooning with great zeal, and introduced it into their military tactics, and the battle of Theurus was gained by means of observations taken from a balloon.

Let us, in imagination, ascend, not emulating the birds on their air-cleaving pinions, but in the only way available to us wingless and heavy-boned bipeds, dragged up by the imprisoned gas. Let us ascend, not for our amusement only, but to observe *more closely*[6] the phenomena of the air and sky. Just so Gay-Lussac and Biot ascended in 1804; and Welsh four different times in 1852, guided by the veteran Green, who first made use of the *coal gas*[6] with which our streets are lighted to inflate his gigantic air-ships. In one of these ascents Welsh attained the height of 22 930 feet, more than four miles, and nearly as high as the summit of the loftiest mountain on our globe.

As it is on a scientific expedition that we are going, we must take with us all requisite instruments, a barometer, thermometer, hygrometer, electrometer, *and any thing else we may suppose of service*[8]. We must first see that we rightly understand all our instruments.

There is the barometer; it is intended to measure the weight of the air. "What! *has the air any weight*[9]," cries one of my readers, and is astonished when gravely assured *that it is pressing with a weight of*[10] 15 pounds on every square inch of his body. A fish would find it difficult to believe that the element through which he is gliding has any weight. The diver too, when reminded of the pressure of water, would answer, that so far from feeling heavy upon him, it actually buoys him up; and yet we all know for a certainty that water has weight

---

[6] more closely, *de plus près.*

[7] coal gas, *gaz d'éclairage.*

[8] and any thing else we may suppose of service, *et tout autre chose qu'on peut croire utile.*

[9] has the air any weight, *l'air est-il donc pesant.*

[10] that it is pressing with a weight of, *qu'il exerce une pression de.*

and exerts no small pressure on any vessel containing
it. Thus it is with the atmospheric ocean. In both
cases, the reason why a body immersed does not experience this pressure, is, that the fluid presses equally
on all sides. That air has weight may be easily proved
by exhausting a vessel by an air-pump[11], *when it will
weigh less than it did when full of air*[12]. Many proofs
will the air-pump give of the prodigious force of the
atmosphere when not counterbalanced by air at a similar
tension; bladders or glass vessels being broken to pieces
by it, and *the exhausted receiver*[13] fixed so *that no
man could lift it*[14]. If we immerse the open end of a
tube, perfectly empty of air, in any liquid, this liquid
will be forced up the tube by the external pressure of
the atmosphere. Water will thus be raised even till it
form a column of thirty three feet in height, before its
weight counterbalances the pressure from below. Mercury,
or as it is frequently called quicksilver, will, on account
of its greater weight, rise in such a tube only to the
height of about thirty inches; and were we to weigh
an inch column of water of thirty inches[15], we should
find both alike to be fifteen pounds. This, then, is the
measure of the atmospheric pressure exerted upon *a
superficial inch*[16]. Our barometer is essentially the instrument just described—an exhausted glass tube closed
at the upper end dipping into mercury, the height to
which the liquid metal rises, indicating the actual pressure
of the atmosphere. The thermometer, as every one knows

---

[11] by exhausting a vessel by an air-pump, *en faissant le vide
dans un vase au moyen de la machine pneumatique.*
[12] when it will weigh less than it did when full of air, *ce vase
pesera moins que quand il était plein d'air.*
[13] the exhausted receiver, *le récipient où l'on a fait le vide.*
[14] that no one man could lift it, *qu'aucun homme ne saurait le
soulever.*
[15] an inch column of water of thirty inches, *une colonne d'eau
d'un pouce de diamètre et de 30 pouces de hauteur.*
[16] a superficial inch, *un pouce de superficie.*

is intended to measure heat and cold. *Advantage is taken of the fact*[17], that bodies, especially metals, expand when heated, and so by placing liquid quicksilver in a glass bulb, and making it as it expands ascend a thin tube of the same material properly graduated, the degree of temperature is easily read off.

We take the hygrometer with us for the purpose of measuring the amount of moisture in the air. This instrument is of very various construction, but it generally depends on determining the dew point, as it is termed, that is to say, the degree of cold which is necessary *to cause moisture in the air to be deposited in dew*[18]. The amount of vapour of water which the air is capable of holding uncondensed increases in a certain proportion as the temperature rises, and this affords the data for the calculation.

Now the cords which fix us to the earth are cut asunder, and we rise majestically. It is the weight and pressure of the atmosphere, of which we were just speaking, that are forcing us up; our imprisoned gas is lighter than *the air around*[19], and thus we rise, even as a cork would rise through the watery ocean. But our barometer is telling us that this pressure is diminishing; the air is becoming thinner or rarer. We too learn the same, from the difficulty of breathing we are beginning to experience, and from the expansion of gas in the balloon *which necessitates our opening the valve for the escape of some of it*[20], lest the silken envelope should be rent. In about 11,000 feet of perpendicular ascent the mercury has sunk to only half its previous height. We must not howewer, rashly conclude that at double that

---

[17] advantage is taken of the fact, *on profite de ce que.*

[18] to cause moisture in the air to be deposited in dew, *pour que l'humidité de l'air se dépose en rosée.*

[19] the air around, *l'air ambiant.*

[20] which necessitates our opening the valve for the escape of some of it, *qui nous force à ouvrir la soupape pour en laisser échapper.*

altitude the air would be so thin as to exert no pressure;
we are sure that there is a limit to the atmosphere, but
the rarefaction of it proceeds at a decreasing ratio as
we ascend, and there are reasons for believing that it
extends to somewhere about forty-five miles from the
earth's surface.

The thermometer too, is indicating a diminution of
the temperature as we rise; *so, indeed, are our feelings,
making us wrap ourselves up*[21] in our great coats. Rising
above the region of clouds we get into a space where
the temperature is *below the freezing point*[22] ; and this
explains to us why, even *in the height of summer*[23], lofty
mountains are always covered with snow. Floating
majestically through the cold, clear air of these upper
regions, with the sun shining in unbroken splendour
across the deep blue heavens which have never known a
cloud, we descend not to terra firma till prudence renders
it necessary.

92. CONSCIENCE.

A stranger came recommended to a merchants' house
at Lubeck. He was hospitably received; but, the house
being full, he was lodged at night in an apartment
handsomely furnished, *but not often used*[1]. There was
nothing that struck him particularly in the room, when
left alone, till he happened to cast his eyes on a picture,
which immediately arrested his attention. It was a single
head; but there was something so uncommon, so frightful
and unearthly, in its expression, though by no means
ugly, that he found himself irresistibly attracted to look
at it. In fact, he could not tear himself from the

---

[21] so, indeed, are our feelings, making us wrap ourselves up,
de même que nos sensations qui nous font nous envelopper.
[22] below the freezing point, *au dessous de zéro.*
[23] in the height of summer, *au fort de l'été.*

92. CONSCIENCE.
[1] but not often used, *mais qni ne servait pas souvent.*

fascination of this portrait, till his imagination was filled by it, and his rest broken. He retired to bed, dreamed and awoke from time to time, with the head glaring on him. In the morning, his host saw by his looks that he had slept ill, and inquired the cause, which was told. The master of the house was much vexed, and said *that the picture ought to have been removed*[2], that it was an oversight, and that it always was removed when the chamber was used. The picture he said, was, indeed terrible to every one; but it was so fine, and had come into the family in so curious a way, that he could not make up his mind to part with it, or to destroy it. The story of it was this: "My Father," said he, "was at Hamburgh on business, and, whilst dining at a Coffee-house, he observed a young man of a remarkable appearance enter, seat himself alone in a corner, and commence a solitary meal. His countenance bespoke the extreme of mental distress, and every now and then, he turned his head quickly round as if he heard something, then shudder, grow pale, and go on with his meal after an effort as before. My father saw this same man at the same place for two or three successive days, and at length became so much interested about him, that he spoke to him. The address was not repulsed, and the stranger seemed to find some comfort from the tone of sympathy and kindness, which my father used. He was an Italian, well informed, poor but not destitute, and living economically upon the profits of his art as a painter. Their intimacy increased; and at length the Italian, seeing my father's involuntary emotion at his convulsive turnings and shudderings, which continued as formerly, interrupting their conversation from time to time, told him his story. He was a native of Rome, and had lived in some familiarity with, and been much patronized by a young nobleman; but upon some slight

---

[2] that the picture ought to have been removed, *qu'on aurait dû enlever le tableau.*

occasion, they had fallen out, and his patron, besides
using many reproachful expressions, had struck him.
The painter brooded over the disgrace of the blow. He
could not challenge the nobleman on account of his rank;
he therefore watched for an opportunity, and assassinated
him. Of course he fled from his country, and finally
had reached Hamburgh. He had not, however passed
many weeks from the night of the murder, before, one
day, in the crowded street, *he heard his name called
by a voice familiar to him*[3]; he turned short round, and
saw the face of his victim looking at him with a fixed
eye. From that moment he had no peace; at all hours
and in all places[4], and amidst all companies, however
engaged he might be, he heard the voice, and could
never help looking round; and, whenever he so looked
round, he always encountered the same face staring close
upon him. At last, in a mood of desperation, he had fixed
himself face to face, and eye to eye, and deliberately drawn
the phantom visage as it glared upon him; and this was
the picture so drawn. The Italian said, he had struggled
long, but life was a burden which he could no longer
bear; and he was resolved when he had made money
to return to Rome, *to surrender himself to justice*[5], and
expiate his crime on the scaffold. He gave the finished
picture to my father, in return for the kindness he had
shown him."

93. THE FISHERMAN OF THE DOURO.

The name of our hero was Antonio[1]: *he went by no
other*[2], but by that he was known on the banks of the

---

[3] he heard his name called by a voice familiar to him, *il entendit prononcer son nom par une voix qui lui était familière.*
[4] and in all places, *et en tous lieux.*
[5] to surrender himself to justice, *de se livrer à la justice.*

93. THE FISHERMAN OF THE DOURO.

[1] The name of our hero was Antonio = *Antonio was the name.*
[2] he went by no other, *on ne lui en connaissait pas d'autre.*

Douro; there were many Antonios, but he was the Antonio. He was somewhat better and more compactly put together, if we may use the expression, than the generality of the Portuguese; and although he could not boast a much fairer complexion than usually falls to the lot of his countrymen, it was somewhat relieved by the dark hair, which curled in profusion about his swarthy brows. He had an eye black as jet, but it was large and full, and combined with a high and broad forehead, gave an expression of openness and honesty which at once created confidence.

Regarded professionally[3] he had a quick eye, a ready hand and a stout heart, and was celebrated for the skill and dexterity with which he managed his little craft; insomuch that even in the fastidious judgment of the English sailors who frequented the port, he was rated a smart fellow; and was looked upon with a covetous eye, by many a lieutenant of his Britannic Majesty's navy, who thought it a thousand pities, that the energies of so fine a fellow were not displayed on the deck of a man of war, instead of in a washing tub of a fishing boat.

That man is born to die, is a truth which none can gainsay, and that he is also born to fall in love, is a maxim next in infallibility; thus Antonio fullfilled his destiny and was married. If ever man had excuse for so rash a step, it was to be found in the mild eyes and sweet smile of Teresa. Antonio was a man without guile; he had no craft but that by which he gained his living, to wit his fishing boat: he preferred his suit to the damsel and was made happy.

Matrimony is, after all, the grand test of character; a man may gloss over his infirmities, or to speak in plain terms his sins to the world; but he cannot hide them long from his wife; and she will be very happy or (*whatever face her good sense may induce her to put*

---

[3] Regarded professionally, *au point de vue du métier.*

upon the matter)[4] very miserable, according as she draws a prize or a blank in the great lottery. *Teresa's ticket came up a prize*[5]. *Neither is there anything like matrimony*[6] for bringing out a man's energies, be they those of the mind or of the hand; the feeling that the support and the happiness, as far as that may be within human control, of another are committed to his charge, will rouse into action powers which have hitherto been dormant, *and of which it may be he was unconscious*[7] ; and as he will become a more useful, so will he be, if his mind be rightly constituted, a better man for the exertion of them. *Thus was it with Antonio*[8], and on occasions where before he incurred the responsibilities of a husband, his little bark would have been *"high and dry"*[9] upon the beach, it was breasting the billow at the mouth of the Douro.

Weeks, months, a year passed away and Antonio, if he did not increase in riches, acquired an additional title, that of parent, and he was the happiest fisherman in the universe. It was about a month after this acquisition, *that on a remarkably unpromising day*[10], Antonio with six adventurous comrades, put their little barks to sea, *in a state of weather*[11] which the majority of the fishermen of the Douro prudently perhaps, *declined to face*[12]. Teresa, anxious throughout the day, the most wearisome she had

---

[4] whatever face her good sense may induce her to put upon the matter, *de quelque manière que son bon sens puisse la porter à considérer la chose.*

[5] Teresa's ticket came up a prize, *le billet de Téresa fut un numéro gagnant.*

[6] Neither is there anything like matrimony, *il faut dire aussi qu'il n'y a rien de tel que le mariage.*

[7] and of which it may be he was unconscious, *et dont il peut se faire qu'il n'ait pas eu conscience.*

[8] Thus was it with Antonio, *il en fut ainsi d'Antonio.*

[9] high and dry, *à sec.*

[10] that on a remarkably unpromising day, *qu'un jour qui s'annonçait mal.*

[11] in a state of weather, *par un temps.*

[12] declined to face, *ne voulurent pas affronter.*

ever spent, repaired at evening to the lookout on the Freixo, an hour before the return of the little fleet could be reckoned upon. That hour wore heavily away, and then another; at last a sail hove in sight—it was not Antonio's; a second, a third and so on, until she had counted six, but her husband's was not of the number. She continued to watch with an anxiety which every moment increased, until at length, unable longer to contain herself, she rushed down to the bank of the river to inquire if any of *the returned fishermen*[13] had tidings of her husband. She approached one and then another, but they all avoided her; *they who would under other circumstances, have gone some furlongs out of their way*[14] for a smile from the pretty Teresa.

Then her heart sank within her, and as the Scripture saith, which hath a phrase and, blessed be God! a balm for every human suffering, "a horrible dread overwhelmed her." At last came the fatal truth, and when it came, the shriek of agony and the fixed look of despair and that utter prostration of the spirit, *which none can conceive but they who have seen*[15] the gulph of the grave suddenly open between them and those they most loved on earth. Oh! if there be a picture of desolation on which we gaze with more anguish *than another*[16], it is the widow! Man, whatever may be the intensity of his grief, is in most instances, prevented from brooding over it by the bustle of the world into which he is of necessity flung; and though "honour's voice" cannot "provoke the silent dust" it is still music to the ears of living clay, and the "noble infirmity of ambition may beguile the softest heart of its sorrows. But to the majority of

---

[13] the returned fishermen, *des pêcheurs qui étaient rentrés.*

[14] they who would under other circumstances, have gone some furlongs out of their way, *dans d'autres circonstances ils se seraient écartés d'un quart de lieue de leur route.*

[15] which none can conceive but they who have seen, *que, seuls peuvent concevoir ceux qui ont vu.*

[16] than another, *que sur une autre.*

women the path of ambition is closed; *and it is well that it is so*[17], since few of them tread in its briary paths without losing much of the bloom which constitutes the chief charm of the feminine character.

The account brought by the fisherman who had accompanied Antonio was, that he had ventured further to sea than the rest; that a violent squall had come on, and that his little bark had been capsized in sight of them all; that from the fury of the tempest, they had been unable to render him any succour, but that when its rage had somewhat abated one of the boldest ventured to the spot, and found the boat keel uppermost on the wide ocean.

Teresa however, was not quite alone; there was yet left to her a child, and while she had something to love, the world was not a blank to her. *True it was*[18], that she had to work for the subsistence of herself and her orphan babe, and the harvest of her labour was scant; but the deficiency was made up by the kindness of those neighbours who regulated their alms by the pious maxim, that he who giveth to the poor, lendeth to the Lord. Thus it was, that notwithstanding her adverse circumstances, she was still enabled to keep, not only the house over her head, but the gaunt wolf from the door.

It was at the close of one of those lovely days with which Portugal is so abundantly blessed, that Teresa, the labour of the day being over, was sitting in her cottage, with no other companionship than that of her sleeping babe and her own melancholy thoughts. Her dwelling was at some distance from the village and removed a few paces from the common path; so that she was startled by the approach of footsteps at that hour of the evening, for it was growing dusk. She looked from the window, and by the imperfect light,

---

[17] and it is well that it is so, *et il est bien qu'il en soit ainsi.*
[18] True it was, *il est vrai.*

perceived a person in the trim dress of an English sailor approaching the door, which she instinctively as it were, immediately fastened; *and had scarcely done so, before an attempt was made on the outside, to open it*[19]. Aware that the door was incapable of resisting much violence, and feeling the utter helplessness of her situation, she sunk into a chair almost paralysed by fear.

"Teresa!" exclaimed a voice. Was that voice from the grave?—First came a superstitious, fear over her spirit, then passed over it a gleam of reviving hope, and then the cold damp of doubt, till her name was again uttered by the same voice: The door suddenly flew open and Antonio stood before her!

The reader will imagine the rest of the scene, but may desire to know *the manner of the poor fisherman's deliverance*[20]. It was true that his little craft had been capsized in the storm, and that so suddenly, that he was scarcely aware of the fact until he found himself struggling among the waves. By dint of great exertion he contrived to regain his boat, but was unable *to right her*[21]. After some difficulty he managed, as his only chance of immediate safety, to mount upon her keel, where he remained for a considerable time, making signals to his comrades, *whose attention however, he could not succeed in attracting*[22].

At length an English brig descried him and, at considerable hazard, bore down to his relief. *To lower a boat*[23] in such a sea would have been but a wanton

---

[19] and had scarcely done so, before an attempt was made on the outside, to open it, *et elle venait à peine d'en agir ainsi qu'on essaya de l'ouvrir du dehors.*

[20] the manner of the poor fisherman's deliverance, *de quelle manière le pauvre pêcheur fût sauvé.*

[21] to right her, *de le redresser.*

[22] whose attention however, he could not succeed in attracting, *dont il ne put cependant, réussir à attirer l'attention.*

[23] To lower a boat, *mettre une embarcation à la mer.*

sacrifice of life; and thus all they could do was to fling
him a rope, of which he made *such good use*[24], that he
was speedily upon the deck of the brig.

No sooner was he safe from the peril of drowning,
than his thoughts reverted to Teresa and to the agony
which his absence would occasion to her. The captain
of the brig however, in reply to his frantic supplications
to be set on shore[25], represented to him the impossibility
of compliance, and there was nothing left for him, but
to make the voyage *to*[27] England and get back to Portugal *as best as he could*[26].

It happened that the passage was a remarkably rough
one, and the vessel, as is too frequently the case, *being
but shortly manned*[28], the activity of Antonio was often
called into requisition and was duly appreciated, not only
by the captain, but by the only passenger, a merchant
of London, who had *chartered*[29] the ship, and having been
to Oporto on a visit of business, took that opportunity
of returning to England.

The vessel arrived at Gravesend, where the merchant
had Antonio called aft, and told him that he had heard
his story, *by which he had been greatly interested*[30],
and moreover felt personally indebted to him for his
exertions, to which he in some degree attributed, the
safety of the ship, that he would take upon himself
to procure him a free passage back to Oporto; but as
several days might possibly elapse before he could
accomplish this, and as Antonio's scanty knowledge of
the language and entire ignorance of the country might
expose him to inconvenience if left alone in the metro-

---

[24] such good use, *si bon usage.*
[25] to be set on shore, *d'être mis à terre.*
[26] to == *of.*
[27] as best as he could, *du mieux qu'il pourrait.*
[28] being but shortly manned, *n'étant pas bien garni de monde.*
[29] chartered, *affrété.*
[30] by which he had been greatly interested, *qui l'avait grande-
ment intéressé.*

polis, he offered him, what he called *the "run of his house"*[81] until he could find him a ship.

Antonio was sufficiently alive to the advantages of such an offer to embrace it immediately, which he did with expressions of the sincerest gratitude; and in the course of the next six hours found himself installed in *the servants' hall*[32] of one of the most opulent merchants in the city.

The worthy merchant's kindness did not stop *here*[33]: for willing that his humble guest should see as many of the lions in the metropolis as possible during his short stay, he committed him to the ciceroneship of his butler, whom he also commissioned to make such a metamorphosis *in Antonio's outward man*[34], as would render him a less conspicuous object "to fix the gaze of idiot wonder," than he would have been in the garb of a Portuguese fisherman. The said butler had a kind heart, but withal *an eye to his own dignity*[35], and accordingly, when he took him to the shop *of an outfitter, so called, because they are usually out in their fitting*[36], he took especial care to rig him in jacket and trowsers of super-fine blue cloth, *of a fancy cut*[37], such as were worn by old Incledon, when he sang "the Storm" *on the boards*[38] of Drury Lane.

Nor were the cares of the butler thrown away upon Antonio, who independently of his handsome face and fine figure was, unlike his countrymen, naturally of tidy

---

[31] the run of his house, *l'entrée de sa maison.*
[32] the servants' hall, *l'office.*
[33] here = *there.*
[34] in Antonio's outward man, *dans l'extérieur d'Antonio.*
[35] an eye to his own dignity, *soucieux de sa dignité personnelle.*
[36] of an outfitter, so called, because they are usually out in their fitting, *d'un confectionneur, ainsi nommé parce qu'en général il ne confectionne rien de bien.* NB. It is impossible to render the English into a perfectly equivalent French expression.
[37] of a fancy cut, *d'une coupe de fantaisie.*
[38] on the boards, *sur la scène.*

habits and looked the beau ideal of a sailor. Indeed it
is perhaps well, that his sojurn in the merchant's family
was not prolonged, for he became such a huge favorite
among the females of the establishment, that had he
not left a wife in Portugal, he might have suited himself
to his heart's content in England: but alas! the recollection of poor Teresa, whom he justly pictured in
despair for his loss, was a sad drawback upon the pleasure
he derived from the novelties which London presents to
the eye of a foreigner.

He saw the Bank and the Royal Exchange, and the
Monument, St. Paul's, and, sight of sights! the Lord Mayor's
coach, and the Tower and Westminster Abbey, and in fact
every accessible lion in London. Among other gratifica-
tions and not the least of them, was a visit to the
merchant's country house, where he had an opportunity
of witnessing rural life in England, which however it
may be the fashion to decry in these days of emigration,
must to the eye of a foreigner of whatever condition,
present a striking contrast, to the filth and wretchedness
one sees abroad.

A gentleman not less distinguished by his genius,
than his rank in society, once mentioned to the writer,
that while travelling on the continent some years since,
he heard most appalling accounts of the English peasantry,
who were represented to him *as ripe for rebellion*[39]. "But,"
said he, "when I crossed the Channel and saw the
cottager's windows glazed I knew it was all right. These
fellows thought I, will not throw stones, lest their own
windows should suffer in the mêlée.—The merchant *was
as good as his word in every particular*[40] and Antonio
had not been in England a fortnight, *before a*[41] passage
for Oporto was secured for him and he departed for his

---

[39] as ripe for rebellion, *comme prêts à se révolter.*

[40] was as good as his word in every particular, *tint parole
en tout.*

[41] before a, *avant qu'un.*

native land laden with favours and particularly with presents for Teresa and his little girl from the lovely daughters of his generous host.

How true it is, that when relieved from greater evils the mind dwells upon minor ones; thus it was that Teresa, now that her husband was restored to her, and that as it were from the grave, began to bewail the loss of the gallant craft and to express her apprehensions as to their future subsistence.

Antonio with a smile at her fears drew from his pocket a paper saying; "the kind Englishman has provided against that; see, here is that which will build me the finest boat on the Douro."

When our friend had finished his story, we accompanied him to the dwelling of the hero of it, and our national predilections were highly gratified by observing in the neatness and order which pervaded it, that Antonio had profited by his visit to the villages of England. Indeed so far had his prejudices been overcome by his reception in the land of strangers, that we are informed, he has had something like a quarrel with his priest, for presuming to doubt that all heretics must infallibly go to the place, not to be mentioned to ears polite.

94. BRUTUS ON THE DEATH OF CÆSAR.

Romans, Countrymen, and Lovers! *hear me for my cause*[1] : and be silent, that you may hear: believe me for mine honour: and have respect to mine honour, that you may believe: censure me in your wisdom: and awake your senses, that you may the better judge. If there be any in this assembly, any dear friend of Cæsar's, to him I say, that Brutus' love to Cæsar was no less than his. If then that friend demand why Brutus rose

---

94. BRUTUS ON THE DEATH OF CÆSAR.
[1] hear me for my cause, *écoutez-moi, pour l'amour de ma cause.*

against Cæsar, this is my answer,—Not that I loved
Cæsar less, but that I loved Rome more. Had you
rather Cæsar were living, and die all slaves; than that
Cæsar were dead, to live all freemen? As Cæsar loved
me, *I weep for him*[2]; as he was fortunate, I rejoice at
it; as he was valiant, I honour him: but, as he was
ambitious, I slew him: There are tears for his love;
joy for his fortune; honour for his valour; and death for
his ambition. Who is here so base, that would be a
bondman? *If any*[3], speak; *for him have I offended*[4].
Who is here so rude, that would not be a Roman? If
any, speak; for him have I offended. Who is here so
vile, that will not love his country? If any, speak; for
him have I offended. I pause for a reply.—None—Then
none have I offended. I have done no more to Cæsar,
than you should do to Brutus. The question of his
death is enrolled in the Capitol: his glory not extenuated,
wherein he was worthy; nor his offences enforced, for
which he suffered death.

Here comes his body, mourned by Mark Antony:
who, though *he had no hand in his death*[5], shall receive
the benefit of his dying, a place in the Commonwealth;
as which of you shall not?[6]

With this I depart,—that, as I slew my best lover
for the good of Rome, I have the same dagger for
myself, when it shall please my country to need my
death.—*Shakspeare.*

95. DEBATE OF FOX AND BURKE

*on the subject of the French revolution, in the memorable discussion,
which in 1796 broke up the friendship of the two leaders of the*

---

[2] I weep for him, *je le pleure.*

[3] If any, *s'il y en a.*

[4] for him have I offended, *car celui-là je l'ai offensé.*

[5] he had no hand in his death, *quoiqu'il n'ait pas eu part à
sa mort.*

[6] as which of you shall not, *et quel est celui d'entre vous qui
n'en aura pas?*

opposition, while discussing a bill proposed by Pitt for the organi-
sation of Canada. Burke brands the French Revolution with infamy;
Fox speaks in its defence.

...... On the French Revolution I did indeed differ
from *my right honourable*[1] friend; our opinions, I have
no scruple to say, *are as wide as the poles asunder*[2] ;
but what has a difference of opinion on that, which to
the House is only matter of theoretical contemplation,
to do with the discussion of a practical point, on which
no such difference exists? On that revolution I adhere
to my opinion, and never will retract one syllable of
what I have said. I repeat that I think it, on the
whole, one of the most glorious events in the history
of mankind. But when I on a former occasion mentioned
France, I mentioned the revolution only, and not the
constitution; the latter remains to be improved by
experience, and accommodated to circumstances. The
arbitrary system of government is done away; the new
one has the good of the people for its object, and this
is the point on which I rest. I have no concealment
of my opinions; but if anything could make me shy of
such a discussion, it would be the fixing a day to
catechize me respecting my political creed, and respecting
opinions on which the House is neither going to act,
nor called upon to act at all. Were I do differ from
my right honorable friend on points of history, on the
constitution of Athens or of Rome, is it necessary that
the difference should be discussed in this House? Were
I to praise the conduct of the elder Brutus, and to say
that the expulsion of the Tarquins was a noble and
patriotic act, would it thence be fair to argue that I
meditate the establishment of a consular government in

---

95. DEBATE OF FOX AND BURKE.

[1] right honourable, *très honorable.*

[2] are as wide as the poles asunder, *sont aussi éloignées les unes
des autres que les pôles.*

this country? Were I to repeat the eloquent eulogium of Cicero on the taking off of Cæsar, would it thence be deducible that I went with a knife about me for the purpose of killing some great man or orator?

When the proper period of discussion comes, feeble as my powers are, compared with those of my right honorable friend, whom I must call my master, for he taught me every thing I know in politics (as I have declared on a former occasion, and I mean no compliment when I say so), yes, feeble as my powers comparatively are, I shall be ready to maintain the principles I have asserted, even against my right honorable friend's superior eloquence, and maintain that "the rights of man," which my right honorable friend has ridiculed as chimerical and visionary, are in fact the basis and foundation of every rational constitution, and even of the British constitution itself; as our statute-book proves; since, if I know any thing of the original compact between the people of England and its government, as stated in that volume, it is a recognition of the original inherent rights of the people as men, which no prescription can supersede, no accident remove or obliterate. If such principles are dangerous to the constitution they are the principles of my right honorable friend, from whom I learned them.

I cannot help feeling a joy ever since the constitution of France became founded on the rights of man, on which the British constitution itself is founded. To deny it, is neither more nor less than to libel the British constitution; *and no book my right honorable friend can cite, no words he may deliver in debate, however ingenious, eloquent, and able, as all his writings and all his speeches undoubtedly are, can induce me*[3] to change or abandon

---

[3] and no book my right honorable friend can cite, no words he may deliver in debate, howewer ingenious, eloquent, and able, as all his writings and all his speeches undoubtedly are, can induce me, *et mon très honorable ami ne pourra ni citer un livre, ni prononcer une parole dans ce débat, quelque ingenieux, quelque eloquents*

that opinion: I differ upon that subject with my right honorable friend toto cœlo.

96. REPLY OF BURKE.

I asserted that dangerous doctrines are encouraged in this country, and that dreadful consequences may ensue from them, which it was my sole wish and ambition to avert, by strenuously supporting the constitution of Great Britain as it is, which, in my mind, can better be done, by preventing impending danger, than by any remedy that can afterwards be applied; and I think myself justified in saying this, because I know, that there are people in this country, avowedly endeavouring to disorder its constitution and government, and that in a very bold manner. The right honorable gentleman, in the speech he has made, treated me in every sentence with uncommon harshness. *In the first place*[1], after being fatigued with the skirmishes of "order," which were wonderfully managed by his light troops, he brought down the whole strength and heavy artillery of his own judgment, eloquence and abilities upon me, to crush me at once, by declaring a censure upon my whole life, conduct and opinions. Notwithstanding this great and serious, though on my part, unmerited attack and attempt to crush me, I shall not be dismayed; I am not yet afraid to state my sentiments in this House, or any where else, and I will tell all the world, that the constitution is in danger. It certainly is indiscretion at any period, but much greater *at my time of life*[2], to provoke enemies, or to give my friends cause to desert me; yet if that is to be the case, by adhering to

---

et quelque habiles qu'ils puissent être, comme le sont, assurément tous ses écrits et tous ses discours, qui puisse m'amener &c.

96. REPLY OF BURKE.

[1] In the first place, *tout d'abord.*
[2] at my time of life, *à mon âge.*

the British constitution, I will risk all, and as public
duty and public prudence teach me, in my last words
exclaim: "Fly from the French constitution." (It was
whispered by Mr. Fox, there was no loss of friends.)
Yes (exclaimed Mr. Burke), there is a loss of friends;
I know the !price of my conduct; I have done my
duty at the price of my friend; our friendship *is at
an end*[3]. I have] been told that it is much better
to defend the English constitution by praising its own
excellence, than by abusing other constitutions, and certainly the task of praising is much more pleasant than
that of abusing; but I contend that the only fair way
of arguing the merits of any constitution is by comparing
it with others. I warn the right honorable gentlemen,
who are the great rivals in this House, that whether
they should in future move in the political hemisphere
as two flaming meteors, or walk together as brethren,
that they should preserve and cherish the British constitution; that they should guard against innovation, and
save it from the danger of these new theories.

97. THE REJOINDER OF FOX.

However events may have altered the mind of my
right honorable friend (for so I must call him, notwithstanding what has passed, because grating as it is to
any man to be unkindly treated, by those to whom we
feel the greatest obligations, and whom, (notwithstanding
their harshness and severity, we find we must still love
and esteem), I cannot forget, that when a boy almost,
I was in the habit of receiving favors from my right
honorable friend; that our friendship had grown with
our years, and that it had continued for upwards of
twenty five years, for the last twenty of which we have
acted together and lived on terms of the most familiar

---

[3] is at an end, *est finie.*

intimacy. I hope, therefore notwithstanding what has happened on this day, the right honorable gentleman will think on past times, and however any imprudent words or intemperance of mine may have offended him, it will show that it has not been, at least intentionally my fault...... I have, as every other man must have, a natural antipathy to being catechised as to my political principles. Because I admire the British constitution, is it to be concluded that there is no part of the constitution of other countries worth praising, or that the British constitution is not still capable of improvement? I therefore can neither consent to abuse every other constitution, nor to extol our own so extravagantly as the right honorable gentleman seems to think it merits.

Nothing but the ignominious terms which my right honorable friend has this day heaped upon me— "Mr. Burke said loud enough to be heard, that he did not recollect the epithets;"—they are out of his mind; then they are completely and for ever out of mine. I cannot cherish a recollection so painful, and, from this moment, they are obliterated and forgotten.

I admit that no friendship should exist in the way of public duty: and if my right honorable friend thought he did service to the country by blasting the French revolution, he must do so, but at the same time he must allow others who thought differently to act in a different manner.

98. CHARACTER OF THE RIGHT HONORABLE CHARLES FOX.

Mr. Fox's eloquence was of a kind *which, to comprehend you must have heard him yourself*[1]. When he

---

98. CHARACTER OF THE RIGHT HONORABLE
CHARLES FOX.

[1] which, to comprehend you must have heard him yourself, *qu'il fallait avoir entendu pour le comprendre.*

got fairly into his subject, *was heartily warmed with it*[2], he poured forth words and periods of fire that smote you, and deprived you of all power to reflect and rescue yourself, while he went on to seize the faculties of the listener, and carry them captive along with him whithersoever he pleased to rush. It is ridiculous to doubt that he was a *far closer*[3] reasoner, a much more argumentative speaker than Demosthenes; as much more so, as Demosthenes would perhaps have been than Fox, had he lived *in our times*[4], and had to address an English House of Commons. For it is the kindred mistake of those who fancy that the two were like each other, to imagine that the Greek's orations are long chains of ratiocination; like Sir William Grant's arguments or Euclid's demonstrations. They are close to the point; they are full of impressive allusions; they abound in expressions of the adversary's inconsistency; they are loaded with bitter invective: they never lose sight of the subject; and they never quit hold of the hearer by the striking appeals they make to his strongest feelings and his favorite recollections: to the heart, or to the quick and immediate sense of inconsistency, they are always addressed, and find their way thither by the shortest and surest road; but to the head, to the calm and sober judgment, as pieces of argumentation, they assuredly are not addressed. But Mr. Fox as he went along, and exposed absurdity, and made inconsistent arguments clash, and laid bare shuffling and hypocrisy, and showered upon meanness, or upon cruelty, or upon oppression, a pitiless storm of the most fierce invective, was ever forging also the long, and compacted, and massive chain of pure demonstration.

There was no weapon of argument which this great orator more happily or more frequently wielded than

---

[2] was heartily warmed with it, *qu'il s'y était echauffé.*
[3] far closer, *bien plus vigoureux.*
[4] in our times, *de nos jours.*

wit, the wit which exposes to ridicule—the absurdity or inconsistency of an adverse argument. It has been said of him that he was the wittiest speaker of his times; and they were the times of Sheridan and of Windham. This was Canning's opinion, and it was also Mr. Pitt's. There was nothing more awful in Mr. Pitt's sarcasm, nothing so vexatious in Mr. Canning's light and galling raillery, as the battering and piercing wit with which Mr. Fox so often interrupted, but always supported, the heavy artillery of his argumentative declamation.

In most of the external qualities of oratory, Mr. Fox was certainly deficient, being of an unwieldy person, without any grace of *action*[5], with a voice *of little compass*[6], and which, when pressed in the vehemence of his speech, *became shrill almost to a cry or squeak*[7]; yet all this was absolutely forgotten in the moment when the torrent began to pour. Some of the undertones of his voice were peculiarly sweet; and there was even in the shrill and piercing sounds which he uttered, *when at the more exalted pitch*[8], a power that thrilled the heart of the hearer. His pronunciation of our language was singularly beautiful, *and his use of it pure and chaste to severity*[9]. As he rejected, from the correctness of his taste, all vicious ornaments, and was most sparing indeed in the use of figures at all, so in his choice of words, he justly shunned foreign idiom, or words borrowed, whether from the ancient or modern languages, and affected the pure Saxon tongue, *the re-*

---

[5] action, *geste.*

[6] of little compass, *de peu d'étendue.*

[7] became shrill almost to a cry or squeak, *devenait aiguë au point de n'être qu'un cri ou qu'un glapissement.*

[8] when at the more exalted pitch, *au comble de l'enthousiasme.*

[9] and his use of it pure and chaste to severity *et l'usage qu'il en faisait si correct et si pur qu'il allait jusqu'à la sévérité.*

sources of which are unknown to so many who use it, both in writing and in speaking.—Broughham[10].

99. THE FALL OF RIENZI.

The balcony on which Rienzi had alighted, was that from which he had been accustomed to address the people; it communicated with a vast hall, used on solemn occasions for state festivals, and on either side were square projecting towers, whose grated casements looked into the balcony. One of these towers was devoted to the armoury, the other contained the prison of Brettone, the brother of Montreal. Beyond the latter tower was the general prison of the Capitol; for then the prison and the palace were in awful neighbourhood.

The windows of the hall were yet open, and Rienzi passed into it from the balcony. The witness of the yesterday's banquet was still there; the wine, yet undried, crimsoned the floor, and goblets of gold and silver shone from the recesses. He proceeded at once to the armoury, and selected from the various suits that which he himself had worn when, nearly eight years ago, he had chased the barons from the gates of Rome. He arrayed himself in the mail, leaving only his head uncovered, and then taking in his right hand, from the wall, the great gonfalon of Rome, returned once more to the hall. Not a man encountered him: in that vast building, save the prisoners and the faithful Nina, *whose presence he knew not of*[1], the senator was alone.

On they came, no longer in measured order, as stream after stream from lane, from alley, from palace, and from hovel—the raging sea received new additions. ·

---

[10] the resources of which are unknown to so many who use it, both in writing and in speaking, *dont les ressources, tant pour écrire que pour parler sont inconnues de beaucoup de ceux qui s'en servent.*

99. THE FALL OF RIENZI.

[1] whose presence he knew not of, *dont il ignorait la présence.*

On they came—their passions excited by their numbers—
women and men—children and malignant age; in all
the awful array of aroused, released, unresisted physical
strength and brutal wrath. "Death to the traitor! Death
to the tyrant! Death to him who has taxed the people!"
("*Mora il traditore che ha fatta la gabella! Mora!*")²
Such was the cry of the people—such the crime of the
senator! *They broke over*³ the low palisades of the
Capitol — they filled with one sudden rush the vast
space, a moment before so desolate, now swarming with
human beings athirst for blood! Suddenly came *a dead
silence*⁴, and on the balcony above stood Rienzi; his
head was bare, and the morning sun shone over that
*lordly brow*⁵, and the hair, grown grey before its time,
in the service of that maddening multitude. Pale and
erect he stood—neither fear, nor anger, nor menace,
but deep grief and high resolve upon his features; a
momentary shame—a momentary awe seized the crowd.

He pointed to the gonfalon, wrought with the
republican motto and arms of Rome, and thus he began:
"I too am a Roman and a citizen, hear me!"

"Hear him not, hear him not, his false tongue can
charm our senses, cried a voice louder than his own;
and Rienzi recognized Cecco del Vecchio.

"Hear him not! down with the tyrant!" cried a more
shrill and youthful tone; and by the side of the artizan
stood Angello Villani.

"Hear him not! Death to the death-giver," cried
a voice close at hand, and from the grating of the
neighbouring prison glared near upon him as the eye
of a tiger, the vengeful gaze of the brother of Montreal.

---

² Mora il traditore che ha fatta la gabella! Mora! *Qu'il meure
le traitre qui a introduit la gabelle, qu'il meure!*
³ They broke over, *ils franchirent.*
⁴ a dead silence, *un silence de mort.*
⁵ lordly brow, *front noble.*

Then from earth to heaven rose the roar—„Down with the tyrant! down with him who taxed the people!"

A shower of stones rattled on the mail of the senator; still he stirred not. No changing muscle betokened fear. His persuasion of his own wonderful powers of eloquence, if he could but be heard, inspired him yet with hope; *he stood collected in his own indignant but determined thoughts*[6]—but the knowledge of that very eloquence was now his deadliest foe. The leaders of the multitude trembled lest he should be heard; "and doubtless," says a contemporaneous biographer, *"had he but spoken*[7], he would have changed them all, and the work been marred."

The soldiers of the barons had already mixed themselves with the throng; more deadly weapons than stones aided the wrath of the multitude; darts and arrows darkened the air: and now a voice was heard shrieking, *"Way for the torches!"*[8] and red in the sunlight the torches tossed and waved, and danced to and fro above the heads of the crowds, as if the fiends were let loose amongst the mob! And what place in hell hath fiends like those a mad mob can furnish? Straw and wood and litter were piled hastily round the great doors of the Capitol, and the smoke curled suddenly up beating back the rush of the assailants.

Rienzi was no longer visible, an arrow had pierced his hand—the right hand that supported the flag of Rome—the right hand that had given a constitution to the Republic. He retired from the storm to the desolate hall. He sat down—and tears springing from no weak and woman source—but tears from the loftiest fountain of emotion—tears that befit a warrior when his troops

---

[6] he stood collected in his own indignant but determined thoughts, *il était là, recueilli dans ses pensées pleines d'indignation quoique pleines de résolution.*

[7] had he but spoken, *s'il avait seulement parlé.*

[8] Way for the torches, *place aux torches.*

desert him—a patriot when his countrymen rush to their own doom—a father when his children rebel against his love; tears such as these forced themselves from his eyes, and relieved, but they changed also his heart!

"Enough, enough!" he said, presently rising and dashing the drops scornfully away, "I have risked, dared, toiled enough, for this dastard and degenerate race. I will yet baffle their malice. I renounce the thought of which they are so little worthy! Let Rome perish! I feel at last, that I am nobler than my country!— she deserves not so high a sacrifice."

With that feeling, death lost all the nobleness of aspect it had before presented to him, and he resolved, in very scorn of his ungrateful foes—in very defeat of their inhuman wrath, to make one effort for his life. He divested himself of his glittering arms—his address, his dexterity, his craft returned to him. His active mind ran over the chances of disguise—of escape. He left the hall, passed through the humbler rooms, devoted to the servitors and menials, found in one of them a coarse working garb, *indued himself with it*[9], placed upon his head some of the draperies and furniture of the palace; as if escaping with them, and said, *with his old "fantastic rise,"*[10] "When all other friends desert me, I may well desert myself."

With that he awaited his occasion. Meanwhile the flames burnt fierce and fast—the outer door below was already consumed; from the apartment he had deserted the fire burst out in volleys of smoke, the wood crackled, the lead melted, with a crash fell the severed gates.— The dreadful entrance was opened to all the multitude —the proud Capitol of the Cæsars was already tottering to its fall! Now was the time! He passed the flaming door—the smouldering threshold; he passed the outer

---

[9] indued himself with it, *s'en revêtit.*
[10] with his old "fantastic rise" *avec son emphase fantasque.*

gate unscathed—he was in the middle of the crowd. "Plenty of pillage within," he said to the bystanders in the Roman patois, his face concealed by his load,— *"Suso, suso a glie traditore!"*[1 1] The mob rushed past him; he went on; he gained the last stair descending into the open streets: he was at the last gate—liberty and life were before him.

A soldier (one of his own) seized him.

"Pass not—whither goest thou?"

"Beware lest the senator escape disguised!" cried a voice behind—it was Villani's. The concealing load was torn from his head—Rienzi stood revealed.

"I am the senator!" he said in a loud voice. "Who dare touch the representative of the people?"

The multitude were round him in an instant. Not led, but rather hurried and whirled along, the senator was borne to the Place of the Lion. With the intense glare of the bursting flames, the grey image reflected a lurid light, and glowed (that grim and solemn monument!) as if itself of fire.

There arrived, the crowd gave way, terrified by the greatness of their victim. Silent he stood, and turned his face around; nor could the squalor of his garb, nor the terror of the hour, nor the proud grief of detection, abate the majesty of his mien, or re-assure the courage of the thousands who gathered gazing round him. The whole Capitol wrapped in fire, lighted with ghastly pomp the immense multitude. Down the long vista of the streets extended the fiery light and the serried throng, till the crowd closed with the gleaming standards of the Colonna—the Orsini—the Savelli! Her true tyrants were marching into Rome! As the sound of their approaching horns and trumpets broke upon the burning air, the mob

---

[1 1] Suso, suso a glie traditore, is probably intended for, suso, suso allo traditore. *sus, sus au traître.*

seemed to regain their courage. Rienzi prepared to speak; his first word was as a signal of his own death.

"Die, tyrant!" cried Cecco del Vecchio; and he plunged his dagger into the senator's breast.

"Die executioner of Montreal!" muttered Villani; „thus the trust is fulfilled!" and his was the second stroke. Then, as he drew back and saw the artisan, in all the drunken fury of his brute passion, tossing off his cap, shouting aloud, and spurning the fallen lion; the young man gazed upon him, with a look of withering and bitter scorn, and said, while he sheathed his blade, and slowly turned to quit the crowd, "Fool! miserable! thou, and thou at least hadst no blood of kindred to avenge!"

They heeded not his words—they saw him not depart; for as Rienzi, without a word, without a groan, fell to the earth, as the roaring waves of the multitude closed over him, a voice shrill, sharp, and wild was heard above all the clamour. At the casement of the palace (the casement of her bridal chamber) Nina stood; through the flames that burst below and around, her face and outstretched arms alone were visible! Ere yet the sound of that thrilling cry passed from the air: down with a crash thundered that whole wing of the Capitol—a blackened and smouldering mass. At that hour a solitary boat was gliding swiftly along the Tiber. Rome was at a distance, but the lurid glow of the conflagration cast its reflection upon the placid and glassy stream—*fair beyond all art of painter and of poet*[12], the sunlight quivering over the autumnal herbage, and hushing into tender calm the waves of the golden river.

Adrian's eyes were strained towards the towers of the Capitol, distinguished by the flames from the spires and domes around; senseless and clasped to his guardian breast, Irene was happily unconscious of the horrors of the time.

---

[12] fair beyond all art of painter and of poet, *d'une beauté qui surpasse l'art du peintre ou du poëte.*

"They dare not, they dare not," said the brave Colonna, "touch a hair of that sacred head! If Rienzi fall, the liberties of Rome fall for ever! As those towers that surmount the flames, the pride and monument of Rome, he shall rise above the dangers of the hour. Behold, still unscathed amidst the raging element, the Capitol itself is his emblem."

Scarce had he spoken, when a vast volume of smoke obscured the fires. Afar off, a dull crash travelled to his ear; and the next the towers on which he gazed 'had vanished from the scene, and one intense and sullen glare seemed to settle over the atmosphere, making all Rome itself the funeral pyre of the last of the Roman Tribunes!—Sir *E. Bulwer Lytton.*

100. THE LAST DAYS OF GEORGE LORD JEFFREYS.

Among the many offenders whose names were mentioned in the course of these enquiries, as exceptions to the Bill of Indemnity, *was one who stood alone and unapproached in guilt and infamy*[1], and whom Whigs and Tories were equally willing to leave to the extreme rigour of the law. On that terrible day which was succeeded by the Irish Night*), the roar of a great city disappointed of its revenge had followed Jeffreys to the drawbridge of the Tower. His imprisonment was not strictly legal: but he at first accepted with thanks and blessings the protection which those dark walls, made

---

*) It was said that the Irish whom Feversham had let loose were marching on London and massacreing every man, woman, and child on the road. At one in the morning the drums of the militia beat to arms. During many years the Londoners retained a vivid recollection of what they called the Irish night.

---

100. THE LAST DAYS OF GEORGE LOLD JEFFREYS.

[1] was one who stood alone and unapproached in guilt and infamy, *il y en avait un dont le crime et l'infamie étaient uniques et dont sans parallèle.*

famous by so many crimes and sorrows, afforded him against the fury of the multitude. Soon, however, *he became sensible*[2] that his life was still in imminent peril. For a time he flattered himself with the hope that a writ of Habeas Corpus would liberate him from his confinement, and that he should be able to steal away to some foreign country, and to hide himself with part of his ill-gotten wealth from the detestation of mankind: but, till the government was settled, there was no court competent to grant a writ of Habeas Corpus; and, as soon as the government had been settled, the Habeas Corpus Act was suspended. *Whether the legal guilt of murder could be brought home to Jeffreys may be doubted*[3]. But he was morally guilty of so many murders that, if there had been no other way of reaching his life, a retrospective Act of Attainder would have been clamourously demanded by the whole nation. A disposition to triumph over the fallen has never been one of the besetting sins of Englishmen: but the hatred of which Jeffreys was the object was without a parallel in our history, *and partook but too largely*[4] of the savageness of his own nature. The people, *where he was concerned*[5], were as cruel as himself, and exulted in his misery, as he had been accustomed to exult in the misery of convicts listening to the sentence of death, and of families clad in mourning. The rabble congregated before his deserted mansion in Duke street, and read on the door, with shouts of laughter, the bills which announced the sale of his property. Even delicate women, who had tears for highwaymen and housebreakers, breathed nothing but vengeance against him. The lampoons on him which were hawked about

---

[2] he became sensible, *il comprit*.
[3] Whether the legal guilt of murder could be brought home to Jeffreys may be doubted, *on peut douter si on aurait pu prouver contre lui la culpabilité légale de meurtre*.
[4] and partook but too largely, *et ne tenait que trop*.
[5] where he was concerned, *en ce qui le concernait*.

the town were distinguished by an atrocity, rare even in those days. Hanging would be too mild a death for him: a grave under the gibbet too respectable a resting place: he ought to be whipped to death *at the cart's tail*[6]; he ought to be tortured like an Indian: he ought to be devoured alive. The street poets portioned out all his joints with cannibal ferocity, and computed how many pounds of steaks might be cut from his well fattened carcass. Nay, the rage of his enemies was such that, in language seldom heard in England, they proclaimed their wish, that he might go to the place of wailing and gnashing of teeth, to the worm that never dies, to the fire that is never quenched. They exhorted him to hang himself in his garters, and to cut his throat with his razor. They put up horrible prayers that he might not be able to repent, that he might die the same hardhearted, wicked Jeffreys that he had lived. His spirit, as mean in adversity, as insolent and inhuman in prosperity, sank down under the load of public abhorrence. His constitution, originally bad, and much impaired by intemperance, was completely broken by distress and anxiety. He was tormented by a cruel internal disease, which the most skilful surgeons of that age were seldom able to relieve. One solace was left him, brandy. Even when he had causes to try and councils to attend, he had seldom gone to bed sober. Now, when he had nothing to occupy his mind save terrible recollections and terrible forebodings, he abandoned himself without reserve to his favourite vice. Many believed him to be bent on shortening his life by excess. He thought it better they said, to go off in a drunken fit than to be hacked by Ketch, *or torn limb from limb*[7] by the populace.

Once he was roused from a state of abject despondency by an agreeable sensation, speedily followed by a

---

[6] at the cart's tail, *dérrière une charrette*.

[7] or torn limb from limb, *ou déchiré*.

mortifying disappointment. A parcel had been left for him at the Tower. It appeared to be a barrel of Colchester oysters, his favourite dainties. *He was greatly moved*[8] : for there are moments when those who least deserve affection are pleased to think that they inspire it. "Thank God," he exclaimed, "I have still some friends left." He opened the barrel; and from among a heap of shells out tumbled a stout halter.

It does not appear that one of the flatterers or buffoons whom he had enriched out of the plunder of his victims came to comfort him in the day of trouble. But he was not left in utter solitude. John Tutchin, whom he had sentenced to be flogged every fortnight for seven years, made his way into the Tower, and presented himself before the fallen oppressor. Poor Jeffreys, humbled to the dust, behaved with abject civility, and *called for wine*[9]. "I am glad, Sir," he said, "to see you." "And I am glad," answered the resentfull Whig, "to see Your Lordship in this place." "I served my master," said Jeffreys: "*I was bound in conscience to do so.*"[10] "Where was your conscience when you passed that sentence on me at Dorchester?" said Tutchin. "It was set down in my instructions," answered Jeffreys fawningly, "that I was to show no mercy to men like you, men of parts and courage. When I went back to court I was reprimanded for my lenity." Even Tutchin, acrimonious as was his nature, and great as were his wrongs, seems to have been a little mollified by the pitiable spectacle which he had at first contemplated with vindictive pleasure. He always denied the truth of the report, that he was the person who sent the Colchester barrel to the Tower.

A more benevolent man, John Sharp, the excellent

---

8 He was greatly moved, *il fut très ému.*
9 called for wine, *demanda du vin.*
10 I was bound in conscience to do so, *en conscience il fallait que je le fisse.*

Dean of Norwich, forced himself to visit the prisoner. It was a painful task: but Sharp had been treated by Jeffreys, in old times, *as kindly as it was in the nature of Jeffreys to treat any body*[11], and had once or twice been able, by patiently waiting till the storm of curses and invectives had spent itself, and by dexterously seizing the moment of good humour, to obtain for unhappy families some mitigation of their sufferings. The prisoner was surprised and pleased. "What," he said, "dare you own me now?" It was in vain, however, that the amiable divine tried to give salutary pain to that seared conscience. Jeffreys, instead of acknowledging his guilt, *exclaimed vehemently*[12] against the injustice of mankind. "People call me a murderer for doing what at the time was applauded by some who are now high in public favour. They call me a drunkard because I take punch to relieve me in my agony." He would not admit that, as President of the High Commission, he had done any thing that deserved reproach. His colleagues, he said, were the real criminals; and now they threw all the blame on him. He spoke with peculiar asperity of Sprat, who had undoubtedly been the most humane and moderate member of the board.

It soon became clear that the wicked Judge was fast sinking under the weight of bodily and mental suffering Doctor John Scott, prebendary of Saint Paul's, a clergyman of great sanctity, and author of the "Christian Life," a treatise once widely renowned, was summoned probably on the recommendation of his intimate friend Sharp, *to the bedside of the dying man*[13]. It was in vain however, that Scott spoke, as Sharp had already spoken, of the hideous butcheries of Dorchester and Taunton. To the

---

[11] as kindly as it was in the nature of Jeffreys to treat any body, *avec autant de bonté qu'il était dans le naturel de Jeffreys de traiter quelqu'un.*

[12] exclaimed vehemently, *se récria.*

[13] to the bedside of the dying man, *au chevet du moribond.*

last Jeffreys continued to reply, that those who thought him cruel did not know what his orders were, that he deserved praise instead of blame, and that his clemency had drawn on him the extreme displeasure of his master. Disease assisted by strong drink and by misery, did its work fast. The patient's stomach rejected all nourishment, *he dwindled in a few weeks from a portly, and even corpulent man to a skeleton.*[14] On the eighteenth of April he died, in the forty first year of his age. He had been Chief Justice of the King's Bench at thirty five, and Lord Chancellor at thirty seven. In the whole history of the English bar there is no other instance of so rapid an elevation, or of so terrible a fall. The emaciated corpse was laid, with all privacy, next to the corpse of Monmouth in the chapel of the Tower.

---

[14] he dwindled in a few weeks from a portly, and even corpulent man to a skeleton, *en quelques semaines, de corpulent et même de gros qu'il était, il fut réduit à l'état de squelette.*

101. LOVE OF COUNTRY.

Breathes there the man, with soul so dead,
Who never to himself hath said
  This is my own, my native land?[1]
Whose heart hath ne'er within him burn'd
As home his footsteps he hath turn'd,
  From wand'ring[2] on a foreign strand?
If such there breathe[3], go mark him well;
For him no minstrel raptures swell[4] ;
High though his titles, proud his name,
Boundless his wealth as wish can claim,
Despite those titles, power, and pelf,
The wretch concenter'd all in self,
Living[5], shall forfeit fair renown,
And, doubly dying, shall go down
To the vile dust, from whence he sprung,
Unwept, unhonour'd and unsung.

Walter Scott.

---

101. LOVE OF COUNTRY.

[1] Breathes there the man with soul so dead . . . . my native land? = *does he breathe the man, with soul so dead, who has never said to himself, this is my own land, my native land.*

[2] From wandering, *après avoir erré.*

[3] If such there breathe, *si un tel homme respire.*

[4] For him no minstrel raptures swell, *pour lui le poète ne chantera pas.*

[5] Living, *pendant qu'il vit.*

102. WHAT IS FAME?

What is *the end*[1] of fame? 'Tis but to fill
    A certain portion of uncertain paper.
Some liken it to climbing up a hill,
    Whose summit *like all hills*[2] is lost in vapour.
For this men write, speak, preach, and heroes kill,
    And bards burn what they call their midnight-taper,
To have, when the original is dust,
A name, a wretched picture, and worse bust.

What are the hopes of man? old Egypt's king
    Cheops erected *the first pyramid,*
And largest[3], thinking it was just the thing
    To keep his memory whole, and mummy hid;
But somebody or other rummaging,
    Burglariously[4] broke his coffin lid:
Let not a monument give you or me hopes,
Since not a pinch of dust remains of Cheops.

Byron.

103. HOME.

I've roamed through many a weary round[1],
    I've wander'd *east and west*[2];
Pleasure in every clime I've found,
    But sought in vain for rest.

---

102. WHAT IS FAME.

[1] the end, *le but.*
[2] like all hills, *comme celui de toutes les collines.*
[3] the first pyramid, and largest = *the first and largest pyramid.*
[4] Burglariously, *comme un voleur de nuit.*

103. HOME.

[1] I've roamed through many a weary round, *J'ai erré pendant bien des voyages ennuyeux.*
[2] east and west, *d'orient en occident.*

14 *

While glory sighs for other spheres,
   I feel that one's too wide,
And think the home that love endears
   Worth all the world beside.

The needle[3] thus too rudely moved,
   Wanders, unconscious where;
Till having found the place it loved,
   It trembling settles there[4].

Moore.

104. THE TORCH OF LIBERTY.

I saw it all in Fancy's glass—
Herself, the fair, the wild magician,
That bid this splendid day-dream pass,
And named each gliding apparition.

'Twas like a torch-race, such as they
Of Greece perform'd *in ages gone*[1],
When the fleet youths, in long array,
Pass'd the bright torch triumphant on.

I saw th' expectant nations stand,
To catch *the coming flame*[2] in turn—
I saw from ready hand to hand,
The clear, but struggling glory burn[3].

---

[3] The needle, *l'aiguille aimantée*, that is to say *la boussole*, 'the compass'.

[4] It trembling settles there, *elle s'y fixe en tremblant*.

104. THE TORCH OF LIBERTY.

[1] in ages gone, *dans les siècles passés*.

[2] the coming flame, *la flamme qui s'approche*.

[3] The clear, but struggling glory burn, *brûler la gloire brillante, qui luttait*.

And, oh, their joy, as it came near,
'Twas, in itself, a joy to see—
While Fancy whisper'd in my ear,
"That torch they pass is Liberty!"

And each, as she received the flame,
Lighted her altar with its ray;
Then, smiling, to the next who came,
Speeded it on its sparkling way[4].

From Albion first, whose ancient shrine
Was furnish'd with the fire already,
Columbia caught the spark divine,
And lit a flame like Albion's steady.

The splendid gift then Gallia took,
And like a wild Bacchante raising
The brand aloft, its sparkles shook,
As she would set the world a-blazing[5]!

And when she fired her altar[6], high
It flash'd into the redd'ning air
So fierce, that Albion, who stood nigh,
Shrunk[7] almost blinded by the glare.

Next Spain[8], so new was light to her,
Leap'd at[9] the torch—but ere the spark
She flung upon her shrine could stir,
'Twas quench'd, *and all again was dark*[10].

---

[4] Speeded it on its sparkling way, *la faisait passer rapidement sur sa route étincelante.*

[5] As she would set the world a-blazing, *comme si elle voulait mettre la terre en feu.*

[6] And when she fired her altar, *et quand elle alluma le feu sur son autel.*

[7] Shrunk, *se recula.*

[8] Next Spain, *après elle l'Espagne.*

[9] Leap'd at, *s'élança sur.*

[10] and all again was dark, *et tout redevint ténèbres.*

Yet, no—not quench'd—a treasure worth
So much to mortals rarely dies—
Again her living light *look'd forth*[11],
And shone a beacon in all eyes!

Who next received the flame? alas!
Unworthy Naples,—shame of shames,
That ever through such hands should pass
That brightest of all earthly flames[12]!

Scarce had her fingers touch'd the torch,
When frighted by the sparks it shed,
Nor waiting ev'n to feel the scorch[13],
She dropp'd it to the earth and fled.

And fall'n it might have long remain'd,
But Greece, *who saw her moment now*[14],
Caught up the prize, tho' prostrate, stain'd
And wav'd it round her beauteous brow.

And Fancy bid me mark where, o'er
Her altar, as its flame ascended,
Fair, *laurell'd spirits*[15] seem'd to soar,
Who thus in song their voices blended:

"Shine, shine for ever, glorious flame,
"Divinest gift of Gods to men!
"From Greece thy earliest splendour came,
"To Greece thy ray returns again.

---

[11] looked forth, *se montra.*

[12] That ever through such hands should pass that brightest of all earthly flames = *that that brightest of all earthly flames should ever pass through such hands.*

[13] Nor waiting ev'n to feel the scorch, *et sans même attendre d'en sentir l'ardeur.*

[14] who saw her moment now, *qui alors vit le moment venu.*

[15] laurell'd spirits, *des esprits couronnés de lauriers.*

"Take, Freedom, *take thy radiant round*[16] :
"*When dimm'd*[17], revive; *when lost*[18], return;
"*Till not a shrine through earth be found*[19],
"On which thy glories shall not burn."

Thomas Moore.

105. ÆNEAS RELATING THE SACK OF TROY TO DIDO.

'Twas now the dead of night[1], when sleep repairs
Our bodies worn with toils, our minds with cares,
When Hector's ghost before my sight appears;
Shrouded in blood he stood, and bath'd in tears[2],
Such as when by the fierce Pelides slain,
Thessalian coursers dragg'd him o'er the plain;
Swoln were his feet, as when the thongs were thrust
Through the pierc'd limbs: his body black with dust,
Unlike[3] that Hector, who return'd from toils
Of war triumphant in Æacian spoils,
Or him[4] who made the fainting Greeks retire,
Hurling amidst their fleets *the Phrygian fire*[5].
His hair and beard *were clotted stiff with gore*[6] ;
The ghastly wounds he for his country bore,
Now *stream'd afresh*[7].

---

[16] take thy radiant round, *accompli ton brillant voyage.*
[17] When dimm'd, *quand tu seras obscurcie.*
[18] when lost, *quand tu seras perdue.*
[19] Till not a shrine through earth be found, *jusqu'à ce qu'on ne puisse trouver un autel sur la terre.*

105. ÆNEAS RELATING THE SACK OF TROY TO DIDO.

[1] 'Twas now the dead of night, *Nous étions alors au milieu de la nuit.*
[2] Shrouded in blood he stood, and bath'd in tears, *Enseveli dans le sang et baigné de larmes, il était devant moi.*
[3] Unlike, *différent de.*
[4] Or him = *or of him.*
[5] the Phrygian fire, *le feu grégeois.*
[6] were clotted stiff with gore, *étaient collés et raidis par le sang.*
[7] stream'd afresh, *saignèrent de nouveau.*

I wept to see the solitary man,
And, whilst my trance continued, thus began:
"O light of Trojans and support of Troy,
Thy father's champion, and thy country's joy!
O, long expected[8] by thy friends! from whence
Art thou so late return'd to our defence?
Alas! what wounds are these? What new disgrace
Deforms the manly honours of thy face?
The spectre, groaning *from his inmost breast*[9],
This warning in these mournful words express'd:
"Haste, *goddess-born*[10]! *Escape*[11], by timely flight,
The flames and horrors of this fatal night.
The foes already have possess'd our wall,
Troy *nods from high*[12], and totters to her fall.
Enough is paid to Priam's royal name,
Enough to country, and to deathless fame.
If by a mortal arm my father's throne
Could have been saved—this arm the feat had done.
Troy now commends to thee her future state[13],
And gives her gods companions of thy fate.
Under their umbrage hope for happier walls,
And follow where thy various fortune calls[14]."

He said[15] and brought forth from the sacred choir
The Gods and relics of the immortal fire.
Now peals of shouts came thund'ring from afar,
Cries, threats, and loud laments, and mingled war.

---

[8] O, long expected, *O toi longtemps attendu.*
[9] from his inmost breast, *du fond de son cœur.*
[10] goddess-born, *toi, né d'une déesse.*
[11] Escape, *échappe aux.*
[12] nods from high, *tremble de toute sa hauteur.*
[13] Troy now commends to thee her future state, *Troie remet son avenir entre tes mains.*
[14] And follow where thy various fortune calls, *et va où t'appelera la fortune inconstante.*
[15] He said, *il dit ces mots.*

The noise approaches, though our palace stood
Aloof from[16] streets, *embosom'd close with wood*[17] ;
Louder and louder still I hear th' alarms
Of human cries distinct and clashing arms.
Fear broke my slumbers.
I mount the terrace, thence the town survey,
And listen what the swelling sounds convey.
Then Hector's faith was manifestly clear'd,
And Grecian fraud in open light appear'd.
The palace of Deiphobus *ascends*
In smoky flames[18], *and catches on*[19] his friends.
Ucalegon burns next; the seas are bright
With splendour not their own, and shine with sparkling
New clangours and new clamours now arise,   [light.
The trumpet's voice with agonizing cries.
With frenzy seiz'd I run to meet th' alarms,
Resolv'd on death, resolv'd to die in arms[20],
But first to gather friends with whom t'oppose,
If fortune favour'd, and repel the foes,
By courage rous'd, *by love of country fired*[21],
With sense of honour and revenge inspired.
Pantheus, Apollo's priest, a sacred name,
Had 'scaped the Grecian swords, and pass'd the flame;
With relics loaded *to my doors he fled*[22],
And by the hand his tender grandson led.
"What hope, o Pantheus? Whither can we run?
Where make a stand[23]? Or what may yet be done*[24]?
Scarce had I spoke, when Pantheus, with a groan,

---

[16] Aloof from, *éloigné.*
[17] embosom'd close with wood, *caché au sein des bois.*
[18] ascends in smoky flames, *s'élève en flammes fumeuses.*
[19] and catches on, *et communique le feu à.*
[20] Resolv'd on death, resolv'd to die in arms, *résolu à mourir, et à mourir sous les armes.*
[21] by love of country fired, *enflammé par l'amour de la patrie.*
[22] to my doors he fled, *il dirige sa fuite vers mon palais.*
[23] Where make a stand, *où résister.*
[24] what may yet be done, *que peut-on encore faire.*

"Troy is no more! her glories now are gone.
The fatal day, th' appointed hour is come,
When wrathful Jove's irrevocable doom
Transfers the Trojan state to Grecian hands:
Our city's wrapt in flames: the foe commands.
To several posts their parties now divide[25];
Some block the narrow streets: some scour the wide;
The bold they kill, th' unwary they surprise;
Who fights meets death, and death finds him who flies[26]."

Dryden.

106. THE GREEKS BEFORE TROY.

Now had the Grecians *snatch'd*[1] a short repast,
And buckled on their shining arms in haste.
Troy rous'd as soon; *for on that dreadful day
The fate of fathers, wives, and infants lay*[2].
The gates unfolding pour forth all their train;
Squadrons on squadrons *cloud*[3] the dusty plain;
Men, steeds, and chariots shake the trembling ground;
The tumult thickens and the skies resound.
And now with shouts *the shocking armies clos'd*[4],
To lances lances, shields to shields, opposed;
Host against host their shadowy legions drew;
The sounding darts in iron tempests flew[5];

---

[25] To several posts their parties now divide, *alors leurs bandes se divisent pour aller à leurs différents postes.*

[26] Who fights meets death, and death finds him who flies, *qui combat trouve la mort et qui s'enfuit: le trépas.*

106. THE GREEKS BEFORE TROY.

[1] snatch'd, *prirent à la hâte.*

[2] for on that dreadful day, the fate of fathers, wives, and infants lay, *car des événements de ce jour affreux dépendait le sort de pères, femmes et enfants.*

[3] cloud, *obscurcissent.*

[4] the shocking armies clos'd, *les armées qui s'entre choquent en viennent aux mains.*

[5] The sounding darts, in iron tempests flew, *les traits résonnants volent comme une tempête de fer.*

Victors and vanquish'd join promiscuous cries:
Triumphant shouts and dying groans arise;
With streaming blood the slippery fields are dyed,
And slaughter'd heroes swell the dreadful tide.
Long as the morning beams in increasing bright[6]
O'er heav'n's clear azure spread the sacred light,
Promiscuous death the fate of war confounds,
Each adverse battle gored with equal wounds.
But when the sun the height of heav'n ascends,
The sire of Gods his golden scales suspends
With equal hand; in these explores the fate
Of Greece and Troy, and poised the mighty weight.
Press'd with its load the Grecian balance lies
Low sunk on earth; the Trojan strikes the skies.
Then Jove from Ida's top his horrors spreads;
The clouds burst dreadful o'er the Grecian heads;
Thick lightnings flash; the mutt'ring thunder rolls,
Their strength he withers, and *unmans*[7] their souls.
Before his wrath the trembling hosts retire,
The god in terrors, and the skies on fire.

Pope.

107. MILTON'S SONNET ON HIS OWN BLINDNESS.

When I consider *how my light is spent*
Ere half my days[1], in this dark world and wide,
And that one talent which is death to hide,
Lodg'd with me useless, though my soul more bent
To serve therewith my Maker, and present
My true account, lest he, returning, chide.

---

[6] Long as the morning beams increasing bright, *Tant que les rayons du matin augmentent en splendeur.*
[7] unmans, *amollit.*

107. MILTON'S SONNET ON HIS OWN BLINDNESS.

[1] how my light is spent ere half my days, *que ma vue est éteinte avant d'avoir atteint le milieu de ma vie.*

,,*Doth God exact day-labour, light denied*² ?"
I fondly ask; but Patience, to prevent
That murmur, soon replies, ,,God doth not need
Either Man's work, or his own gifts; who best
Bears his mild yoke, they serve him best; his state
Is kingly; thousands at his bidding speed,
And post o'er land and ocean without rest;
They also serve, who only stand and wait!"

108. INGRATITUDE.

Blow, blow thou winter wind,
Thou art not so unkind
   As man's ingratitude:
Thy tooth is not so keen,
Because thou art not seen,
   Although thy breath be rude.

Freeze, freeze, thou bitter sky,
Thou dost not bite so nigh,
   As benefits forgot:
*Though thou the waters warp*¹,
Thy sting is not so sharp,
   As friend remembered not.

Shakespeare.

109. THE SEVEN AGES.

All the world's a stage,
And all the men and women mere players:
They have their entrances and their exits:
And one man, in his time, plays many parts,
*His acts being seven ages*¹. At first the infant,

---

² Doth God exact day-labour, light denied? *Dieu demande-t-il un travail quotidien à celui qui est privé de la lumière?*

108. INGRATITUDE.
¹ Though thou the waters warp, *quoique tu déformes les eaux.*

109. THE SEVEN AGES.
¹ His acts being seven ages, *ses actes sont sept âges.*

Mewling and puking in his nurse's arms.
And then the whining school-boy, with his satchel
And shining morning face, creeping like snail
Unwillingly to school. And then the lover,
Sighing like furnace, with a woful ballad
Made to his mistress' eyebrow. Then a soldier,
Full of strange oaths, and bearded like the pard,
Jealous in honour, sudden and quick in quarrel;
Seeking *the bubble reputation*[2]
Even in the cannon's mouth[3]. And then the Justice,
In fair, round belly, with good capon lined[4],
With eyes severe, and beard of formal cut,
Full of wise saws and modern instances;
And so he plays his part. The sixth age shifts
Into the lean and slippered pantaloon,
With spectacles on nose and pouch on side;
His youthful hose, well saved, *a world too wide*[5]
For his shrunk shank; and his big, manly voice,
Turning again toward childish treble, pipes
And whistles in the sound. Last scene of all;
That ends this strange, eventful history —
Is second childishness and mere oblivion;
Sans[6] teeth, sans eyes, sans taste, sans every thing!

Shakespeare.

110. HAMLET'S SOLILOQUY.

To be, or not to be, that is the question:
Whether 'tis nobler in the mind, to suffer

---

[2] the bubble reputation, *la réputation chimérique.*
[3] Even in the cannon's mouth, *même à la gueule des canons.*
[4] In fair, round belly, with good capon lined, *au joli ventre rebondi, garni de bon chapon.*
[5] a world too wide, *bien trop larges.*
[6] Sans = *without.*

The slings and arrows of outrageous fortune;
Or to take arms against a sea of troubles,
And by, opposing, end them?[1]—To die;—to sleep;
No more;—and by a sleep, to say we end
The heart-ache, and the thousand natural shocks
That flesh is heir to[2],—'tis a consummation
Devoutly to be wished. To die:—to sleep;—
To sleep! perchance to dream;—Ay, *there's the rub*[3] ;
For in that sleep of death what dreams may come,
When we have shuffled off this mortal coil,
Must give us pause: *there's the respect*[4],
That makes calamity of so long life[5] :
For who would bear the whips and scorns of time,
The oppressor's wrong, the proud man's contumely,
The pangs of despis'd love, the law's delay,
The insolence of office[6], and the spurns
That patient merit of the unworthy takes,
When he himself might his quietus make
With a bare bodkin[7] ?   Who would fardels bear,
To groan and sweat under a weary life;
But that[8] the dread of something after death,—
The undiscover'd country, from whose bourn
No traveller returns, puzzles the will,
And makes us rather bear those ills we have,
Than fly to others that we know not of?
Thus conscience does make cowards of us all:

---

110. HAMLET'S SOLILOQUY.

[1] And by, opposing, end them, *et en y resistant, y mettre fin.*
[2] That flesh is heir to, *auxquels la chair et sujette.*
[3] there's the rub, *c'est là l'embarrassant.*
[4] there's the respect, *c'est là la difficulté.*
[5] That makes calamity of so long life, *qui fait une calamité d'une vie si longue.*
[6] The insolence of office, *l'insolence des gens en place.*
[7] With a bare bodkin, *rien que d'un coup de poinçon.*
[8] But that, *si ce n'est que.*

And thus *the native hue*[9] of resolution
Is sicklied o'er with the pale cast of thought;
And enterprises of great pith and moment,
With this regard[10], their currents turn awry
And lose the name of action . . . .

Shakespeare.

---

[9] the native hue, *la teinte naturelle.*
[10] With this regard, *à cet aspect.*